MW01146462

A GROOM WITH A VIEW

A Groom with a View

Sophie Ranald

A Groom with a View © Sophie Ranald 2014
All rights reserved in all media. No part of this book may be reproduced
or transmitted in any form by any means, electronic or mechanical (including but not limited to: the internet, photocopying, recoding or by
any information storage and retrieval system), without prior permission
in writing from the author and/or publisher.
The moral right of Sophie Ranald as the author of the work has been
asserted by her in accordance with the Copyright Designs and Patents
Act 1988.

ISBN-13: 9781499705409

For my wonderful friends at STBC,
the drinking group with a book problem

CHAPTER ONE

From: nick@digitaldrawingboard.com
To: iain.coulson@coulsoncreative.com
Subject: Last night of freedom

Mate

Just a quick one to say all the best on your last day as a single man. If your stag night was anything to go by, tomorrow is going to be one hell of a party! See you at noon – I'll keep my hip flask handy and resist finishing the contents until my ushering duties are over. Shout if you need anything. Hope you get some kip tonight.

Nick

I don't remember very much about the night it happened, because we were a bit pissed. That sounds so bad, doesn't it? I know a proposal's meant to be right up there in the high points of a girl's life, along with the wedding it leads to, but there you have it – I was wankered and so was Nick. And neither of us can clearly remember, even now, exactly when he demanded to make an honest woman of me, popped the question, went down on one knee (actually, that was when he tripped up the stairs coming out of the Tube station), or asked for my hand in marriage.

Nick loves to quote some rock god idol of his who apparently once said, after some or other shameful rock god antics on stage at a gig, that everyone, from time to time, behaves badly and everyone, from time to time, gets drunk. I'm afraid that was us at Iain and Katharine's wedding. Okay, there were no screaming groupies involved and no mic stand to wave around in a manner contrary to all health and safety guidelines, but we worked with what we had. We behaved as badly as we could have, really, considering it was your typical civilised London wedding.

Iain is Nick's former business partner, and the two of them used to play in a band together before they got respectable and started a graphic design agency, and although they certainly didn't set the world on fire, they were quite well thought of at one stage, opening for Snow Patrol back in 2004 (admittedly only at a tiny gig in a pub in Bournemouth, but still). Since then, Iain's gone via more respectable to extremely respectable – the old Iain, with his waist-length hair and squat in Dalston, wouldn't have stood a chance with Katharine; the new one, with his designer suits and penthouse in Shoreditch, married her.

In all the years I'd known him, Iain had never been single. First there were groupies who he'd take to bed, take to his gigs, then invariably cheat on and be dumped by amid screaming rows. Later there were work experience girls who he'd dazzle with expense-account lunches at Itsu, sleep with and then part from with some relief when their three-week stint at the agency ended. Then, about three years ago, Katharine came on the scene. She's the marketing manager at Brightside.com, a toe-curlingly stylish interiors e-tailer that's one of the agency's biggest clients. I'm not sure if it was fear of losing the account or fear of losing Katharine, but Iain seemed to clean up his act and stop shagging around, and in due course he proposed. I liked Katharine – she was sweet and a bit kooky but had a will of iron and an impressive ability to get what she wanted.

Anyway, the point is that there was no expense spared at Iain and Katharine's wedding. They hired the ballroom at The Mortimer. They had gulls' egg canapés with gold leaf stuck to them. I overheard two girls talking in the ladies' saying the flowers cost six thousand pounds, but they must have been joking, because of course no one spends that on flowers for a wedding. Do they?

There were two hundred of the bride and groom's closest friends there, some of whom were Nick's and my old mates from school and from the Deathly Hush days. And there was free-flowing Krug and lethal cinnamon mojitos (Nick had five. I counted). It was a bloody brilliant day, and by the time Nick and I sprinted for the last Jubilee Line train home, making it with seconds to spare, we were, as I've said, a bit the worse for wear.

"That was so cool," I said, lifting my hair and fanning my sweating neck.

"Wicked," agreed Nick, swaying slightly, out of synch with the motion of the train. "We're never going to do it, right?"

Nick and I have always said marriage isn't for us. When we first got together, when I was only sixteen, we said it was because we didn't want to do anything that would make us in any way at all like our parents. Then when we got together the second time, Nick said that marriage was a bourgeois construct aimed at commodifying women and entrenching Judeo-Christian morality, and I agreed vehemently (then went off and googled what all that meant). Then after a few more years together, we'd bought our first flat and Nick had had his thirtieth birthday and we were fine as we were. Even if our relationship wasn't perfect, what relationship is? We were happy and settled we saw no reason to change anything. We weren't into soppiness and romance. We thought what we had worked just fine.

So all our friends had more or less given up asking, "Are you two going to be next?" at every single one of the weddings we'd been to that summer (and there had been lots; last time I counted I had seventeen hats).

"No chance," I said to Nick, as the train pulled out of Southwark, sending him lurching off balance again. "Not a hovering batfuck."

He grinned at me and I grinned back, and we moved together and had a proper full-on snog on the train, in front of everybody, until some teenagers shouted at us to get a room, and the sudden, jerking stop at Bermondsey almost sent us flying. We snogged some more on the escalator, and again when we stepped out of the station and the hot September night hit us like a sponge, and again when I stopped to take off my shoes because my toes felt like they were bleeding.

By the time we got upstairs to the flat, I was dizzy with desire for him. You know what it's like, if you've been with someone for ages. Some days the only conversation you have is a one-liner about whose turn it is to take out the bins. There are weeks when you don't have any physical contact more meaningful than a kiss goodbye in the morning and the warmth of their back against yours at night. And then there are times when you're knocked sideways by lust, like Nick and I were that night.

Of course, he is absolutely gorgeous. Properly hot – but I've got so used to seeing him every day that sometimes I just don't notice. That night, though, I was devouring the sight of him like someone on the 5:2 diet slavering at the window of Greggs. His dark hair is slightly wavy and always shiny and, back in his lead-guitarist days when he had it long, was considerably nicer looking than my own. His steely grey eyes still manage to be warm and smiley even though their colour is cold as a winter sky. Deep dimples press into his cheeks when he smiles his special, wicked grin that's just for me. He's tall and broad-shouldered, and his legs are all muscly from running.

It sounds like I'm showing off. I don't mean to. I'm not some model-gorgeous stunner who automatically assumes she'll get the best-looking guy, I'm just averagely pretty, if you don't mind short girls, so it amazes me that I was able to pull Nick in the first place, let alone be his girlfriend for more than a decade. So that night I was truly swept away by how lucky I was to have him, and by the knowledge that he wanted me as much as I wanted him.

We ran up the stairs to our flat together, holding hands, and tumbled into the hallway, and Nick swept my hat off and whizzed it like a frisbee on to the kitchen table (he's always had impressive aim). We didn't even make it as far as the living room before he'd unzipped my dress and let it fall to the floor in a puddle of silvery satin. And you'll appreciate the intensity of the moment when I tell you that I didn't even consider saying, "That's Anglomania! I need to hang it up or Spanx will sleep on it!" like I normally would.

(Spanx is our ginger cat. We couldn't decide what to call him when we first got him, and we were in the middle of a heated argument about it when he came trotting into the room with a pair of my suck-it-all-in knickers, which he'd retrieved from the washing basket, in his mouth. And that settled it.)

Soon Nick's jacket had joined my dress on the floor and we were both gasping with desire and laughter, our hands and mouths all over each other's bodies. Nick and I have been together for ages, as I said, and you know how you sort of get into a routine? Not this time. This was filthy. At one point he... but that's too much information. I will say that we fell off the sofa, which made us laugh so much I could hardly breathe, and then we went upstairs to bed and service, as they say, resumed. It was totally amazing, the way sex sometimes is when you've had a lot to drink and have no inhibitions left to speak of.

And that's pretty much all I can remember. I suppose there must have been a moment – maybe when I was on top of him, my hair falling in a tangle over his face, his hands gripping my waist; maybe when we were lying together after-wards, sweaty and sated – when one of us said it. Or perhaps it was more of a team effort – I quite like to imagine that.

Me: You know, I bloody love you.

Him: You're not too shabby either, Pip.

Me: Iain and Katharine looked really happy today.

Him: They did. You know, you don't make me suicidally miserable either.

Me: I know what you mean. Some days, being with you is almost bearable.

Him: So this marriage malarkey...

Me: Maybe it's not actually...

Him: Such a bad idea...

Me: So should we...?

Him: So will you...?

Kind of like that. You get the idea. Spontaneous. A sort of joint proposal. But unfortunately I can't say for sure what happened, because I genuinely don't remember a thing about that night beyond our tumble off the sofa and stum-ble up the stairs, and the rush of love and pleasure flooding over me.

What I do remember is waking up the next day with about as awful a hangover as I've ever had in my life, cuddling up to Nick's warm bare back for comfort and kissing his neck, and him saying sleepily, "Did what I think happened last night really happen, Pippa?"

And me saying, "Oh fuck, I'm going to be sick," and legging it to the bathroom just in time.

Like I said, that's Nick and me. A right pair of old romantics.

Foolishly, I'd arranged to meet Callie that day for breakfast and I was already late, so I didn't have time to question Nick further about what had or hadn't taken place between us the previous night. I showered at top speed, left my hair to dry on its own (even though I knew it would mean my head would look like the aftermath of an explosion in a cotton wool factory by lunchtime), dragged on a pair of jeans and went out, bashing out a quick text to Callie as I ran to the bus stop to tell her I'd be there in half an hour.

I don't see Callie as much as I used to, nor as much as I'd like to, but she's still my best friend. We grew up together, after all. It was Callie who punched Lauren Davidson in the nose for bullying me when we were eight, and then was made to sit in the corner, and her parents got called in for a meeting with the Head. It was Callie who showed me how to paint my nails when we were eleven, and to whom I owe my current shamefully excessive nail enamel collection (last count: one hundred and seventy-two colours, plus base and top coats, and my nails still look shite. I've learned that having nail polishes sat in a drawer doesn't do anything to improve the appearance of your nails – you have to actually use them. But still I keep buying them). It was Callie who I told when I got my first period and when I lost my virginity.

So even though there'd been a weird distance creeping in between us recently, I wanted Callie to be the first person I told about Nick's non-proposal, and not even the most vicious hangover would have stopped me taking advantage of her being in London, for some conference about legal aid that was starting the next day. I was really excited about seeing her, especially as she'd be on her own, without her flatmate Phoebe. Phoebe's lovely and a proper good laugh, but recently it had seemed a bit like every time I arranged to see Callie, she was there too, and sometimes I felt a bit left out. So I was glad to have Callie to myself for once.

Callie was already waiting when I arrived at the café I'd chosen, a former greasy spoon that had recently chi-chi'd itself up and started describing the weekend fry-up as 'brunch'. Even though it was Sunday, she was wearing tailored trousers and a white shirt and her blonde hair was perfectly straightened.

"What's up?" I said, once I'd ordered a sorely needed Diet Coke. "How's work? How's Southampton? How's Phoebe? How's Phoebe's dad?"

It always comes as a surprise to people who were at school with Callie and me that, rather than moving to London and setting the world of law alight with her brilliance, she chose to stay in the town where we grew up, working in a small high-street practice and learning to draw up wills and sort house purchases and defend people in court when they fail to abate a smoking chimney, and whatever else solicitors in small firms do.

"Work's great," Callie said. "Really good. One of the senior partners, Jeremy Gardner, who's been there so long his office chair is practically welded to his flesh, has finally decided to retire. Which means there might be a vacancy for a junior partner. Which means..." She crossed her fingers.

"Callie, that's fantastic news! Really great! When will you find out?"

"Hopefully early next year, but I'm not going to get excited about it until I know for sure. Phoebs is fine," she went on. "Her dad's not. So no change there."

"Poor Phoebe," I said. "It's utterly shit for her. Having to be a part-time carer is tough anyway, but how much tougher must it be when the person you're caring for is vile Vernon?"

At first I'd felt really sorry for Phoebe's dad, because being in constant pain must be an awful thing. But then I began to realise that his pain seemed to mysteriously get worse whenever Phoebe was planning something she was looking forward to, or was under lots of pressure at work, or had just finished being under lots of pressure at work and was planning to spend a weekend vegging in front of the telly. I actually went so far as to google the condition she told us he had. I forget its name now but it's some distant and horrible member of the arthritis family, and I learned that it was one of those things that are meant to get better the more active you are. As far as I could tell, the only form of physical activity Vernon practised was pressing the keys of his mobile to summon Phoebe and her mum to do his bidding.

"And Phoebs and her mum won't admit it," Callie said. "Not even to each other. Not even to themselves. All Phoebe will say is that he gets depressed sometimes. But he's depressed most of the time, and he's a fucking nightmare all the time. Anyway. It's awful but there's nothing we can do to change it. Shall we order some food?" She smiled at the waitress who'd been discreetly hovering for the past few minutes. "I'd like an egg white omelette with tomato and another black coffee, please."

"May I have another Diet Coke?" I said. "And a toasted bacon, egg and cheese ciabatta and a custard Danish?"

"Ouch," Callie reached over and stroked my hand, very gently. "Poor suffering Pippa. How was the wedding?"

"Great. Katharine's really brought Iain into line. She's got such amazing taste, I think she chose pretty much everything and it was all terribly stylish and a bit… you know. Too perfect, I suppose. Very 'here's how Shoreditch hipsters do weddings'. But fabulous all the same." I spent a few minutes telling her all about the five-course meal, the tiny replicas of the bride's bouquet positioned at all the women's place settings, the art deco styling on all the stationery to fit the *Great Gatsby* theme, and the person whose job it was to stand in the cloakroom with a basket of red rose petals and scatter a few in the toilet bowl after you'd flushed. "Anyway, we had a great time and the food was lush and we drank way too much. And then…"

"Then what? Did you do the Sexy Dance again?"

"Yes," I blushed furiously into my breakfast at the memory. "And snogged Nick on the Tube home. But then after that, it got really weird."

"Weird how?"

"I think Nick and I might be engaged. I think he asked me last night, or possibly I asked him. But I definitely woke up somehow knowing we are, and it wasn't a dream because he thinks so too."

"You're engaged!" Callie shrieked. "You and Nick… That's just the best news ever. It doesn't matter if you were pissed when he asked you, you weirdo. You guys are perfect together. You had 'happily ever after' written all over you back when you were sitting A-levels and now you're getting married." She sniffed, and a little tear rolled down her cheek, taking a smear of mascara with it. Bless Callie, she cries at absolutely anything. Sometimes I hum the theme tune to *Watership Down* deliberately to set her off – it never fails.

She accosted the waitress. "Two glasses of champagne, please. My friend got engaged last night! Can I be your chief bridesmaid, Pippa? Please? We said we'd be each other's when we were eight, remember?"

"I do remember. But, Callie, the thing is, even if Nick doesn't change his mind, I don't think we'd want to have that kind of wedding. We've been to so many weddings together and they've all been lovely but I can't imagine us doing it. I mean, why would we? We were never going to get married at all. We'll just... I don't know. Elope or something. Or go to a registry office. Or a tropical island."

"You'll still need a bridesmaid, though," Callie objected. "Otherwise who's going to untie the sheets from your bedpost after you've climbed out of the window to meet him? Or sign the register, or protect you from falling coconuts?"

I laughed. "If I need any of those things, I promise I'll ask you. No one else would be nearly as good, especially at the coconut bit. But seriously, it'll be a tiny wedding, if it even happens. Microscopic. And really, like, low-key."

"Pippa, come on. You say that now, but just wait and see what will happen to you. How many weddings have you been to? At least a dozen in the past year, maybe more. And how many of them have been low-key? Don't rush, I'll give you a minute to think about it."

I didn't really need a minute, but I tried to look thoughtful anyway, and finished the champagne in my glass. "Er... Simon and Deborah's was quite low-key. It was in a village church, then a marquee in her parents' garden."

"Low-key, my arse," Callie said. "You told me about that wedding. You said it was fabulous, and there was a bonfire and a cake made out of cheese and all the men wore matching ties from Liberty."

"Only the best man and the groom's brothers," I said.

"Pippa," Callie gave my hand another squeeze, a firmer one this time. "I'm four whole months older than you and I have more life experience, and I can guarantee that you will become obsessed with this wedding. All brides do, sure as night follows day. I give it two months before you're on the phone to me and Phoebe telling us we have to match our knickers to your table napkins. It. Is. Going. To. Happen. And now I'm off to be a lawyer."

She put thirty pounds down on the table and gave me another hug and a kiss on both cheeks. "Go and buy a few wedding magazines. You need to start lusting over frocks and wondering if a grand is too much to spend on invitations. And give my love to Nick. Tell him congratulations, and to beware of the bridezilla lurking in his future."

After Callie had gone and I'd paid the bill, I left the café and wandered aimlessly around a bit, thinking about what she'd said. I couldn't detect even a hint of bridezilla-ness in myself. Deep inside me, a small, warm flame was glowing with excitement at the idea of being married to Nick (although I'd already decided I was going to remain Pippa Martin, thank you very much, none of this Mrs Pickford business for me). But I also felt a sense of deep trepidation. Would marrying Nick mean that things between us would change? Did I want them to change?

And the actual wedding?

It all struck me as an awful lot of fuss for just one day. I cook for a living and I've catered plenty of weddings and I've seen the waste of food, of drink, of money they cause, not to mention the stress and the strops. One reception dinner we did at Falconi's involved a ten-course tasting menu for a hundred and twenty people, followed by fireworks, with an ice rink set up in the square outside, and the couple split up after six weeks.

That wouldn't happen to Nick and me, obviously. But the obsession that Callie had mentioned? I like to think I'm quite a level-headed person, but what if it was inevitable?

I spotted a newsagent further along the street and went in and bought a packet of wine gums and another Diet Coke. A shelf stacked with glossy wedding magazines caught my eye, and I thought I might as well buy a representative sample, just to see if Callie was right. I sat on a bench in the park and ripped the plastic cover off the first one, and a stash of leaflets spilled out: 'Bespoke Suit Hire for Him'; 'Have you considered a faux bouquet?'; 'Fancy Favours for Everyone'; 'DON'T FORGET YOUR WEDDING INSURANCE!'

Wedding insurance? What the very fuck was that?

I selected a red, black and green wine gum and put them all in my mouth at once, opened the first of the magazines and scanned the contents page. 'Lose weight for your big day'; 'The season's most dramatic dresses'; 'Our fairytale Nantucket nuptials'. The pages were full of pictures of impossibly perfect women in gorgeous frocks, fantastically elaborate cakes and cherubic pageboys. None of it looked like anything to do with me or Nick, I reassured myself. We simply weren't interested in stuff like this – we'd do it our own way. We'd have our relaxed, low-key, small wedding, with just a handful of guests. Maybe Erica, Nick's mother, might even decide not to come, if it was going to be small enough and informal enough? But that was probably too much to hope for.

Still, I felt confident as I boarded the bus home that Callie was wrong. I wasn't going to turn into some spoiled brat insisting that it must be all 'My Day, My Way' (which appeared to be the mantra of Lacy Garter, the agony aunt at *Inspired Bride* magazine). Well, I would actually want things my way, and Nick's, because that's what it was about: our future together, moving forward from where we'd been before. Not custom-made basques and ombré icing.

And anyway, there was a really good chance that Nick hadn't meant it and would change his mind. Or I would. In which case we'd just carry on as we'd been before. It was all fine. We didn't need a wedding – we just needed to be together.

I'd take the magazines home to Nick, I decided, along with the rest of the wine gums (all five of them), and we could read them and have a good laugh about Highland castles and croquembouches, and then talk about last night, and decide what to do. Whether we carried on as we were or went ahead with the smallest wedding ever, it would be fine with me.

"Hello!" I called, opening the front door.

"Hi, Pip," said Nick. "I'm in the office with Spanx. Come and have a look at this, and tell me how it went with Callie."

Nick works from our spare room, where just about every inch of space is taken up by his iMac, his scanner, printer, graphics tablet and all the rest. Usually when I look over his shoulder as he works, I'm dazzled by edgy magazine layouts, modernist logo designs or sleek website treatments (when I can see anything past the furry ginger body of Spanx, Nick's self-appointed junior designer). Now, though, I could see a complex grid of words and figures.

"What are you up to?" I asked.

"I'm doing a spreadsheet," he said proudly. "For the wedding. I've got about two hundred names so far. We might have to cut down a bit."

"Two hundred…" I leaned against the door frame, clasping the glossy magazines to my chest like armour. "Nick, what on earth are you…?"

"Hey, did you know we need to take out wedding insurance?" he said. "And is that *Inspired Bride* magazine? Awesome! Let's have a read."

Chapter Two

From: nick@digitaldrawingboard.com
To: enquiries@brockleburymanor.co.uk
Subject: Booking enquiry

Hello

I'm getting in touch to find out what availability you have for weddings in the next 12 months. My fiancée and I would like a Saturday ideally, although we could consider other days, and we'll have in the region of 120-200 guests.

Please get in touch by email or on the mobile number below and let me know.

Many thanks
Nick Pickford

I don't want to give the impression that my average day's food intake consists of fat-laden fry-ups, pastries and sugary confectionery – far from it. If it did, I'd be the size of a house, rather than… well, the size of an average London flat aimed at the first-time buyer. Luckily, working around food means that quite a lot of the time I'm thoroughly sick of it before I get around to eating it. I know it sounds implausible, but trust me, when you've spent three months in meetings discussing the launch of an ostrich lasagne, another six weeks cooking and tasting countless variations of it and then three days looking at cold slabs of it on different coloured plates while a photographer complains that your tomatoes aren't red enough and your béchamel isn't white enough... Let me just say it puts Slimming World to shame.

So my working day got off to a pretty standard start nutritionally when I bought a black coffee and an apple on my way to the office later that week. When I arrived, Guido, my boss, was on the phone.

"No, Matthew. I don't care if it's Gwyneth fucking Paltrow, we're not doing a macrobiotic menu. My grandmother would turn in her grave! Tell her to go somewhere else, or eat linguine with pesto like the other vegetarians. No, it isn't! Turning away celebrities is great PR! Right. Ciao, ciao.

"Morning, Pippa. Good weekend? God, I've got a fucking shite hangover. You couldn't get me a sausage sandwich, could you, sweetheart?"

"Get it yourself, you lazy git," I said, but I put my jacket back on and retraced my steps to Kaffee Klatch.

Guido's story is really impressive. You're probably familiar with it from his autobiography, *Searing Ambition*. He's the eighth son of a Tuscan peasant, and he followed his dream to Rome, where he spent five years scrubbing pans and mussels at various restaurants before eventually being allowed to learn to cook. He often held down two jobs at once, getting by on three hours' sleep a night, in order to save every lira he could towards his coach ticket to London.

Then he spent the eighties and nineties working his way up to head chef and learning English from Rosetta Stone CDs and from being shouted at. In due course he found a backer to finance the opening of Osteria Falconi in Marylebone, which went on to win first one, then two Michelin stars. Since then, the Falconi empire has expanded to nine restaurants and the brand has gone supernova.

If you've got even the faintest interest in food and cooking, you know who Guido is. If you haven't eaten at one of his restaurants, chances are you own one of his cookbooks, or at any rate you'll have seen him on telly, cooking coconut-based curries in *Guido Goes Bamboo* or returning to his roots in *Guido's Italian Legacy*. And even if your idea of cooking is shoving something in the microwave, there's a good chance that ends up being one of the range of posh ready-meals we do for Thatchell's – you know, the organic spelt risotto with natural smoked haddock and the fragrant pork loin with lemongrass and so on? The ostrich lasagne was the latest addition to the range, its launch planned to coincide with the first episode of *Guido's African Safari* and publication of the accompanying book.

Of course, it's done Guido's career no harm at all that he's seriously easy on the eye. He's tall and just the right side of chunky, keeping himself in shape by dint of ruthless, if intermittent, self-discipline and ten hours a week with his personal trainer. His hair and his designer stubble are generously flecked with silver and there are crow's feet around his warm, smiley brown eyes, but evidently the consensus is that he's improving with age, like a fine wine. The other day some columnist in the *Daily Telegraph* described him as 'the thinking woman's totty'.

Thanks to the CDs and the years working in posh restaurants, Guido speaks better English than I do. But his cooking talents are nothing compared to his gift for self-promotion, and he still plays up the Italian accent when he's talking to diners, and when he's on telly obviously. I guess he thinks it reminds people of his roots.

I started working at Osteria Falconi as a lowly chopper of garlic and roller of pasta. By the time Guido promoted me to chef de partie, I'd moved in with Nick. I loved the tension and testosterone of being in a professional kitchen, the mayhem and camaraderie of a busy service, the satisfaction of wiping down my station after a hectic night. But I hated never seeing Nick – well, only seeing him for ten minutes first thing in the morning and the top of his sleeping head on the pillow when I got home at night. I know it makes me a bit of a traitor to the sisterhood, but I'd more or less decided to hand in my resignation and look for a job with less antisocial hours when the Thatchell's deal came along. Guido asked me if I fancied doing a few months in the development kitchen working on the launch of their ready-meals and I jumped at the chance.

And four years later, there I still was. Don't get me wrong, it's not uninteresting. Thatchell's are great partners to work with and more importantly have seriously deep pockets and are committed to promoting the range. And even though I sometimes find the endless whittling away at the amount of salt and saturated fat we're allowed to use a bit soul-destroying and miss working in a proper kitchen, I know I'm really lucky to have Guido as my boss and mentor. He's nurtured me through my whole career and given me so many chances, and I try to pay him back by working my arse off and being loyal. And fetching him sausage sandwiches, obviously.

"So, Pippa," he said, around a mouthful of sliced white and unmentionable bits of processed pig, "We've got the Thatchell's people coming in later. They said they want an in-depth discussion about the ostrich lasagne and I suspect it isn't going to be pretty. They're bringing their nutritionist. They said something about there being too much butter in it. Too much fucking butter! That's not even possible."

A couple of years ago, Guido was slated in an article in the *Daily Mail* shaming chefs for the disgracefully high calorie content of some of their signature dishes. If I remember correctly, our osso bucco was dissed for having enough saturated fat per serving to last a prop forward a week, and the tiramisu packed about nine hundred calories per serving. We called an emergency meeting with our PR people, and they advised Guido to declare unrepentantly that these dishes were treats, to be consumed on special occasions only and then offset by several days' hard work herding goats in the Appenine foothills. This approach worked for a while, but Thatchell's had become increasingly twitchy recently, sending doom-laden emails warning us about government traffic-light labelling systems and taxes on junk food.

Guido and I might chunter about it in private, but he is as malleable as gnocchi dough when faced with Zelda, the Thatchell's nutritionist, a rail-thin, immaculately groomed woman in her late thirties who wields her nutritional analysis software to deadly effect. We mustered our forces well in advance of the meeting. Tamar, who works with me on recipe development but is more focussed on the books and television stuff, Guido and I carefully arranged bottles of water and platters of fruit on the boardroom table, together with piles of plates, forks and napkins ready for tasting the reduced-fat, reduced-salt, reduced-flavour lasagne.

Thatchell's marketing manager Bryn and the terrifying Zelda arrived early, as they were wont to do, but we were ready for them. I gratefully disappeared into the kitchen to prepare the plates of food for tasting, but even through the closed boardroom door I could hear Zelda bollocking Guido.

"The Thatchell's customer chooses ostrich because of its nutritional benefits and ethical credentials," she said. "It's a lean meat, high in essential amino acids and trace elements and of course is organically and extensively farmed. Our shoppers care as much for the environment as they do for their waistlines. Which is why it is absolutely imperative that we reduce the saturated fat content in this product."

"Sì, sì," Guido agreed. "We have worked on the recipe. It is superb, delicious – yet so low in fat and salt. We have used skimmed milk for the béchamel, extra virgin olive oil has replaced the butter, yet the flavour is exactly like my mamma used to make for me when I was a boy in Tuscany." I heard a sound that could only be him kissing his fingers. "Pippa will bring it for you now to taste."

Right on cue, the microwave pinged.

By the time I left the office that night, I honestly felt like I never wanted to see, taste or talk about food again. But as soon as I walked through the door I knew that Nick was having one of his cooking nights – there was a strong smell of frying onions wafting through the front door and Guns n'Roses playing at full volume.

I walked through to the kitchen. Nick hadn't heard me come in, so I was able to stand in the doorway without him noticing. He was wearing a comedy apron with a woman's naked torso on it, which I'd given him last Christmas along with a Nigel Slater book as a not-so-subtle hint that he needed to do his share of the cooking (I'm not sure which of them did the trick, but the desired effect had apparently been achieved). His eyes were closed, and he was playing air guitar on a cheese grater.

"Oi, Axl," I shouted over the music. "What's for tea?"

Nick's eyes snapped open. He turned the volume down and wrapped me in a tight hug, still holding the grater.

"Hello, beautiful," he said. "Mac and cheese. With onions in it, and bacon. Because everything tastes better with bacon, right?"

"Everything tastes better with a large glass of rioja," I said. "Mind if I go and watch *EastEnders*?"

"Off you go," he said. "I'll bring you your wine." Okay to eat in an hour?" As I turned around, he thwacked me on the bottom with a wooden spoon.

"So," he said later, as we sat at the table surrounded by the remains of our meal (in case you don't already know this, I can confirm that mac and cheese is greatly improved by the addition of bacon and of course given added savour when cooked by someone who isn't you), "I spoke to Mum today."

"Did you? What, in Liberia?" Nick's mother is a nurse specialising in ophthalmic surgery. She works for a charity in West Africa, training other nurses to assist surgeons with cataract operations in remote areas of the region. It's incredibly noble, important work and I admire her greatly for doing it. I also happen to think that remote West Africa is the best place for Erica.

"Yep. It was a terrible line but I managed to tell her we're getting married, after we'd been cut off about five times."

"And what did she say?" I felt a cold knot of anxiety in my stomach. Even though Nick and I had been together for a decade, Erica had never forgiven me for our first break-up when we were teenagers – for, as she saw it, selfishly swanning off to pursue my career in That London and thinking that my ambitions were more important than her darling boy, along with other, worse transgressions. I'm sure when she's training Liberian nurses she's a model of professionalism, but as soon as she sets foot on English soil Erica reverts to a sort of Stepford wife demeanour, and apparently expects me to be one too. So despite me having made compromises in my career to be with Nick, and despite me being a bloody model girlfriend in a lot of ways, still, in Erica's eyes, I just couldn't get it right.

"She seems to be cool with it," Nick said, looking down at his empty plate. "I'm sure she said she knows we'll be very happy. It was a really bad line."

"She probably said she thinks the idea's very crappy," I said.

Nick laughed. "I'm pretty sure it wasn't that, Pip. Anyway, she did say that she's going to be here for the wedding, and we must let her know as soon as we've decided on a date so she can arrange it. And she said she wants to help us pay for stuff, so, you know, you don't have to feel we can't have the kind of day you want."

When Nick's dad died shortly after Nick moved to London, Erica sold their modest three-bedroom house for an absolute fortune, and announced that she was off to make far-flung climes better far-flung climes. She spent some time at an ashram in India and some in a Tibetan Buddhist collective in Cumbria, before deciding that her skills would be put to best use in tented hospital compounds in the middle of nowhere, rather than having massages on luxury cruise ships, which is what I'd do if I found myself suddenly loaded after slaving away in an NHS hospital for thirty years. But then, I'm not Erica.

"Nick," I said. "I really don't think we need to have a massive wedding. Those magazines we were looking at last night – don't you think some of it's a bit, like, excessive?"

"Oh, God, yes, of course!" he said. "That couple that hired the whole island. Crazy. And the ones that got Robbie Williams to sing for their first dance. Just nuts. I mean, Robbie Williams, for fuck's sake. Now if it had been Radiohead, or even the Arctic Monkeys…"

"Nick! It's not about that. It's the whole way it seems to take over people's lives, to the exclusion of everything else. It seems like they stop being people and start being… just a bride and groom. Worse – a plastic bloody plastic cake topper. You know what Katharine was like, she didn't talk about anything else for months."

"She was a bit tedious about it," Nick agreed. "Speaking of which, they've invited us to go round there for dinner and, apparently, the official photograph viewing. I've said yes. It's the Saturday after next, when they're back from the Maldives."

"Exactly!" I said. "That's exactly my point! It doesn't even stop with the wedding, it carries on afterwards. Official photograph viewings and honeymoons that have to be at some stupid beach resort where they don't allow gay people and keeping the bottom tier of your cake for your child's twenty-first birthday and…" I stopped. Nick and I don't really discuss children.

"Pippa, steady on. Are you sure you're not overthinking this? It's just a day, it's just a way of celebrating us being together with the people we love. You said even Callie thinks we should make a big thing out of it."

No, she didn't, I wanted to say. She said I'd turn into a bridezilla wedding obsessive, because everyone does. But then I thought, Nick has a point. It's about us, and us means him as well as me, and what if a massive wedding is what he wants? How selfish would it be of me to stop him from having one?

"So what do *you* think?" I asked. "What would you like to do?"

"Well, of course I haven't thought about it much." Nick was looking down at his plate again. "I wanted to discuss it with you first."

"Bollocks!" I said. "You so have thought about it. And what have you thought?"

"Okay, okay," he said. "I have had a few ideas. I thought maybe we should have it near home, you know, where we first got together. Maybe in the New Forest somewhere. There was that wedding in *Inspired Bride* that was near there, at a stately home. It looked cool. I know you're mad busy at work, Pip, I don't want you to stress about it. I don't want to be one of those men who sits on his arse and lets his fiancée do all the work, and says, 'I don't mind,' when she asks about flowers and... er... stuff. I want to be involved, I want to be as much a part of it as you. That's what I thought."

He looked excited and a bit embarrassed, and the dimple in his cheek was disappearing then appearing again. I felt a rush of love for him.

"Callie would be pleased if we got married there," I said. "And Mum and Dad would be too, I suppose. I haven't spoken to them yet." I realised I'd been avoiding telling people, avoiding anything that would make it all seem too real. "I'll call Mum. I'll call her this week and arrange to go round and we can tell them, and why don't you ring that place... what was it called again? And see when they've got a free Saturday, because I bet they get booked ages in advance. It might be months away, probably a year."

"Brocklebury Manor," said Nick. "Actually, Pip, I emailed them today. You know, just to see what they said. And they've had a cancellation in February. It gives us almost four months to plan everything."

"This is utterly ridiculous," I complained to Nick as we made our way through the seemingly endless corridors leading to Iain and Katharine's penthouse apartment in a converted corset factory in East London. "I mean, having a wedding photo reveal party is bad enough, but insisting that everyone wears the same outfit they wore to the wedding is just beyond bonkers. I look like a total prat in this hat."

"I know, Pippa," Nick adjusted the carnation in his buttonhole. "But apparently Katharine cried when she realised she wasn't going to get to wear her wedding dress again, and then she had the idea of asking everyone else to wear their wedding kit so she could. Iain's none too pleased about it either."

I could imagine that, just as I could imagine Iain having had very little say in the matter. I've always known that Katharine's girly demeanour conceals a will of iron.

We tapped the polished steel knocker and Iain opened the front door a second later, red in the face beneath his top hat.

"Glad you could come," he said, a bit sullenly, knocking my own hat askew as he tried to kiss me, and clapping Nick on the back. "Come and have a drink. Katharine's made those cinnamon mojitos you liked so much, or there's fizz, and we got the caterers who did the wedding to recreate the canapés. Grub's through in the dining room."

I caught Nick's eye and tried not to giggle, but he was looking surprisingly serious. Perhaps it was the memory of the cinnamon mojitos.

Walking into Iain and Katharine's living room felt totally surreal. Looking like aliens who'd just landed in the setting of face-brick walls, tank of tropical fish and exposed steel girders were about twenty of their erstwhile wedding guests, the women in floaty frocks and big hats, and the men in morning suits. Katharine herself was holding court at the centre of the group in her sequinned flapper-style wedding dress, complete with veil, bead-encrusted headband and even a bouquet.

"It was just the most special day of my life," she burbled, sipping champagne. "And we've been so excited about getting the photographs back and reliving it all. So when Iain suggested that we ask a few of our closest friends to share the moment with us – well, what could I say?"

A glance at Iain's stony face told me that he'd suggested nothing of the kind.

"Thanks, mate." Nick took a cocktail and passed me a glass of champagne from Iain's outstretched tray. "Look, I know this is probably not the best time, but I wanted to tell you... To ask you... Pippa and I are engaged. Would you mind...?"

Iain enveloped us both in a bear hug, spilling quite a bit of cinnamon mojito down my front.

"Finally!" he said. "I thought you two would never get around to it. Congratulations. I'd be honoured to be your best man." And, bless him, he actually had to blow his nose on his pocket square.

"Just remember, word to the wise," he went on, lowering his voice, "It's just one day. It's very, very easy to get carried away, if you see what I mean? Especially the ladies."

Before I could object to this ridiculously sexist observation, he'd called Katharine over to join our little group. "Darling, Nick and Pippa have fabulous news! They're finally getting around to tying the knot, in... when did you say it was?"

"February," said Nick.

"Oooh, fabulous!" Katharine made 'Mwah, mwah' noises at us. "Congratulations! And more than a year to go – that's plenty of time to get everything organised absolutely perfectly."

"Actually," I said, "We were thinking more of this coming February. Like, the one after December and January?"

Katharine's excited face fell into a look of horror. "*This* February?"

"Well, yes," I said. "We want to keep it all quite simple really, and Nick's seen a potential venue that's had a cancellation, and..."

"Right," Katharine said. "Congratulations! Personally I think you're quite mad to try and arrange a wedding in three and a half months, but I expect it can be done... Come with me."

She took my arm in a vice-like grip and marched me off to their bedroom. I cast a 'rescue me' glance over my shoulder at Nick, but he was listening intently to what Iain was saying.

"I love weddings. Love them! In fact I'm thinking of doing some wedding planning for friends in my spare time and maybe making a career out of it later on, when we have children. So I'd be thrilled to have you as my guinea pig," Katharine said, with what I suppose was meant to come out as a sisterly giggle, but sounded more like a demented cackle to me.

"Katharine, that's absolutely lovely of you," I said feebly. "But really, we want to keep things very low-key. It's sweet of you to..."

"Don't mention it. I would like nothing better than to help. Being part of another person's special day is a pleasure, it's a privilege! Now, the first thing you need is my master USB stick."

She powered up her laptop and inserted a removable storage device. "This baby holds all the secrets to your perfect day," she said. "For a year I took it everywhere with me. Everywhere! If I saw a shop window display that captured my imagination, I'd take a photo and save it on here in the 'Inspiration' folder. All my quotes are here, under 'Finance'. And of course everything feeds into the master spreadsheet, which has pages for the week-by-week and day-by-day countdown, with automatic reminders set to be sent to Iain's, his brother's, my maid of honour's and of course my own phone."

"That's very, er, impressive," I said.

"Impressive? Pippa, it's *essential.* Absolutely essential, if you don't want your big day to disintegrate into chaos. Now, let's have a look at my contacts file – that's the first thing you'll need because a lot of these people will have been booked up for several months already. You may find yourself having to resort to my B- or even C-list suppliers, but of course even they were thoroughly vetted and you never know, for a February wedding, so long as it's not actually the fourteenth, some of the A-list might even be free."

I tried hard not to tune her out. This was important stuff, presumably, if Nick and I were to be saved from wedding disaster.

"It's all alphabetised," she said. "Accessories, bouquets, cakes, dance instructors, evening entertainment, fireworks, groom's outfits, horse-drawn carriages…"

"Wow," I said, interrupting because she looked all set to continue through the remainder of the alphabet. "And where did you find your dress, in the end? It's beautiful."

"That's the fun part." she clasped her hands. "The dresses! I had to password-protect this folder so Iain couldn't hack into it and access my secrets." She scrolled through image after image of almost identical beaded frocks. "Of course, with so little time you may have to go for off-the-peg, but we can give Marissa Beaumont a call and see if there's any way at all she could squeeze you in. She was my second-choice designer, if Sarah Burton hadn't been available."

I looked at Katharine's dress. It was gorgeous, the bodice stiff and heavy with sparkly embellishment, the skirt floating in a layers of ethereal chiffon petals. I'm not exactly the world's most skilled seamstress (in fact the last time I tried to sew on a button I was trying to watch *Breaking Bad* at the same time, and ended up sewing it and the shirt to the arm of the sofa) and I had no idea how long it takes to make a dress. There were an awful lot of beads on Katharine's, but they wouldn't have to be sewn on one at a time, surely? And four *months*? I took a sip of champagne.

"Katharine," I said. My voice came out a bit croaky, so I cleared my throat and tried again. "Katharine, how long did all this actually take you?"

She gave her light, tinkling laugh again. It sounded a bit like other day at work, when Guido dropped a stack of roasting tins on to the kitchen floor.

"Iain proposed to me on the first of September, two years ago. Of course I'd already made some plans before then," her voice dropped to a whisper, "Don't pretend you haven't, it's just between us girls! But after that, it took us a few months to find our venue, exploring different places most weekends. Then things got really quiet for a while, and I only spent maybe a day a week researching things and writing my wedding blog – there's a link to it here – before the dress fittings and the other final preparations started to kick in a year or so ago. But you don't have anything like as long as I did, so it will all be much more intense."

Much more intense? Jesus! What had I let myself in for?

"One thing I will advise." Katharine wagged a manicured finger at me. "Don't let it take over your relationship! Remember, your hubby-to-be is the most important person in your life. Even more important than your dress designer!

I made a rule not to mention the wedding to Iain one day a week – Thursday was my day, because I have a regular breakfast meeting and Iain plays squash in the evenings and we don't actually see each other anyway, so it wasn't as hard as I expected. We also made Tuesdays our date nights. I'd cook us a special low-cal dinner and we'd have a glass of bubbly and then it was time for nookie. You know what men are like – that's the best way to keep them sweet. If there was anything particularly expensive I wanted for the wedding, I'd be sure to raise the subject on... Tuesday," she finished triumphantly.

"Right," I said. "Date nights. What a lovely idea."

"And while we're on the subject," said Katharine (and I thought, no, please, please get off the subject), "You might want to think of a sex diet before the big day."

I let out an involuntary shriek of laughter. "A what diet?"

"Sex diet. No nookie for six weeks before the wedding. Iain grumbled about it at the time, but it was so worth it. It made our wedding night much more magical in that way. Almost like the first time."

As far as I could tell, the only possible consequences of that for us would be Nick wanking himself into an early grave, or things on the wedding night coming to a disappointingly premature conclusion. But I said, "Thanks for sharing that with me, Katharine. That's really interesting and special. I'll keep it in mind. Now what about shoes?" I might be a bit of a dead loss when it comes to flowers and stuff, but there's nothing I like better than a good long chat about shoes.

Just as Katharine was about to open the folder entitled 'Shoe inspiration' (I could see that it contained more than two hundred files and I was leaning forward eagerly for a look), Iain stuck his head round the door.

"Come on, ladies," he said. "Tear yourselves away from the wedding master plan! We're about ready to see the photos and the video."

Katharine ejected the USB stick and pressed it into my hand, actually squeezing my fingers shut around it. "Guard. This. With. Your. Life," she said.

CHAPTER THREE

From: nick@digitaldrawingboard.com
To: erica@visionforliberia.org
Subject: Re: Plans

Hi Mum

Well, tomorrow we're off to see Pippa's folks and break the news. Can't help feeling a bit nervous about it! Am I meant to ask Gerard's permission, or do we just jump right in and tell them it's a done deal, or what? And next weekend we're going to check out a venue, a posh country house hotel. Hopefully Pippa will like it as much as I do from looking at the photos. I'm attaching a link and I can't wait to hear what you think. It's all starting to feel very real now – bet you never thought you'd see me settling down at last! Great that you might be able to come out for a bit longer before the wedding – it sounds like you could do with a break, and I miss you, you know.

Love
Nick

One of the first things I get asked when I tell people I cook for a living is, "Did you learn from your mum?" My reply is generally, "Well, I learned how *not* to cook." Mum's motto in the kitchen is that if you put nice things into food, the end result will be nice too, and to some extent this is true. But then she does tend to get a bit carried away and add rather too many nice things, or forget she's got something in the oven because she's catching up with *The Archers* omnibus or dead-heading the camellias.

As a child I was treated to many birthday cakes that tasted like the aftermath of a house fire, in spite of having had the burned bits scraped off into the sink and the whole thing thickly coated in lurid buttercream. And then there was the time she read an article about the importance of umami and decided a jar of anchovies would make a brilliant addition to spag bol. So Sunday lunches chez Martin tend to be a bit hit and miss, which is why Nick and I bought bacon croissants at Delice de France to eat on our way down to see my parents and deliver our good news.

Not that I care what they give us to eat. As we walked hand in hand from the station to the house where I grew up, I could feel a deep sense of peace descending over me, and I know this is going to sound a bit fanciful and silly, but the closer we got, the more intense it became. By the time we pushed open the garden gate and I could smell the roses and phlox that were blooming in wild profusion, even though it was almost November (since Mum and Dad retired from academia, they've gone completely gardening-crazy, along with discovering amateur dramatics. Their garden is a thing of beauty and the plays put on by the Westbourne Thespians are staggeringly awful), I could feel a huge, happy smile plastering itself on my face. I love coming home.

"Hello, darling," Mum met us at the front door, wearing ancient jeans and a checked shirt that I remembered giving Dad about fifteen Christmases ago. Despite her shabby clothes, her hair and her make-up were perfect as always, and she smelled deliciously of Chanel Number 5 when she hugged me. "Hello, Nick dear. Come in and have a drink. Your father's tidying the shed, he promised he'd be in soon but perhaps you could go and hurry him along while Pippa helps me with lunch. I thought I'd put some beetroots into the stew but they seem awfully hard, and I'm afraid the lamb's a bit tough too. It's the most extraordinary colour though, quite dramatic.

"Did I tell you I'm playing Gertrude?" she went on. "It's our first attempt at Shakespeare and I think perhaps *Hamlet* was a tiny bit ambitious. Stanley, the director, has cut ever so many lines but it's still over three hours long and you know how restive audiences can get when they want to go to the loo and have a drink."

I shuddered inwardly at the thought of the hours that lay in my future watching the Westbourne Thespians transform the tragedy of the Prince of Denmark into farce. "That's brilliant, Mum, you must be really proud! If it's too long surely they can just cut more?"

"You'd think so," she said, "but Dominic Baker is playing the lead and he's really rather good and gets cross if too many of his lines are taken out. So it may end up being one long soliloquy. But how are you, darling? How's work? What shall we do about this lamb?"

As I attempted a rescue job on lunch and Mum opened a bottle of Riesling, I told her all about Guido and Zelda and the ostrich lasagne, and she laughed. She loves hearing my stories about Falconi's. If my parents were disappointed to have a daughter who only just scraped through three A-levels in Food Technology, Creative Writing and French and was clearly never destined to become a mathematician like Mum or a chemist like Dad, they've hidden it really well.

They've always loved Nick, too, ever since he became my First Proper Boyfriend when I was sixteen. By the time I met him, I'd had a few unsatisfactory fumbles at parties and three disastrous dates with Kevin Popplewell, culminating in us going to see *What Lies Beneath* and him pressing my fingers into his lap and urging me to discover what lay beneath the zip of his jeans. Two minutes later he'd spunked all over my hand and I'd stormed out into the night. I still can't see Michelle Pfeiffer's face without wanting to reach for the antibacterial gel.

Anyway, it was a Saturday night and Callie and I were made up to have been invited to Suze Pickford's birthday party. Suze was one of the most popular girls in our year and was rumoured to have a hot older brother who played in a band, so she was way out of our league. However, she'd been at Tabitha Smith's party two weeks before, and I had increased my standing amongst our peer group hugely by making a batch of hash brownies that were not only lethal but actually tasted quite good. So I, together with Callie and a batch of Nigella's finest, liberally laced with weed, had cracked the nod.

Even at sixteen, I knew I was never going to achieve the long-limbed, silky-haired look that was all the rage at the time (thanks for demolishing any confidence I might have had in my appearance as a teenager, cast of *Friends*). I was short and hourglass-shaped, with dark brown hair that would occasionally, for no apparent reason, decide to fall into soft, loose natural curls, but was a mop of frizz the rest of the time. Mum always said I should value my best features, my clear skin and greeny-blue eyes, but at five foot two, all any potential boyfriends got to see of me was the top of my head. So I enlisted Callie's help to prepare me for Suze's party.

We'd done our nails and fake tan the night before. Then it had taken Callie three hours to blowdry my hair straight, in those dark days before GHDs, and we'd both slicked on masses of wet-look lip gloss. As soon as we were out of sight of my parents' house, we pulled down our jeans so our sparkly thongs and my muffin-top showed at the back, and teetered onwards on our platform flip-flops. But within a few seconds of arriving, we realised we'd got it terribly wrong.

The prevailing aesthetic among Suze's friends was more Manic Street Preachers than Steps, and we stood out like deeply uncool, French manicured sore thumbs from the black-clad, smudgy-eyelinered crowd. Humbly, I handed over the hash brownies – our only ticket to any sort of credibility – and we armed ourselves with bottles of warm Smirnoff Ice and tried to look like we belonged.

Callie, of course, had a not-so-secret weapon: her fantastic figure and blonde hair were enough to guarantee that she'd pull, dodgy lip gloss or no dodgy lip gloss, and within about half an hour she was wrapped round Dwayne Roberts on the dance floor, the two of them kissing passionately as they locked pelvises to U2. I leaned despondently against the wall and wondered whether to go and look for another Smirnoff Ice, go and find a bathroom and confirm that my hair was frizzing up again, or head home – I'd already had four drinks in quick succession and was feeling light-headed and furry-toothed.

I'd actually decided to interrupt Callie's snog to tell her I was abandoning her (yes, I was as much of a loser as I sound when I was a teenager), when I got the sense I was being watched. I looked up and there, on the other side of the room, was the boy I realised must be Suze's big brother. He had the same ice-grey eyes as her and the same air of effortless cool. He had shaggy dark hair. He was wearing camo trousers and a faded Iron Maiden T-shirt and smoking a fag. And looking at me. And smiling.

I felt myself start to blush, and pretended to inspect my fingernails intently. But when I glanced up again, he was coming towards me.

He didn't say anything for a bit – not that I would have heard anyway, the music was deafening. But he handed me another drink – a cold one – and stood next to me, and straight away I felt less stupid and out of place. When the music stopped, he smiled again and said, "So, what brings you here?"

I must have been emboldened by alcopops, because instead of staring at my shoes and blushing and stammering something about how I'd come with my mate, that was her over there, the hot one, I looked up at him and said, "I came to meet you."

And that was how it began. For the rest of that night Nick and I talked and danced together. He took my number, and two days later he called and asked me out, and for the next two years we were inseparable, an item, Nick and Pippa, Pippa and Nick. And now we were going to be Mr and Mrs Pickford. Or rather, Mr Pickford and Ms Martin.

"So, that went well," said Nick as we boarded the train home. And it had, as I'd known it would. My parents were thrilled, in their slightly muddle-headed way. Mum recited 'Let me not to the marriage of true minds admit impediment', and Dad insisted that Nick smoke one of his special-occasion cigars. Nick was still looking faintly green, although that may just have been the after-effects of Mum's salted caramel chocolate pudding, which was a bit heavy on the salt – I was feeling rather thirsty myself.

"I knew it would," I said. "They're pretty chilled out generally and they've always loved you to bits. They'll be cool about the wedding anyway – they won't try and take over and invite loads of distant relatives I've never met. Speaking of which…"

Although Nick doesn't have brothers or sisters apart from Suze, who's married and lives in Melbourne, Erica, his mum, is one of eleven siblings. Consequently Nick has an absolute plague of cousins, and they all have wives and husbands and children and even grandchildren, and their name is legion. Seriously, if you ever find yourself in need of a cousin or twelve, Nick's your man. He'll never get through them all.

"We're going to have to talk about who we're going to invite, at some stage," I said. "I mean, I don't want to rush into asking people but if we at least have an idea of who we want to be there…"

"I'm on it," said Nick. "Remember, I did a spreadsheet?" He took out his iPad and tapped away at the screen for a bit. "Here's where I got to. There are three hundred names so far. I've put them in categories to make it easier: friends, family, work people, other."

"What's 'other'?" I said. "Why on earth do we want anyone at our wedding who isn't a friend, family or a colleague?"

"Won't your parents want to invite some of their friends?"

"Er… no, I don't think so. And if they did I'd tell them they couldn't. Why would we want their friends at our wedding? And why would their friends want to come when they haven't even seen me since I was sixteen? Or distant relatives, for that matter. Not that I have any of those, thank God."

"I have no idea, Pippa. But apparently people do invite their whole family and their parents' friends as well. Mum says…"

I started to feel all prickly and defensive, the way I get whenever Nick mentions Erica. "She says what?"

"Hold on, I'll find her email," said Nick. "She sent it the other day. Here you go, just that paragraph there." He pushed the iPad across the narrow train table towards me.

"You're in my thoughts and in my meditation all the time," I read. "And in all the excitement of planning this important day, there is something I would like you to keep in your thoughts, too. A wedding is about more than the frock and the flowers – although I know Pippa will have exciting plans for those."

"I haven't even thought about the fucking flowers," I snapped at Nick. "What did you tell her?"

He laughed. "Steady on, Pip, I didn't tell her anything. She's just making assumptions. You know what she's like."

"Right," I said. "Still, though, it's a bloody cheek that she thinks…" I caught Nick's eye and shut up. I hate slagging off his mother, and I know he hates me doing it, but sometimes I just can't help myself. "Sorry."

I carried on reading. "A wedding is, first and foremost, about the wider community. One day, if Pippa is not too focused on her career to give you children, you will understand that it takes a village to raise a child; for now, please trust my wisdom in the matter. And remember, if you can, how special Susannah and Dylan's wedding was: a true celebration of family love."

I remember Suze's wedding well. Suze and her mother didn't speak for weeks before it. Dylan was so stressed out by the whole thing that he started making plans to emigrate the minute they got back from honeymoon. And on the day, everywhere you looked, were dozens of cousins.

"If she thinks we're going to have her entire bloody family…" I stopped myself and took a breath. "I'm honestly not sure it would work to have that many people at the wedding,

Nick. Three hundred is loads. I haven't even met all your cousins and it's not like you ever really see them."

"I wouldn't mind a cup of tea," Nick said. "Would you like anything? Diet Coke?"

Nick can be maddeningly evasive when we're arguing, especially, I've noticed, if I'm in the right. But I did need to calm down a bit and I was still suffering from low-grade salt poisoning after Mum's dessert. "I'd love one," I said. "Thanks."

Nick swayed off down the carriage and I turned my attention back to his iPad, trying to breathe myself into a state of Zen calm as I reread Erica's email. She was just a woman with a strong sense of family values, I told myself. She just wanted the best for her son. But I couldn't help waves of resentment crashing over me as I read.

"I know you won't lose sight of the preciousness of family bonds when you are planning this day," Erica had written. "Alongside my spirituality, the ties that bind me to my family are the most precious thing in the world to me. Which is why it has been so hard for me to answer the call of duty that has kept me so far away from the people I love best for so many years." Utter bollocks, I thought, she couldn't wait to get on a flight to India when Nick's dad died.

"So I am overjoyed that I will be seeing you again so soon, my precious boy. Thank you for your generous offer of a bed with you and Pippa for the three months leading up to the big day! I am very much in need of a rest but I hope I can help and support you both and be a big part of all your plans.

"Love and peace, Mum.

"PS – have you heard anything from Bethany recently? What a lovely girl she was."

One look at my face must have been enough for Nick to know what I had seen. He put our drinks on the table and sat down.

"Oh shit, Pippa, I'm sorry. I was going to…"

"You were going to tell me. *Tell* me. Do me the courtesy of telling me that you've invited your mother to come and stay for three *months* without actually *asking* me if I minded, and letting her wank on about how wonderful your ex is in the same breath as accepting?"

"Okay, just hear me out, please, before you go off on one." Nick fished the teabag out of his plastic cup. "I really didn't have any choice. Mum told me in her last email that she's completely burned out. She's been working ten-hour days, seven-day weeks for months now. And Vision for Liberia have basically ordered her to go home and get some rest. She said it coincided perfectly with wanting to come out anyway, and helping with the wedding, which she's offered to pay for, remember, out of the money she made selling her house, which is why she has nowhere else to stay when she's here."

"Really?" I said. "I was under the impression that she had one or two nieces and nephews floating about the place. Clearly I was mistaken."

"Pippa," Nick reached out and squeezed my arm. "Please don't be angry about it. I know you and Mum don't always get on. But she's my mother. I haven't seen her for three years, because last time she came home we were on holiday in Greece. I can't just say she can't stay with us, and expect Aunt Dawn or whoever to put her up. Think how that would make her feel."

"How do you think it makes me feel when every time I see her she makes digs at me and finds fault with every-thing I do, and apparently thinks I'm some kind of scarlet woman?" I demanded. "Nick, I have tried, you know I have. But she's just vile to me. She's been vile to me since I was eighteen."

"She's mellowed," Nick said. "Honestly, she has. She's really affectionate about you in that email. And ignore what she said about Bethany. It doesn't mean a thing."

If that was affection, I'd hate to see hostility. Actually, I'd seen Erica's hostility often and knew it well. The thing is, so many of the little things she's done to undermine me over the years have been under the guise of being helpful and supportive. Like when we went to Prague for a long weekend and Nick asked her to pop in and feed Spanx. She did, and it was very kind and generous of her, but then she took it upon herself to defrost our fridge and throw away the fresh white truffle I'd bought at Borough Market for fifty quid. And then she 'forgot' to return our key and I came home from work one day to find her hoovering our mattress, saying brightly that she thought she'd 'pop in and help out with a spring-clean, since you're obviously so busy, Pippa'. And when she sent me a copy of *The Greedy Girl's Diet* for my last birthday. And the time… anyway, as I've said, I was frankly delighted when Erica decided to take herself and her organising ways off to Africa. I felt tears of anger sting my eyes.

"Pippa, I'm really sorry," Nick said. "Can you see where this leaves me, though? What could I do?"

"You could have asked me," I said. "Just asked."

"And what would you have said?"

"I'd have said… I'd have said yes, for fuck's sake. There's nothing else I can say."

"It'll be fine, Pip. I promise it will. Just trust me."

"I do trust you," I said miserably. It was Erica I didn't trust.

"Good," Nick said. "And Pip? I really don't want this wedding to be stressful for you. It's your day. It's not supposed to be a massive drama. So let me do my share, okay? Don't worry about the guest list and the cousins. I'll sort it out."

CHAPTER FOUR

From: nick@digitaldrawingboard.com
To: imogen@brockleburymanor.co.uk
Subject: Re: Booking enquiry

Hi Imogen

Just to confirm our booking for Sunday night. We'll arrive mid-afternoon, and it would be great if you could be there to show us round. I hope that's not too much trouble.

Look forward to meeting you.

Regards
Nick

"So I'm not worrying about the guest list and the cousins," I told Callie and Phoebe. "He's sorting it out."

Phoebe laughed so much she actually snorted wine out of her nose. "He's sorting it out? What's he going to do? Organise a badger-style cull of them? Defriend loads of them on Facebook? Demand DNA tests so he can say some of them aren't actual cousins?"

It was a week later, we were almost three bottles of wine down, and I was ready to see the funny side of it all myself.

"Not invite anyone else?" Callie suggested. "So the only guests at your wedding will be Nick's mum and… *cousins*? Which of them is going to be your chief bridesmaid? Normal for Norfolk cousin Deirdre?"

"Stop!" I bent over the table, laughing so much it hurt. "I don't know what he's going to do. But I'm sure he'll work something out. There's masses of time still, we haven't even booked the venue yet. And anyway, this is supposed to be a wedding planning summit conference, not a mass piss-take." I hiccuped and took another sip of wine, then started to giggle again.

"Not booked the venue? Pippa, I know you're relaxed about these things but surely you need to get something sorted soon?" Callie looked alarmed. "I'm your chief bridesmaid, assuming you don't sack me off and appoint a cousin, and it's my job to worry about stuff like that."

"Well, you're not allowed to worry about cousins or venues. You can worry about…" I racked my brains. "The hen night! Aren't we supposed to go clubbing in Newcastle, and we all wear tiny skirts and hold-ups with the tops showing and no coats, and then pictures of us appear in articles about binge drinking?"

"No, that's not how it works," said Phoebe. "You're going to do it the posh way. You book a week in Ibiza at a villa with a private chef and a yoga instructor and a beautician coming in every day to give us massages and manicures, then you tell your friends it's going to cost two grand each and we have a massive falling out because none of us can afford to go."

Because of having to help out her mum caring for her dad, Phoebe can only work part-time as a teaching assistant, and is consequently skint almost all the time. Still, I thought, two grand for a hen weekend was bonkers in anyone's book.

"Do people really do that?" I said.

"You bet they do," said Callie. "I've been to six hen parties in the past year. One was trying on lingerie and drinking champagne at Victoria's Secret in London, one was a weekend in a country house with a chef, a yoga teacher and three beauty therapists. The other four were abroad: Paris, Las Vegas, Amsterdam and Magaluf. That's why I couldn't have a proper holiday last summer, I'd used up all my annual leave on hen do's."

"Blimey! I'm definitely not up for doing that," I said. "What's the alternative?"

"You can do something that proves how cultured you are," Phoebe said. "Last year that's what they all seemed to be about. Sarah had a salsa class for hers. Rosheen did a thing where we all had to make soap, it was a bit like being on *The Apprentice*. Lisa's was an Italian cookery course. That was a good laugh, wasn't it, Callie?"

"I think it's fair to say I'll pass on the Italian cookery," I said. I hate to admit it, but I was feeling a bit jealous that Callie and Phoebe had been to all these hen weekends and weddings that I hadn't been invited to, and had all these mutual friends who I'd never met – Sarah, Rosheen, Lisa, the Victoria's Secret girl and all the rest of them. Callie was my best friend, but it was beginning to feel a bit like Phoebe was Callie's.

That sort of thing is supposed to stop when you leave school, isn't it? But I couldn't help feeling both sad and slightly annoyed that the friendship I'd carefully kept alive through Facebook and email and text messages and regular nights out, either in London or in Southampton, was being eroded. When Callie advertised for a flatmate to help her pay her mortgage after she split up with David, and Phoebe moved in, I'd been really pleased that the two of them got on so well, and that there was someone to go with Callie to the pub and help mend her broken heart and stop her sending late-night, drunken texts to David.

I'd welcomed Phoebe as a third member of our group, the one slightly on the outside, but now it was me feeling like the sad newbie. "I'll let you decide," I said. "Make it a surprise. I'll give you Katharine's email address, I know she'll have loads of ideas but they'll probably all be completely over the top, so feel free to ignore her. I just want something small though. And no Italian cookery classes. Oh, and I don't want Erica to be there."

Callie burst out laughing again, and we speculated for a bit about the awfulness of having Erica along on my hen night.

"Anyway, we have to find a venue and finalise a date," I said. "We haven't even got that far yet, Nick's starting to get quite stressy about it. He's got this long list of stuff that he calls Wedmin, which we have to follow without deviation. He found it in *Inspired Bride*. And finding a venue is top of the list. So we're going to see this Brocklebury Manor place tomorrow, and stay the night there."

"Oooh, fabulous!" said Callie and Phoebe in unison.

"Bless Nick, he thinks we need to have regular romantic interludes in the run-up to the big day, to keep the passion alive," I explained. "Apparently *Inspired Bride* recommends it. I don't think we need help keeping our passion alive, to be honest, but I'm well up for romantic weekends away."

"Awww!" Callie hugged me. "He's lovely. You two are so good together."

"He's a keeper," Phoebe agreed, and they both beamed at me like proud parents, and I beamed back, suddenly struck by how lucky I was to have Nick, and how fragile and precious our happiness was.

"Nick's all right," I said lightly. "I'm quite glad I didn't let him get away in the end."

People think – well, Erica thinks – that it was me who dumped Nick, but it wasn't really. I almost didn't go to London, in spite of being offered a place at Westminster Kingsway to train to be a chef, because I didn't want to leave him. So it ended up with Nick having to do the dumping.

I've never cried as much as I did that night, sitting with him in my bedroom and listening to him tell me it was over. I'm not proud of it, but I actually begged him to change his mind. He wouldn't.

"Pippa, you're eighteen," he said. "It's been incredible, you're wonderful and special, but we need to move on. A long-distance relationship won't work. It's finished."

"But I love you!" I sobbed.

He wiped the tears off my puffy, blotchy face with his thumbs and held my hands. "I don't love you," he said gently. I realise now that it was the only thing he could say in order to make me let him go. I hoped it wasn't true that he'd stopped loving me, but I knew he wasn't going to change his mind. He got up and left, saying a polite goodbye to Mum and Dad, got on his motorbike and roared off into the night (the story would be much better if it had been a Harley but it wasn't, it was a beat-up old Honda). I cried solidly for about a week and then dusted myself off and went to London with my shiny new chef's knives. It took me a while to get over what had happened, but eventually I did, and turned my focus towards learning to cook, having a good time and shagging anyone who'd stay still for long enough to let me.

It took almost three years and although I hadn't forgotten Nick, I was more or less over him. Then, at the end of a particularly brutal shift, some of my hard-drinking colleagues announced that they were heading out to Soho to catch the last set of an awesome new band. I wanted nothing more than to get the night bus home to my grotty digs in

Archway and snatch four hours' sleep before work began the next day, but I had a reputation as a party animal to uphold. So I didn't say no even though I had no make-up on and my hair smelled of roast beef.

The club we went to was a wall of smoke and sound. We fought our way through the sweating crowd to the bar and bought a bottle of Jack Daniels between the six of us (back in my cheffing days I could properly hold my drink). And Tom and the lads were right – the band was top. I took my glass and moved towards the stage to get a closer look at them and there, unmistakeable in spite of having grown even taller and grown his hair even longer, was Nick. I remember thinking with a brief pang of jealousy how much nicer his hair was than mine, then imagining how it would feel falling over my face when we fucked.

I decided immediately that I wasn't going to let him get away again. I'd found him, he was mine, and I'd keep whatever secrets I had to in order to keep him. This sounds like the kind of romantic bollocks I had no time for, then as now, but it was honestly as if everything stopped, suspended, while I stood by the stage willing him to notice me, notice me, notice me! Then he said something to Iain, standing next to him with his bass guitar, and they played the opening chords of *Beautiful Day*. I knew than that he'd seen me too. It was the song that had been playing the night we first met, and that was the start of us being together again. It wasn't quite as simple as that, but it was the start nonetheless.

"So, the website says it's a moated medieval manor house," said Nick, as we heaved our bags into the back of the taxi (actually, he swung his in quite easily and I heaved mine – travelling light has never been one of my core competencies). He opened the door for me and then scrambled in himself, pulling out his iPad.

"The foundations of Brocklebury Manor date back to the thirteenth century," he read, "when it was first occupied by the De Vere family. The house has played a role in some of the key events of the past eight hundred years, having been used as a place of refuge by the embattled blah blah… Wars of the Roses blah, Mary Queen of Scots blah… Do we want to know all this?"

"Not really," I said, shifting up close so I could see the screen. "Let's see what it says about the food."

"Okay, but don't read over my shoulder, it's annoying." He kissed me.

"I'm not reading, I'm just looking," I said. "Come on, go to the food bit." I pointed at the screen.

Nick elbowed me in the ribs. "Patience! Right, here we go. Brocklebury's head chef is Hugh Jameson – Huge Amazon, great name – who trained with Marcus Wareing before spending six years travelling the world, working in some of the top kitchens in Australia, Hong Kong and Los Angeles. This international exposure has given Hugh's cuisine a truly global flair, allowing you to derive culinary inspiration for your special occasion from the finest blah blah. Doesn't say anything very much, does it?"

"Not much, but if he worked with Marcus he must know his stuff. Let's look at the pictures of the bedrooms again."

"Hold on, I think we're here," Nick said. "Isn't that the maze they were going on about? And there's the moat, complete with 'our pair of unique black-feathered swans'. Don't know what's unique about them but they're kind of cute. Why don't I carry that, Pippa, it looks massively heavy. You take mine."

When Nick's excited, he can't stop talking. I followed him up the stone steps, framed by a lichened balustrade, and into a hallway with a huge, glittering chandelier suspended from the high ceiling and a staircase branching off in two directions in front of us. In the centre of the room was a shiny round table with an enormous flower arrangement on it, and the scent of roses filled the air.

We stood for a second, drinking it all in and wondering where to go. Then a pretty dark-haired woman in a grey suit came clicking over to us on her high heels.

"Mr Pickford? Welcome to Brocklebury Manor!" she said. "I'm Imogen, the events manager. We don't have a check-in desk here, because we like to keep everything totally informal and relaxed. We want our guests, especially our wedding couples, to feel as if this house is their home for the time they spend here. So if you'd like to leave your bags and coats, they'll be brought up to your room in a few minutes. And if I could just swipe a credit card for any additional expenses during your stay? That's lovely. Now, would you like a tea or coffee or something from the bar or shall we get straight into the grand tour?"

"Maybe a Diet…" I began.

"The grand tour, definitely," said Nick.

Imogen paused, smiling.

"Let's do the grand tour then. My fiancé and I are really looking forward to seeing it all." I realised it was the first time I'd referred to Nick as 'my fiancé'. It sounded weird. It made me feel old.

"Lovely," said Imogen. "We'll start here in the Great Hall, which is the bit most couples like to see first, because that's probably where your exchange of vows will take place. If you'd prefer a religious marriage, there's a chapel in the grounds that can comfortably accommodate eighty guests. However, the Great Hall has room for two hundred, so many of our couples choose to solemnise their marriage here. This is the oldest part of the house, and these are regarded as amongst the finest examples of mullioned windows in southern England. But as you're having a winter wedding, you'll be more interested in the fireplace! Despite the height of the ceilings, this room is always wonderfully warm, even in February. Now if you'd like to follow me through to the drawing room, where many of our couples choose to have their post-ceremony champagne and canapés, or tea and scones, or perhaps even mulled cider and roast chestnuts – Hugh will talk through all the catering options with you when you meet him…"

The tour took almost an hour. We were shown the formal gardens, where many happy couples chose to pose for their photographs if the weather was fine. We saw the dining room, which could accommodate two hundred guests for an informal buffet or eighty for silver service. We had a look around the spa, where I and the other ladies in the bridal party might like to indulge in some relaxing pampering before the big day. We saw the ballroom, a Regency addition to the house, where the newlyweds and their guests would dance the night away. We even had a peep into the downstairs cloakroom, where presumably those guests who had overindulged in the canapés, four-course wedding breakfast, cake designed by the in-house pâtissier, and late-night bacon butties or cheese toasties could retire to vom copiously in opulent yet comfortable surroundings. And finally we were escorted to the bridal suite.

"Fortunately, the bride and groom who had their wedding here yesterday left early for their honeymoon. They're off to St Lucia." Imogen lowered her voice confidingly. "Jenny and Greg. Such lovely people, it's been a delight working with them for the past two years. But then all our couples are special! Now, it's up this little spiral staircase, in the medieval turret, which is just so romantic – I think it's my favourite room in the house! Most of our brides stay here the night before the wedding too, so you can have your getting-ready photos here, because, as you see, it's really quite enchanting."

Imogen held open the iron-studded wooden door, and waved us inside. The evening sun streamed in through the leaded windows, which overlooked the rose garden, sweeping green parkland, a graceful silver S of river and, in the distance, hazy blue hills. The four-poster bed was draped with chiffon curtains and covered with a white duvet as puffy as whipped cream. The free-standing bath had massage jets and mood lighting for that in-room spa experience. There was a lounge area where we could enjoy a final glass of champagne or a late-night snack before retiring for the night, because you'd be amazed how many happy couples are too excited to want more than a mouthful on the day.

"I'll leave you two here," Imogen murmured. "If there's anything at all you need, just press the bell and your personal butler will be with you shortly." And she tiptoed out, closing the door as softly and discreetly as if we actually were about to consummate our marriage.

I flopped bonelessly on the bed on my back and bounced briefly upwards before being enfolded in exquisite softness.

"I'd fucking kill for a Diet Coke," I said.

Two hours later, I'd had my Diet Coke and a lovely long soak in the bath, making a big dent in the Molton Brown toiletries. I'd painted my nails a rather fabulous shade of mint green and straightened my hair and put on makeup and a sparkly top over my jeans, and Nick and I were sipping champagne in the drawing room while we perused the dinner menu. He kept looking up from the squashy leather folder and gazing around the room, and every time he did, he'd get this huge, excited grin on his face.

"It's fabulous, isn't it, Pippa? Isn't it fabulous?" he kept asking.

"Totally fabulous," I agreed. "I love the... er... art. Who do you think that painting's by?"

"Turner." Nick identified it within about a nanosecond. Although he studied graphic design and his party trick is being able to identify more than two hundred fonts on the basis of an uppercase G and a question mark, he knows lots about painting too. "And that's a Cunningham over there, that drawing of the hare. But anyway, Pip, what do you really think? Fabulous, isn't it?"

"Nick, it's beautiful, it really is. I'm so excited about tasting the food. Our room's gorgeous and you were so clever to find it." But it doesn't feel right, I wanted to say. It doesn't feel like us – or not like me, anyway. I belong at the other end of places like this – behind the scenes, swearing and sweating and showing off my mad knife skills with the brigade in the kitchen. Not out here with the guests – the guests who we used to mercilessly mock for asking for their steak well done or ordering ketchup to put on their sea trout.

"We have some canapés for you to enjoy with your drinks," said the handsome Spanish waiter, putting down a square of slate and topping up our glasses. "This is a grouse-liver bonbon, and this is a shot of celeriac velouté with a Sussex crumble crisp. Your table is ready whenever you'd like to come through to the dining room."

I took another gulp of champagne and ate my bonbon. It was delicious. Nick watched me expectantly. "It's lush," I said, "that's a technical term." And he looked as proud as if he'd made it himself.

"And how about this? This soup stuff? And the what-chamacallit crisp?"

"Sussex crumble," I said. "It's a cheese. It's gorgeous."

"Pippa, I'm so pleased you like it," he said. "I was really worried you wouldn't. I was worried things wouldn't be right." To be fair to Nick, I do have form. He's banned me from ever ordering steak when we go out for dinner because I send it back if it isn't cooked right, which it hardly ever is.

"Well, they've got seven courses left to fuck up," I teased him. "So shall we go through and let them get on with it?"

But they didn't fuck up any of the courses. Everything was perfect, even the steak I insisted on having in order to put Hugh Jameson through his paces. We ate every bit of all the dishes on the tasting menu, plus the little random palate-cleansers and pre-desserts that weren't on it. Afterwards, replete with food and drink, we went for a wander in the moonlit rose garden and watched the black swans drifting on the moat, their heads tucked under their wings. We found our way to the centre of the maze and Nick kissed me and said, "I'm so glad I'm marrying you, Pip. I still don't know how we decided but I'm glad we did."

I said I was the lucky one, and felt a lump in my throat because it was all so romantic and perfect, and I was being an ungrateful cow for feeling that something, somehow, wasn't right. But I pushed aside my feelings of unease and followed Nick up the spiral staircase to the enchantingly romantic bridal suite and we made love in the four-poster bed and I fell asleep with my head on his shoulder.

The next morning was a bit of a mad scramble. I'd told Guido I was going away for the night but would be in the office by eleven o'clock, and Nick had a lunch meeting with a new client who he wanted to impress. So we gulped down the coffee and croissants that were delivered to our suite by yet another impeccably trained waiter, packed our bags and headed downstairs to arrange a taxi to the station.

Imogen was hovering in the hallway.

"Good morning!" she said. "I do hope you enjoyed your stay with us. Did you have a pleasant dinner last night?"

"Pippa's the one to ask," Nick said. "She's a chef and very hard to please."

I said it had all been absolutely wonderful. Imogen was charmingly interested about my job, and by the time I'd finished telling her where I worked and Nick had finished telling her how much he'd loved the room and admired the art, our cab had arrived.

"Anyway, thanks so much," Nick said, picking up my bag. "It was all brilliant. I'll send you an email this afternoon to confirm the booking and transfer over the deposit."

I stood for a second, gawping at him. We hadn't definitely agreed anything. Had we? "Thanks, Imogen," I said. "We've had a great time. Nick will be in touch and I'll... er... see you soon."

Trying desperately to find the words that would tell Nick that I wasn't sure, that despite its perfection, I wasn't convinced that a wedding there was what I wanted, I climbed into the taxi. But before I could say anything, Nick's mobile rang and it was a client needing to be talked through how to upgrade his content management system, and that took up most of the journey.

By the time we approached Waterloo, I'd made up my mind. I wasn't going to be a spoiled or bratty or a bridezilla or a control freak. This was Nick's day as well as mine, and if what he wanted was to get married at Brocklebury Manor, that was what we would do. I owed it to him, after all.

Chapter Five

From: nick@digitaldrawingboard.com
To: pippa.martin@falconis.co.uk
Subject: Re: Tonight

Cool – I'll be in the Grope & Wanker at 8. Hope all is ok.

Love you.

N xx

I kissed Nick goodbye and headed for the Tube, trying to force myself to stop thinking about the wedding and my ambivalence towards the whole thing, and focus on the job in hand. Literally. It looked like I had a punishing week ahead. Thatchell's had finally given the go-ahead to the reduced-everything ostrich lasagne, but it was just one product in the range, and Guido and I needed to give some serious thought to a pumpkin and baobab soup (whatever the hell baobab was – I'd better find a supplier sharpish and figure out what to do with the stuff, or I would find myself deeply regretting including it on a whim in our original proposal). We also had to finalise the spicing for the boerewors burgers and work out how to cut the fat content of those right down without making them like chewing on heavily seasoned MDF.

And I'd be fighting to get a decent amount of time with Guido actually in the kitchen, because as well as flying to Glasgow twice a week to supervise a new restaurant launch, he and Tamar were nailing down recipes for *Guido's African Safari* and having loads of meetings with the production company about locations and shooting schedules.

And Erica was due to arrive on Wednesday. I felt my jaw clench just thinking about it. I'd better plan some kind of welcome dinner for her – I made a mental note to check with Nick if she was still following a strict vegan diet. Surely it would be beyond even Erica's capabilities to buy quinoa and tofu in Monrovia? I'd call in some favours with our suppliers and see if I could get hold of some morels just in case.

I stopped at Kaffee Klatch, which is just around the corner and has been our coffee shop of choice since we moved to the area, long before it became as achingly cool and hipsterish as it is now. (I'm convinced that Kaffee Klatch has survived the influx of competitors with their chai lattes and bubble tea chiefly thanks to the caffeine requirements of the Falconi team.) Clutching a cappuccino for Guido (he always drinks cappuccino before noon and espresso after – "It's the Italian rules! My pappa would turn in his grave if he saw you drinking espresso with breakfast!") and a Diet Coke for myself, I buzzed open the door and let myself into the office.

"Morning!" I called, depositing Guido's coffee on his desk and my bag on mine. Four of the five desks were empty, but Eloise, Guido's PA, was there.

"Ssssh," she hissed, and made a series of cryptic hand gestures involving the boardroom door, her watch and what looked like a lethal right hook.

I scooted my chair over to her and whispered: "What's going on?"

"Don't know," she whispered back. "Guido, Tamar and Helen have been shut in there for the past hour. I heard loads of shouting a few minutes ago but it's all gone quiet now."

Helen's the HR manager who looks after staffing across the whole group. She mostly spends her time running recruitment drives for waiters in Manchester or conducting disciplinary hearings for chefs caught snorting coke on the job and consequently her visits to the office are rare and greeted with a mixture of fascination and dread.

"Shit!" I said. Tamar's great to work with and a fantastic cook but she can be a bit temperamental. When she joined two years ago she was going through a divorce, poor thing, and her meltdowns were absolutely epic, but things seemed to have settled down quite a lot recently, and she'd been looking really glowy and happy, so Eloise and I had been speculating that perhaps there was a new man in her life.

"I know." Eloise was wide-eyed with the drama of it all. "Anyway, I'd better have that cappuccino and you can tell me all about the fabulous wedding venue."

I handed the coffee over and gave her the executive summary of our night at Brocklebury Manor, including details of the food, the turret bedroom, the rose garden and the rest of it, but leaving out my deep misgivings about it all.

"It sounds amazing," she said. "I'm so jealous. Dean and I had to make do with curling sandwiches in the local pub. You are lucky to have a rich, generous mother-in-law."

I was about to say that if she was faced with the prospect of Erica as a mother-in-law, she'd be changing her mind about that PDQ, when we heard Tamar's voice, raised to a near hysterical pitch, coming through the boardroom door.

"Fourteen-hour flights!" she said. "And yellow fever and malaria! I'm just not…" There was a soothing murmur from Helen and then we could hear nothing more.

Then Eloise's phone rang. "Florence," she said, and rolled her eyes. Florence is Guido's girlfriend. They've been together about five years, and I have the sense that Florence is desperate for Guido to marry her and Guido is desperately resisting. There have been several occasions when Guido's come into the office in a foul temper after one of their many rows and I've been convinced that this is it, Florence is going to be given her marching orders. But somehow she always persuades him to change his mind. She's a former lingerie model and absolutely gorgeous but extremely high maintenance, and has a very annoying habit of treating all Guido's staff like we're her personal team of slaves. Last year I almost got roped into doing the catering for her daughter Tanith's seventh birthday party, but I managed to invent a holiday to Portugal just in time.

"Of course, Florence," Eloise said, "Just a pedicure or a reflexology massage as well, like you had last time? Any time on Thursday? I'll let you know. And I rang the dentist, they say he can't fit Tanith in next Monday but he can do half two on Wednesday or three forty-five on Friday. Friday works? Great. And I have your cardigan back from the cleaners, they say unfortunately there's nothing they can do about a turmeric stain on cashmere. I'm really sorry."

"I'd better get some work done," I said regretfully, and wheeled myself back to my desk, where I switched on my PC and started googling UK sources of baobab, but it wasn't long before I got distracted and found myself composing an email to Mick the mushroom man to ask about morel supplies. Just as I was pressing send, the boardroom door opened and Helen and Tamar emerged. Tamar had been crying. Her eye makeup was smeared all over her face, and her shoulders were hunched beneath Helen's comforting arm. They were followed by Guido, looking about as furious as I've ever seen him.

"I'm going to take Tamar round the corner for a cup of tea," Helen said. "If she's feeling up to it, she'll be back in the office later this afternoon. Hi Pippa, lovely to see you briefly. I'll be in touch on email in a couple of days."

Guido said, "Eloise, please ring Zack at Platinum Productions and postpone our four o'clock. Try and get another date in the diary ASAP, and pass on my apologies. Tell him there's an…"

"Unavoidable complication?" suggested Helen.

"Yes, one of those," said Guido grimly. "Pippa, could I see you in the boardroom for ten minutes?"

"So, Tamar's pregnant," I told Nick. As soon as I got back to my desk, I'd emailed him and suggested we meet in the Hope and Anchor for an emergency summit conference. He was already there when I arrived, and had ordered me a large glass of rioja. I kissed him, sank into the banquette next to him and came straight out with the news.

"She's been having IVF with donor sperm, apparently. She never said a word about it but she's been longing to have a baby since she left Bruce and she decided, to hell with it, she wasn't going to piss about waiting for another man to come along, she was going to crack on with it on her own." I took a big gulp of my wine.

"Wow, that's really exciting for her," Nick said. "But she won't be going on maternity leave for, like, ages, will she?"

"No, she won't," I took another swig of wine and realised the glass was almost empty. "Another pint? And shall we order some food?"

"So what's it got to do with you?" Nick asked, when I got back from the bar. "I mean, obviously you'll have to work with a new person when she does go off to have the baby, but for now?"

"It's *Guido's African Safari*," I said. "It's being filmed in South Africa and Tamar's flat-out refusing to go. She says she's not willing to risk the long-haul flights, and what's more a lot of the filming locations are in high-risk areas for malaria. Apparently the official advice is for pregnant women to stay away. Guido's furious, but Helen says if he were to try and make her go she could claim constructive dismissal and Guido would be in court before you could say 'indirect sex discrimination'. Not that he would, obviously, because he doesn't treat us that way."

"Blimey," Nick said. "But I still don't see what…"

For someone as clever as he is, Nick can be maddeningly dense sometimes. Our burgers arrived and we went through the whole, "Ketchup or mayo? Anything else you need?" conversation with the waitress.

I applied a liberal sprinkling of salt to my chips and ate one. After the low-fat, low-sodium Thatchell's food, it tasted like heaven.

"I'm going to have to go instead," I said. I tried to sound reluctant, but to be totally honest I was absolutely fizzing with excitement about the idea. I mean, filming for national television in an exotic location on the other side of the world and getting paid a substantial bonus for it – you so would, wouldn't you?

"Wow!" said Nick. "Pip, that's absolutely fantastic for you! Awesome! Congratulations." He clinked his glass against mine. "So when do you go?"

"Well, that's where the problem is," I said. "The good news is it doesn't overlap with the date of the wedding. The other good news is that I'll be able to take lots of time off afterwards so we can have a fabulous honeymoon. But the bad news is I'll be away for a week at the beginning of next month, then for two weeks after Christmas and I only get back three weeks before the wedding. So basically there's going to be hardly any time between now and then when I'll be around, and even then work is going to be totally full-on."

"Okay." Nick had another bite of his burger and a sip of lager. "It's not ideal. But you know what? You took the office job with Guido so you could have a life with me instead of working nights. You didn't buy new shoes or have a holiday for two years when I left Iain's agency and started out on my own. You've sacrificed a room in the flat to be my studio. You've never once moaned when clients ring me at ten o'clock at night. And your career's fucking important, Pippa. What kind of dick would I be to mind about taking on a bit more of the planning for our wedding because you're doing something awesome that you care about, that's going to benefit us both in the long term?"

I reached across the table and kissed him, my hair narrowly missing the ketchup. "You're so amazing. I thought that was what you'd say. I hoped it was. But I was worried it might be a problem. It's a hell of a lot of work, planning a wedding. Katharine says it took her five hundred hours, or something, in total."

"Ah, but Katharine's offered to help, remember?" said Nick. "She spent five hundred hours planning a wedding so we don't have to. And we've got her USB stick holding all the secrets of the known universe, and I can rope Iain in too, and Callie will want to be involved, won't she? And of course Mum will be here in a few days and although she needs a break from work, you know what she's like. She'll be scrubbing our kitchen cupboards and arranging all our books in alphabetical order within about three hours, she'll get so bored. She'll love helping out with it all. So don't worry. I'll plan the wedding and it will be the perfect day, just wait and see."

I ate the last of my chips – the extra salty ones at the bottom of the bowl – and finished my wine. It took an absolutely mammoth effort of self-control not to say that if Erica so much as opened one of my kitchen cupboards there would be hell to pay. Because now that Nick was being so lovely and reasonable about work, and offering to singlehandedly arrange our wedding, there was no way I could complain about anything his mum did, was there? I'd just have to suck it up.

"Well, the one thing you can't do is choose my dress," I said. "So I'd better see if Katharine can come shopping with me."

"If she can't, Mum would love to," said Nick. "She really would! She…"

"I'll bear that in mind," I said.

It felt as if I'd barely had time to accept the terrible blow of Erica's approaching visit, when the day of her arrival came. I made sure I left work on time, and stopped at Wholefoods to stock up on out-of-season Peruvian asparagus and avocados, three kinds of tofu, two kinds of quinoa, some sort of superfood breakfast cereal that looked like lip-liner sharpenings, dairy-free carob chocolate, spelt bread, cartons of oat and almond milk and a bottle of sulphur-free champagne. That pretty much covered all bases, I thought, lugging it all home along with the hard-won morels sourced from Mick the mushroom man at vast expense.

Nick was in his studio when I got home, but there was no sign of Erica.

"Hey, Pip," he said. "Mum arrived safely, I met her at Heathrow this afternoon."

"Great!" I said, thinking that she couldn't be as exhausted as all that if she'd already gone gallivanting off somewhere.

Nick lowered his voice. "She's asleep at the moment. She really isn't looking well. I've changed the sheets on our bed for her – I'm really sorry, I forgot to mention it to you last night but I thought it would be a good idea for her to have our room, and you and I can sleep on the sofabed in here for the next couple of months. I thought you wouldn't mind, as you're going to be away such a lot."

"You *what?*" I couldn't believe it, I honestly couldn't. So for the next three months I was going to have to knock on my own bedroom door every time I wanted a clean pair of pants, sleep with my legs under Nick's desk, and shower in the tiny second bathroom while Erica wallowed in luxury in our en-suite. I sound horribly selfish, I know I do, but it was *our bedroom.* Our little haven where we slept and had sex and where Nick brought me breakfast in bed on Sundays.

"I thought it made sense," said Nick, "otherwise I'd disturb her if I have to work late. You don't mind, do you?"

I took a deep breath. "Of course not. As you say, it makes sense. I'd better get on with making dinner." And I flounced off to the kitchen, no doubt leaving a strong smell of burning martyr in my wake.

Two hours later, everything was ready. My morel, tofu and kale filo parcels were keeping warm in the oven. There was an elegant salad of endive, orange and pomegranate with a sumac dressing, and even a vegan chocolate mousse I'd found a recipe for online, made with carob and avocado. I suspected it was going to taste disgusting, but it's the thought that counts. I would have loved to have changed out of my work clothes and into something a bit nicer, but our bedroom door remained firmly closed. I poured myself a glass of wine, sat in front of the telly and seethed.

It was another hour before Erica surfaced, and I'd been practising deep yoga breathing and reminding myself that she was the mother of the man I loved, the work she did was selfless and incredibly challenging and if I made an effort, we might be able to rebuild our relationship. So when she emerged from our bedroom, obviously just out of a hot bath and wearing fluffy slippers and an outsized jumper that looked more suitable for an expedition to the Arctic than for our centrally-heated flat, I greeted her with as enthusiastic a hug as I could muster.

"Hello, Erica, how lovely to see you. Did you have an okay flight?"

"Hello, Pippa. Don't you look well? You've put on weight, haven't you?" she said. "My, but this flat is cold! I do find it difficult to be comfortable in a cold place."

"I expect it's having come from a hot climate," I said. "I'll turn up the heating."

"You'll feel warmer when you've eaten, Mum," Nick said. "Pippa's made a wonderful welcome dinner."

So I thought. But apparently I had forgotten (and Nick, who'd lived with the woman for the first eighteen years of his life, had never known) that Erica had a severe allergy to mushrooms, so my filo parcels went down like a bucket of cold sick. Erica scrutinised the sumac salad suspiciously and then said, "In cold weather, I always find that what I really fancy is some soup. Isn't it funny the things you miss most when you're away from home for a long time? For me, it's Campbells tomato soup! I'm sure you've got some, haven't you? It was always Nick's favourite treat growing up."

In all the time I've known him, I have never known Nick to even mention tinned soup.

"There's some homemade tomato and basil soup in the freezer," I said. "We could warm it up if you like?"

"Oh, no, Pippa, I don't want you to go to any trouble! I'd be quite happy with a tin, but if you haven't got any…"

So of course Nick went out to the corner shop and bought up their entire supply of Campbell's Cream of Tomato and Erica happily slurped some down in spite of it being absolutely packed with cow's milk and gluten. And then when I offered her some of the avocado chocolate mousse she said, "Thank you, Pippa, I've had quite enough. You do have to watch your figure at my age! But you must understand the importance of that, of course, working with food all the time."

And I remembered her earlier comment about my weight and had to say I wouldn't have any pudding either, actually, and watch Nick scoff the lot of it. He said it was really good, too.

That night in the too-narrow-for-two sofabed, made even narrower by Spanx, who settled down sideways between us and stretched out to his full length, I downloaded an event countdown app on to my phone. It was clearly designed for weddings, with lots of animated bells and doves and things, but I set it up to keep track of the days remaining until Erica went back to Liberia. Okay, that happened to be two days after our wedding day, but I knew which event I was looking forward to more.

Chapter Six

From: nick@digitaldrawingboard.com
To: caroline.travis@khanclarkegardner.co.uk
Subject: Friday

Hey Callie

Hope all's good with you. This is a very cheeky request so please say no if it's a problem. Pip and I arranged to go down to Brocklebury Manor for an initial chat about colour schemes etc on Friday afternoon. We were meeting Imogen, the events manager, at 4.30pm. But now Pip's got to go dress shopping on Wednesday and she says there's no way she can do two afternoons off work in one week (I don't know if she's told you about the South Africa trip she's got coming up? It's going to be amazing but take up loads of her time, and she's mega-stressed as it is). Anyway she says I'm the one who knows about design and she's happy to leave all that stuff up to me. But I don't want to screw it up! Any chance you could come along in your capacity as Best Woman and stop me having a rush of blood to the head and saying I want blue and white stripes on everything to match the QPR strip, or something?

No bother if you can't make it, but I'll be pathetically grateful if you can!

Nick x

"**B**ut there must be a particular style you had in mind," Katharine said, sipping her latte. I hoped she wasn't regretting her kind offer to take an afternoon off work to come wedding dress-shopping – so far she had managed to elicit very little meaningful information from me.

"I don't know!" I squirmed in my chair. "It's so difficult. All the dresses I've seen in magazines and on Pinterest are so… I don't know. *Bridal.*"

"But Pippa, you're going to be a bride! What kind of dress do you expect to wear? Business casual? Sexy zombie?"

I laughed. "I know, I'm being stupid. I suppose I never imagined needing to buy a wedding dress. Until recently I thought that if I ever got married – which we weren't going to, remember – I'd be in my jeans down the pub or maybe in a bikini on a beach somewhere. But I don't think that would go down so well at Brocklebury Manor. Maybe when I see The One, I'll know."

"If only you had a bit more time, we could have gone for something bespoke," Katharine sighed. "But it is what it is. You'll find something gorgeous, just you wait and see. And they're very good on trend-led stuff at Bliss Bridal, they won't put you in a meringue. Now, we'd better get going, our appointment is in twenty minutes."

Call me naive, but I genuinely hadn't realised that you had to make an appointment to try on wedding dresses, as if you were viewing a house or something. I'd assumed you just turned up at a shop, tried stuff on, and if you saw something you liked, you bought it. Like, you know, buying a dress. But Katharine soon set me straight when I called her to request moral support. She'd also given me a stern talking-to about how I must make sure to wear a strapless bra and nude-coloured pants, do my makeup and put my hair

up, and then she'd secured us an appointment to view...
sorry, try on dresses at Bliss Bridal.

"They've got a really good range of off-the-peg styles
and they do super-fast alterations," Katharine went on, as
we hurried down South Molton Street. "My friend Linda got
her dress from there and she's five foot eleven and a size six
so she really struggles to find clothes that fit. You're a much
easier shape."

I found it hard to summon up any sympathy for Linda,
because frankly hers was a first-world problem if ever there
was one. All my life I've struggled with jeans that make my
arse look the size of Belgium, tops that look fine on the
hanger but reveal an indecent amount of cleavage on me,
and skirts that are supposed to be elegantly on-the-knee but
hit me unflatteringly at the widest part of my calves. Which
is why my fashion purchases are sparse at best and tend to
centre around nail polish and shoes.

"Here we are." Katharine pushed open the heavy glass
door, which had an ornamental gold handle shaped like a
B. It was like walking into a posh hotel – there was a vast,
glittering chandelier, acres of marble tiles and gold brocade chaise-longues dotted about. And wedding dresses, of
course. Loads of them, in heavy plastic covers on rails and
on an assortment of uniformly tall, thin mannequins.

Katharine accosted a tall, thin woman in a tailored black
dress. "Hello, we've got an appointment for Pippa Martin."

"Let me see." She swiped her tablet to life and tapped the
screen. "Yes, we're expecting you. Welcome to Bliss Bridal!
Chelsea is your consultant today. If you'd like to come over
here and have a seat, I'll get you a glass of sparkling wine
and let her know you're here."

We sat for a bit and watched as girls, accompanied by
the sales assistants – sorry, consultants – and their mums

or their friends, approached the huge, curtained fitting rooms. It was weird to see the transformation that took place in all of them. They'd go into the cubicles in their jeans and boots, looking completely normal, and when they emerged, they were brides. Whether the dresses were white or ivory, straight or meringue-like; whether the girls' faces looked happy and excited or anxious and cross, they were all, quite suddenly, brides. Even the girl who left her Uggs on underneath her frock. I took another sip of sparkling wine and felt a bit sick.

"Sorry to keep you waiting. I'm Chelsea." Our consultant had poker-straight fair hair and the longest eyelash extensions I've ever seen. She looked about twelve. "You must be so excited about finding a dress! With your figure, you can wear absolutely anything!"

"It's not for me, actually," Katharine said. "It's for Pippa."

I could see Chelsea blushing through her layers of concealer. "I'm so sorry," she muttered. "Pippa, lovely to meet you. I'm new here so this is still really exciting for me too. Have you had any thoughts about the sort of thing you're after?"

"I just don't know," I said feebly. "Something plain? Or maybe something in a kind of fifties style? Or maybe something in a colour that's not white or ivory?"

"Some brides have their wedding theme or colour scheme as a starting point," said Chelsea, doing her best to be helpful. "What's yours?"

"Theme?" I said, blankly. It was a wedding – surely that *was* the theme?

"Like mine was inspired by *Gatsby*," Katharine said. "So we had cocktails and the wedding car was a vintage Rolls – I wanted cream but we couldn't find one anywhere and I wanted a cigarette holder but not being a smoker, that would have been a bit pointless – and the dress was flapper-style. You remember, Pippa."

"Lots of brides this year have chosen a Bond theme," said Chelsea. "With the men in dinner jackets. It looks dead glamorous. Also, birds are going to be huge next year. And Scrabble is a key trend."

Scrabble? How on earth did you have a scrabble-themed wedding dress? Would it have lots of squares on it? Would everyone have to stand around me arguing about whether proper nouns were allowed?

"And I remember reading somewhere that laser-cutting is the new lace," said Katharine.

They both smiled hopefully at me. "All those sound really interesting," I said.

"Let's have a little look at some of the styles we have in stock." Chelsea sat down next to me and fired up her tablet.

Half an hour later, I stood in front of the huge, gilt-framed mirror in my fifth dress. I presume it was inspired by the fashion-forward avian trend, because the skirt was covered in feathers in shades of yellow from cream to canary.

"Now that's just stunning on you," Chelsea said.

"Not right with your colouring," said Katharine tactfully. I thought, and I'm sure she did too, that I looked like Big Bird. Which would have been great, obviously, had we opted for the lesser-known Sesame Street theme.

"One of the biggest colour trends of the year is called Radiant Orchid," said Chelsea. "It's a more vibrant, but cooler shade of blush. Have a look at this."

She produced yet another frock, in a colour that I can only describe as mauve. I recoiled slightly, but obediently tried it on and looked in the mirror. Big Bird had been replaced by the Queen. All I needed to complete the look was a pair of clumpy black shoes, gloves and a big handbag.

"Maybe not that one," said Katharine.

Even though it was beginning to look like I'd never find a dress, I was increasingly grateful for Katherine's candour. I'd tried a dress with a high halter neck that made me look like my boobs were somewhere down round my waist, and she'd diplomatically pointed out that I might need something a little more low-cut. I'd tried a corseted, strapless number that gave me an even bigger cleavage at the back than at the front and made my upper arms look like something an all-in wrestler would be proud of, and she'd rejected it with a firm shake of her head. I'd tried a clingy column dress with ruching over the front that Chelsea assured us suited absolutely everyone.

"Well, it doesn't suit Pippa," Katharine said, in a tone that brooked no argument.

"How about something backless?" Chelsea suggested.

"I love backless dresses," I said. It's true – I adore the screen-goddess glamour of gowns with low backs, but I've never been able to wear them because of the necessity of industrial-strength scaffolding to hold my chest in place. I live in hope that someone, some day will invent a strapless, backless bra that actually works, possibly involving cleverly concealed helium inserts, but it has yet to happen.

And sure enough, the backless dress, a sheath of heavy, draped satin in the palest grey, looked marvellous from the back and woeful from the front.

"Of course, when you're standing at the altar, the back is what people will be looking at," said Chelsea hopefully.

"Yes, but she can't spend all day turning her back on her guests. It's lovely, Pippa, but it just doesn't work on you."

By the time we reached dress number fifteen, I could see that Chelsea's patience was beginning to wear thin. All around us, girls were gasping in delight as they found the dress of their dreams, or agonising as they attempted to choose between two near-identical, near-perfect candidates. One actually bought two dresses, saying, "I can't decide! I'll make up my mind on the day!"

I was the problem child, the one who couldn't find a frock.

"That's not quite right either, is it?" said Katharine, looking critically at the full, frilly skirt that made me look like I belonged on top of a roll of loo paper.

"Not quite," I agreed. "I'm sorry, Chelsea, you've been so kind and we've taken up so much of your time but I don't think it's going to happen for me today."

Sunk in deepest gloom, I let Katharine steer me out of the shop.

"I've been so useless," I said. "It's just that none of them were quite right."

"Nonsense!" she said. "Your dress must be perfect for you, otherwise there's no point in buying it. We'll find The One, I promise."

I thought, I've only got a couple of months and I'm not even going to be here for half the time. If The One's out there somewhere it's going to have to hurry up and show itself.

"We could pop into Selfridges or Liberty and have a look there," suggested Katharine. "They don't have quite as wide a range of styles but you never know."

But I'd stopped listening to her. I was staring into the window of a shop where, surrounded by embroidered bags, jewel-coloured velvet scarves and ornate hairpins, were the most beautiful shoes I've ever seen in my life. They were silver lace, with sparkly straps and rows of tiny diamonds on the buckles. Just looking at them made we want to dance, even though I can't dance to save my life.

"Katharine, look at those!"

"What, the shoes?"

"Yes! I have to try them on."

And this time, when I stood in front of the mirror, even though I was just wearing my jeans, rolled up over my ankles, and my outdoor coat, I felt it. The shoes made my legs look long and slim. They made my feet look dainty and perfect. They matched the pewter polish on my toenails.

"I've found my shoes!" I was grinning like a lunatic. Katharine looked faintly bemused.

"Well, whatever dress you end up buying, you'll need to wear something on your feet," she said. "Those are lovely, and they're in amazing condition considering they're vintage." I hadn't even noticed.

"I can get married in a onesie and not care, so long as I get to wear these," I said, happily handing over my credit card to buy my wedding shoes.

"I was just hoping for a cup of tea," Erica said, hovering in the kitchen doorway, "but I don't want to get in your way." It was Friday night and I was in the kitchen chopping up the makings of yet another vegan dinner. This time I was having a stab at a South-East Asian treatment involving a great deal of ginger and a huge pile of bird's-eye chillies. I was thoroughly sick of Erica refusing my cooking for increasingly random reasons ("Oh, thank you, Pippa, but I don't really care for quinoa." "What I really fancy is a rice cake with Marmite. It's impossible to get hold of in Liberia, you know." And the particularly crushing time she simply looked at a bowl of spelt risotto with roast pumpkin and said, "I'm not very hungry, actually. I think I'll go and lie down," as if the very sight of it had sapped her will to live). If she was going to turn her nose up at the fruits of my labour, it might as well be because they were hot enough to blow her annoying head off.

And in case you think I'm being mean to a poor, defence-less widow, I feel compelled to point out that the one time Nick made dinner, Erica devoured two massive bowls of dhal and kept telling me how lucky I was that he was willing to 'help in the kitchen'.

"Why don't you sit down and relax and I'll bring it to you?" I said. Deeply as I resented playing skivvy to my future mother-in-law, I had learned that to allow Erica to do any-thing for herself was to invite disaster. There was the time she asked to iron a pair of her jeans (*who* irons jeans? Who?) and took it upon herself to do all our stuff too, and ironed all the silver foil off my new Traffic People top. There was the time I'd come home from work to find the flat thick with black smoke because she'd tried to make some of 'Nick's favourite peanut butter cookies' and put the oven on to grill instead of bake. There was the time she bought some flowers to brighten up the place, except they were lil-ies and could have poisoned Spanx. And in spite of this, Spanx, the traitor, had adopted Erica as some sort of idol, following her around slavishly and leaping on to her lap the second she sat down.

I was laying the table, plonking down plates and cutlery with an undue amount of crashing, when Nick came home. He hung up his coat and kissed Erica, then kissed me.

"So how did it go at Brocklebury Manor?" I asked, when I'd finished dishing up bowls of rice and Thai curry.

"Brilliant," Nick said. "Callie was a total star, she's got all sorts of great ideas that we discussed with Imogen. Because the wedding's going to be in February, she thought it would be good to have a winter theme – not that we've got much choice; if we wanted peonies and roses and things it would cost a fortune. But anyway, Callie suggested going for lots of bare, silver branches and white-on-white textural stuff. Imogen also thinks simple is the way to go."

"Perhaps little galvanised pots with live snowdrops in them as table centrepieces," said Erica, to my surprise. She'd barely mentioned the wedding to me.

"Great idea," said Nick. "And Callie found a tutorial on YouTube that shows you how to make wreaths out of white paper flowers with fake pearls, so she says she's going to try that and see if they look any good."

"I was reading *Martha Stewart Weddings* on the flight here," said Erica. "There was an article in there about hand-stitching embellishment on to card in wool for invitations and placecards. They looked charming." If Erica's embroidery skills were anything like her ironing skills, I thought, our wedding invitations would literally be writ in blood.

"Cool!" said Nick. "Oh, and Hugh's going to put together some suggested menus. As soon as he sends them over, I'll forward them to you, Pip, because I know you'll want to be in charge of the food. But anyway, Imogen also showed us pictures of a winter wedding they did where they made, like, a tent of fairy lights suspended from the ceiling in the hall, which looked wicked, so I think we should have that. And mirrors on all the tables to reflect the light."

"Queen Anne's lace is in season in winter," Erica said. "It's very useful for bouquets. Creates a lovely ethereal effect, a bit like mist." Well, who knew? The woman is a florist as well as a nurse and a food critic, I thought sourly.

"Let me make a note of that," Nick put his iPad on the table. "Queen Mary's what?"

"Queen Anne's lace," Erica said. "And of course, you'll want to think about your attendants and what they'll wear."

"Callie says she has to wait until Pippa's chosen a dress before she even thinks about hers," Nick said. "She suggested you two meet up and go shopping next week sometime, Pip. I think she's worried about running out of time."

"I've chosen my shoes," I said defensively. "And there's plenty of time. It's only a dress."

"And of course you'll have Susannah's little ones as flower girls, won't you? So fortunate to have twins in the family and Bella and Katniss look like little angels. And Deirdre's tot, Albie, for your page boy?"

Erica was addressing all her remarks to Nick, not even looking at me.

"Good idea," Nick said. "You're up for that, aren't you, Pip?"

No, I wasn't. The shameful truth is I'm not great with kids. Mum says that if I have my own some day, I'll change my mind, but I'm not convinced. To be honest, all my encounters with other people's babies leave me feeling a bit bewildered. When they aren't crying they're cute enough, I suppose, when they're just warm, heavy weights in your arms, like cats only floppier and less squirmy, without the purring. So like cats, only not as good. But then they poo or start crying or whatever and it's a relief to give them back to their parents. And then when they get a bit bigger they're all about needing to be entertained and having screaming meltdowns for no reason, and I never know what to do with them and am constantly worrying about saying or doing something that will trigger a meltdown. And then when they get bigger than that, they make inappropriate comments in loud voices, like, "Mummy, why has that lady got funny hair?" (Yes, I speak from experience.)

So, no, Nick, I don't particularly want your nieces and your second cousin twice removed or whatever he is to take centre stage at our wedding, I thought. But it wasn't a conversation I wanted to have – in fact, the subject of children was one I studiously avoided raising with Nick.

I felt a familiar, horrible stab of guilt, and realised that while Nick and Erica had been excitedly making their plans, I'd basically been sitting there sulking. I was worse than a child myself. These were Nick's family, his only nieces. And Nick doesn't share my ambivalence about kids – he absolutely adores them. He spends an hour on Skype to Suze every Sunday and most of that is cooing over Bella and Katniss. And besides, he was doing all the organising of the wedding while I buggered off to South Africa. Okay, it was work, but the fact was, I really wanted to go. And Nick and Callie were taking on all this hard work so that I could.

"That's an absolutely lovely idea," I said. "Little flower girls, and a pageboy! Cute!"

When Nick got up to clear away the plates, and I noticed that Erica had eaten every bit of her curry, and even cleaned out the little dish of extra chopped chilli I'd put on the table. Frankly, I was impressed. Even Nick, who eats phall without flinching and always asks for extra naga chilli when we get takeaway from the Ivory Arch, had had to wipe his eyes before wading back into my Thai curry that night. Perhaps there's some genetic factor at play when it comes to heat tolerance, I reflected.

"Thank you, Nicky," Erica said to Nick as he removed her plate. Then she turned to me. "Pippa, that was delicious. Thank you so much."

You could have knocked me down with a bird's-eye chilli. I said it was a pleasure, and we had a quite civilised chat about Liberian cuisine (wall-to-wall cassava and plantain, apparently, and something called 'beef internal soup', which Erica actually shuddered when she mentioned). She said she'd got into the habit of buying lethally hot sauce and eating it with pretty much everything.

I resolved there and then to make more of an effort not only to make Erica feel welcome, but actually to get to know her, and even, if such a thing were possible, to learn to like her again.

That night, as we curled up on the sofabed and I writhed around trying to get myself in the only position in which the spring didn't dig into my back, I said to Nick, "You know, I think your Mum might be warming to me, just a tiny bit."

Nick looked up from his iPad and said, "Have a look at this. There's someone on the *Inspired Bride* forum who's having a winter wedding, and she's posted loads of cool ideas. What do you think about painting pinecones white and using them in with the flowers and stuff?"

I said, "Mmm, very pretty," trying to imagine a world in which I might have the time and inclination to spray gloss enamel on to the reproductive organs of conifers. I put my head on his chest and he squeezed me close.

"Where's Spanx?" I said sleepily. "He hasn't come to bed with us."

Nick said, "I think he's in with Mum. He really seems to like her."

And I realised that in my campaign to get on better with Erica, I was going to have to deal not only with my long-standing mistrust of her, but also with being jealous of my own cat.

CHAPTER SEVEN

From: nick@digitaldrawingboard.com
To: pippa.martin@falconis.co.uk
Subject: Strict instructions

Hey beautiful

Guess what? Mum's off to see Deirdre in Norfolk so we have the flat to ourselves tonight. And I'm going to take you out for dinner then take you home and we can take advantage of her absence! I also have a surprise for you. So:

1. Don't work too hard.
2. Meet me in the Aqua bar in the Shard at half seven.
3. Wear... actually, I'll leave that up to you.

(Do you reckon this counts as one of those date nights you said Katharine was on about? I do.)

N xx

"Hi Florence," said Eloise. "No, they didn't have it in a size eight, I'm afraid. They've got a ten or a six. Would you still like me to order it for you? Okay, I'll ring them back and check whether it comes up small. No problem. Just a second, I'll see if he's free."

Guido made furious 'cut her off' gestures, then said, "All right, I'll take it. Thanks Eloise."

For the next ten minutes he listened with a face like Kevin the Teenager. Then he put the phone down on his desk and went to the fridge and poured a glass of San Pellegrino, then wandered back and picked the phone up again and listened for another few seconds. Then he went outside and had a fag before returning to his desk.

"You're quite right, darling. It won't happen again. Of course I was! I listen to everything you say. All right, darling. No, I won't be late. Nine thirty latest. Ciao ciao.

"For fuck's sake," he muttered. "Right, I'm going to the restaurant for evening service." I caught Eloise's eye. We both knew this would mean Guido getting home well after midnight and facing Florence's fury. "You girls knock off early. You deserve it." He put on his coat, turned off his mobile and left.

"Great!" said Tamar. "I'll be on time for my yoga class for once."

"I can meet Dean and go to the pub," said Eloise. "What about you, Pippa?"

"Nick's taking me out for dinner," I said. "But we're not meeting until half seven, so I may as well stay here and see if I can nail that soup recipe." I thought for a moment. "Actually, to hell with it. I'm going shopping. There's no way these jeans are worthy of the Shard."

So I got the Tube to Stratford and splashed out on a gorgeous, butter-soft leather pencil skirt that was actually the right length for a change, a cranberry-coloured cashmere jumper and a new lipstick that matched, because I'd read on one of the beauty blogs recommended by Katharine that this was currently a Thing. I bought a bra and matching knickers in black satin, trimmed with little frills, shoved my old underwear into the Victoria's Secret carrier bag and replaced my warm, comfy opaque tights with hold-ups, trusting that they'd do what they said on the tin. And although all that lot made me twenty minutes late to meet Nick, I reckoned he'd probably think it was worth the wait.

The elevator swooshed me up to the thirty-first floor, and I stepped out to see the lights of London spread out beneath me. I felt a huge grin spread over my face, and spotted Nick waiting at a table for two, watching me take it all in. I was glad of my new clothes and make-up; everyone in the room looked impossibly glamorous and even Nick had abandoned his usual leather jacket and was wearing a charcoal blazer over one of his less shabby pairs of jeans and a purple shirt.

"Bit of a step up from the Grope and Wanker," I said, kissing him.

Nick adopted a cheesy, husky voice. "Because you're worth it," he said. "And you are, too. You look bloody gorgeous. Every man in the room was eying up your arse when you walked to the table."

"Shut up!" I rolled my eyes at him, feeling secretly pleased.

"Now, you need a drink. I'm having a Sazerac, no pints of lager tonight."

"In that case, I'll have..." I scanned the cocktail menu. "A cucumber martini. No – I want to try the one made with tea. Or the one that's supposed to taste like scones with jam. Or..."

"You can have them all, as far as I'm concerned. We're celebrating."

"We are?"

"Pip, you're very beautiful and I love you very much, but sometimes you can be a bit dense. We're getting married, remember? We've booked our venue, you've tried on dresses, I've appointed a best man... But isn't there something I left out? Something that normally happens quite early on in the process?"

I took a sip of my drink and ate an olive. "The bit where my Dad says you'll marry me over his dead body?"

"Pippa!" Nick laughed. "No, not that. The bit where I take your hand," he took it, "and you close your eyes," I closed them, "and I say something about this being just a small token to express how I feel about you."

I felt the cool touch of metal on my hand, and opened my eyes. Sparkling on my third finger was the most beautiful ring I've ever seen. It was a delicate platinum band, and in the centre were two sparkling diamonds, one on either side of a clear, blue-green stone.

"It's a tourmaline," Nick said. He looked down at my hand and smiled. "I took a photo of you to a jeweller and asked for something the same colour as your eyes. I could have used a chart – Pantone 2229 is closest, I reckon. But I thought a photo would be better."

"Thank you," my voice came out a bit croaky, so I tried again. "Thank you, Nick. It's perfect. I love it. I love you."

"Just as well," Nick said, "Or I would've had to find someone else with the same colour eyes to give it to, and that might have taken me a while."

All through dinner, I was conscious of the new weight of the ring on my hand, its hardness against my skin. Every now and then I'd catch myself looking down at it, tilting my hand so it caught the light, and smile, and when I looked up I'd see Nick watching me and smiling too. Even though the food was gorgeous, I couldn't eat very much and nor did he.

"Shall we walk home?" said Nick, when he'd paid the bill.

"Let's."

We strolled along the river in the chilly darkness, the lights of Tower Bridge reflecting in the water. We didn't talk about the wedding. I told Nick about Guido letting Florence complain to an unlistened-to phone for quarter of an hour and he laughed and promised he'd never do that to me. He told me that Spanx had brought him another pair of my pants from the drawer as a present, and we congratulated ourselves on the cuteness and cleverness of our cat.

When we got home, Nick put the kettle on for tea and I took off my makeup and my uncomfortable boots, and we sat on the sofa with my feet in his lap and watched a couple of episodes of *EastEnders* that I'd missed. Gradually Nick slid down the cushions until he was lying next to me, and I turned away from the screen and kissed him.

His warm hands slid under my jumper and he pulled it over my head, then he unzipped my skirt and eased that off too. I lay back in my new underwear and smiled at him, and saw his face go all sort of still with desire.

"Pippa." His voice sounded a bit croaky.

"Yes?"

"God, you look… you're amazing."

I sat up and slowly undid his belt. I ran my hands over his familiar hardness, breathing in the smell of him, the juniper shower gel he likes mixed with something that was just Nick. I took him in my mouth, my eyes never leaving his face, and heard him gasp with pleasure.

Then two things happened at once. Spanx came trotting through from our bedroom, carrying a pair of long thermal knickers in his mouth, which definitely weren't mine. He dropped them at Nick's feet and miaowed proudly, just as we heard Erica's key in the front door.

"So I've been making an effort," I told Mum. She and Dad were in London to see Benedict Cumberbatch do Shakespeare and 'gain inspiration', Mum said, or 'see how it ought to be done', according to Dad, and we were having lunch at Wagamama, which is Mum's favourite restaurant in the whole world, bless her. "I thought things were going a bit better but then the last couple of days Erica has been totally off with me again. She hates me."

"She doesn't hate you, darling," Mum loaded her chopsticks with ramen. "She just feels threatened that another woman is taking her son away from her, as she sees it. It's difficult for mothers, you know. That's partly why I'm glad we only had you. I would have made a rotten mother-in-law to another woman, although of course we adore Nick."

"And that's the other thing," I said. "I wish he'd stand up to her sometimes. He sees her constantly criticising me and just ignores it."

"Does she constantly criticise you, or is that just how it feels to you?" Mum asked.

"Yes!" I said. "The other day she asked me, 'What's your day for high-level dusting, Pippa?' I don't even know what that is! I thought she meant, like, intensive dusting, with Mr Sheen and stuff. I never do that, obviously. But she meant dusting cobwebs off the ceiling. Does anyone actually *dust the ceiling*? If there's a cobweb or something up there I make Nick spend two hours searching the flat for spiders, and then maybe a week or so later we'll get around to hoovering the cobweb. But we don't do *high-level dusting*. And then she asked me where I kept my hand tea towels. As opposed to dish tea towels. And when I told her that all tea towels are alike to me she looked at me like I was the scuzziest person ever. And she's doing a massive charm offensive on Spanx and he won't sleep on our bed when she's there. And the way she sneezes is really annoying. She gets this expression on her face like a dying frog for about two minutes and then she just goes 'tfffp' through her nose instead of sneezing properly. It drives me *mad*. And every time she sends a text, she writes it down on paper first before she types it into her phone. Why would you do that?"

Mum had stopped eating her ramen, and she was laughing at me.

"You know, when your father and I were first married, his mother came for tea," she said. "I'd got everything carefully ready, with a hideous embroidered tray cloth she'd given us as a wedding present out on the table. I even baked a cake. When I poured the tea, I asked her if she wanted milk and sugar, and she peered into my sugar bowl and said, 'Do you not have sugar cubes, Justine?' Exactly like that. So the next time she came round, I'd bought sugar cubes. And then she said, 'Do you not have brown sugar?' And so it went on. By the time we'd been married a year I had every kind of sugar known to man in my kitchen: cubes, two different kinds of brown, golden caster sugar, those wooden sticks with crystallised sugar on them – everything. And then she announced that she'd stopped taking sugar in her tea."

When I was growing up, I remember there always being about eight different kinds of sugar in the kitchen, even though Mum and Dad both drink their coffee black and unsweetened. It was great when I was teaching myself to bake. And now I knew why.

"What did you do?" I asked.

Mum shrugged. "I smiled sweetly, and gave her what she wanted. And when she was being really impossible, I used to write 'fuck you' on the roof of my mouth with my tongue."

"Mum!" I burst out laughing.

"I did," Mum said, a bit smugly. "And after forty years of marriage, I have a good relationship with your grandmother. I just had to pick my battles, and try to find common ground with her. And of course, we had the most important common ground there is: we love your father and we love you.

You have that with Erica. So try and find other common ground too, and things will improve. I promise."

"She does like chillies," I said grudgingly. It was something. Not enough to make me overlook why I really detested Erica so much, but something.

"There you go then!" Mum said. "It might not feel like much, but it's a start. 'O gentle daughter, upon the heat and flame of thy distemper sprinkle cool patience,'" she declaimed to me and the rest of Wagamama.

So I took that as my cue to ask her how the play was going, and she told me about that and the garden.

Then she said, "I bumped into dear Callie in Waitrose last week, with her flatmate. She's looking very thin, poor girl. Is something the matter?"

I said, "She's stressed about something, but she won't talk about it. When I ask she says everything's fine, she's just busy at work. But I'm not sure. It can't still be about David, they split up almost two years ago."

"Her flatmate – Phoebe – she seems like a lovely girl," said Mum.

"She is nice," I said. "She has an awful time, though. Her dad's a bit of a monster. He's disabled, apparently he has a bad back, and he can't work or even walk very far. He spends most of his time in bed doing crossword puzzles, Phoebe says, and making Phoebe's Mum's life hell. He's got a horrible temper. Callie told me that when Phoebe comes back from seeing them she cries, almost every time."

"Pain can make people extremely bloody-minded," said Mum. She looked at me shrewdly. "Don't let their friendship make you feel any less close to Callie, Pippa. Old friends are far too precious to let slip away. Now, I must be off and meet your father for our matinée."

And, with her wise words (and another of Gertrude's speeches) ringing in my ears, I went back to the office. I resolved to ring Callie and arrange to meet up soon, and I was determined, too, to make even more of an effort to be friends with Erica again. After all, it wasn't like she hadn't liked me in the beginning. She did – she'd been really warm and sweet when Nick and I first started going out. She treated me like a grown-up. She asked me about myself, my beliefs, my ambitions and seemed to actually listen to my answers. By the time Nick and I had been going out for two years, I thought of her as a friend. I even thought, as teenagers do, how much cooler and prettier and generally better she was in every way than my own unreasonable, embarrassing mother who didn't understand me. And that was what led to the lapse of judgement that scuppered my relationship with Erica, for which I apparently still hadn't finished paying the price.

Despite Mum's good advice, when I got home that night and Nick and Erica were out, I felt quietly relieved. I remembered Nick saying that were going to visit a cousin in East Finchley and would be back late, so Spanx and I played a game of Hunt the Socks and then I had a luxurious hot bath, painted my toenails lilac and ordered a pizza. Lacy Garter of *Inspired Bride* would have been shocked by my gluttony, I thought – she was all for pre-wedding diets, or rather 'healthy eating programmes' as she called them. I opened a Diet Coke to go with it (at least Lacy would approve of that), and sat down at Nick's desk to eat. I found the USB Stick of All Knowledge underneath the gas bill, and decided to have a quick look and see what he'd added.

Alongside Katharine's master folder, 'Iain and Katharine September Wedding', Nick had created his own, imaginatively labelled 'Nick and Pippa February Wedding'. I clicked on it.

Blimey, he'd been busy. Inside were sub-folders for flowers, food, entertainment, attendants, decor, favours, speeches, vows, transport, photographers, videographers, cakes – it went on and on. There was even one for bride's dresses. I felt a prickle of resentment. In his emails, I'd noticed, there was a thread of about thirty messages between him and Imogen, another of about forty between him and Iain, and a third of about sixty between him and Callie, all entitled 'Wedding'. I hovered over them with the mouse, then stopped myself. Even if these were emails about my wedding, they were private, they were Nick's and it would be wrong to read them. If he wanted to tell me about them, he would. I'd snooped before, and I was going to stick to my resolve never to do so again.

It took me a couple of minutes to get on to the internet, because Nick works on a Mac and I've never quite got the hang of it. I thought I'd have a look at inspiredbride. com and have a good laugh at the wedding obsessives on the discussion forum. But then, instead of Nick's usual Digital Drawing Board website, where he showcases his latest work and blogs about design ideas, a new homepage came up.

It was a blog and, typically of Nick, a sleek and elegantly designed one. The header was an image of frosty pinecones, and it was called 'A Groom With A View'. Well, this wasn't private, was it? It was a blog. I was allowed to read it, just like anyone else. And people were reading it. I skimmed down through the posts and they all had loads of responses – about thirty for the most recent, dwindling to four or five for the earlier ones, with the inaugural one having garnered an impressive fifty-eight. Eloise writes Guido's blog at work and she's happy if she gets twenty responses to a post, and he's an actual celebrity. I clicked on the first link.

The title was 'A Planning Man'.

Hi, blog followers (all none of you, lol) I'm Nick, and I'm a graphic designer living and working in south London. A week ago I got engaged to my gorgeous partner, Pippa. It was all a bit unexpected, to say the least. But now we've got just four months to plan a wedding. Not long, is it (fnar)? Since our proposal (more about that later!) I've realised that there's far more to planning a wedding than I'd ever imagined. And I want to make sure we (okay, I – but that's another one for a future post, I think) get it right. So I'm going to use this blog, along with Pinterest and the advice of the good people on Inspired Bride online (where's the Inspired Groom site, hey?) to plan the amazing day Pippa deserves.

I hadn't got a clue there would be such a lot to think about. But after buying a few magazines and browsing online, I've realised I've got one hell of a busy few weeks ahead of me. I hope this blog will help me keep track of it all, and I'll be using it, along with all the other great resources out there, to look for inspiration and – like, duh, obviously – advice when I start to lose the plot! So, first off, if anyone's reading this, what did you love about your wedding and what sucked? And what does a clueless bridegroom-to-be (God, typing that feels bollock-shrinkingly scary!) need to know?

He'd obviously linked to the post on Twitter or on the *Inspired Bride* forum or something, because there was a rash of gushy comments from people saying things like, "OMG, it's tremaze to see a man so involved in wedding planning! Wish I could get my H2B to think beyond how many strippers he's going to have on his stag night, rofl." And from someone calling herself Hipster Bride, "Loving your blog, Nick! Can't wait to see how the planning progresses, I've signed up for updates." And, "You go, dude! Heather and I got married last summer and we did all the planning together. It was awesome and such a special day. Well done, I'll look forward to future posts. Matt."

Most recently, the quality of the comments seemed to have deteriorated a bit. There was, "Hi, I'm Damian and Im a profesional weding photographer based in Grimsby. I offer a bispoke service that will produce an unforgetable record of you're big day for not much £. Visit my website for details and prices." Then, "Hot cum sluts in grl-on-grl action live online NOW!". And one that said, "You cuntin loser, grow a pare of balls & tell ur bitch to get back in the kitchen were she belogns." And finally, "Well, hello there! Check your PMs, I've inboxed you. Bxx."

Then I realised that the last few had all been posted in the last half an hour, which meant that Nick hadn't had a chance to moderate them, which in turn meant that he was weeding out unwanted content pretty frequently. The last post, though, there was something about it that was different from the others, and something familiar about the way it made me feel. But then, I remembered, I shouldn't really be reading any of it. I felt as if I was simultaneously spying and being spied on. Quickly, I closed the window, willing Nick's computer to go the fuck to sleep.

I put my pizza box in the recycling bin and got under the duvet with Spanx, and lay awake until Nick and Erica came home. Then the cat jumped out of my arms and ran to say hello to them, and I pretended to be asleep.

CHAPTER EIGHT

From: nick@digitaldrawingboard.com
To: theamazingarchibald@hotmail.com
Subject: Wedding booking

Hi

I was given your email address by Matt Price. He mentioned that you took care of the kids' entertainment at his and Lisa's wedding earlier in the year, and recommended you very highly. I know it's short notice, but is there any chance you're free on the first Saturday in February? Our wedding is at Brocklebury Manor in Hampshire and there will probably be about twenty kids there, aged from 11 down to 2. What I had in mind was a few magic tricks and then maybe some games, just to keep them busy during the speeches and first dance. We'd need you for about two hours in total – I'm hoping that most of them will have been taken off to bed by about 8pm.

If you could let me know your availability and quote, that would be great.

Many thanks
Nick

"**O**ooh, that feels amazing," Callie said, her voice muffled by the massage bed. "Mmm. I actually think I'm about to slip into a coma of bliss."

We were lying next to each other, with two therapists simultaneously gliding hot stones over our skin. There was whale music wafting away in the background and the room smelled strongly of neroli oil. Nick had practically had to force me to take a day off work and take advantage of the 'Ladies' Pamper Package' that Brocklebury Manor had thrown in for free with our wedding booking, but I was glad he had. After two weeks of working eleven-hour days, I was knackered and the wallow in the hot tub, session in the steam room and now the massage had made me feel gorgeously relaxed. I was even looking forward to the light and healthful salad lunch with unlimited fruit tea and still or sparkling water that would follow.

Callie deserved a treat too. She'd been with Nick to appointments with the photographer, the video guy, the florist and three different bands before Nick deemed one acceptable. She'd even said she would go with him to meet the registrar, but I'd declined that kind offer on the basis that people must already be starting to think that it was her Nick was marrying, not me.

And she was clearly stressed to the max about my dress, poor love. Every couple of days another email would come through from her entitled 'Frocks' with links to yet more one-shouldered Grecian-style satin sheaths and blush-pink tulle prom dresses. Although I always replied thanking her and saying I'd take a look and make a decision really really soon, I promised, the dress thing was beginning to freak me out a bit.

I'd spent a Thursday evening in Selfridges, watched over by scary salesladies who made me put on special white gloves before I was allowed to touch anything. I'd ventured out in my lunch hour and explored the vintage shops of Spitalfields, but they were full of hipsters and made me feel ancient, deeply uncool and a bit of a fraud, so I'd sloped shamefacedly back to the office without trying anything on. I'd even had a look on eBay, but then I was distracted by a link to a website set up by some guy who got off on taking pictures of women weeing in their wedding dresses, and it was so grim I'd closed the browser window in horror, never to return.

And every evening, the first thing Nick and Erica said to me when I stumbled through the front door after nine o'clock, before even, "How was your day, Pippa?" was, "Have you found a dress yet, Pippa?" That's how it felt to me, anyway.

"Now, if you'd just like to turn over on to your back," said the masseuse, and I rolled over, catching Callie's eye and grinning happily at her as I felt the hot stones pressing into my feet.

"So, have you found a dress yet, Pippa?" said Callie.

"Oh, God, Cal, it's a living nightmare," I said. "I just can't make up my mind. I tried loads of different ones when I went shopping with Katharine and none of them were right, and now I seem to have developed some sort of mental block about it. Every time I even hear the words 'wedding dress', I want to run away screaming."

"Well, that's no good, is it?" Callie said. "What are you going to do?"

"I'm meeting Katharine again in a few days for a second attempt," I said. "But if I don't find something then, I don't know what I'll do. It's not like none of the dresses I've seen are okay. Lots of them are okay. But it's my wedding dress. If I'm going to spend six months' mortgage payments on it, it needs to be some sort of transformative miracle garment that makes me look like Alexa Chung and feel like Cinderella. And I haven't found anything that does that yet."

"Phoebs is the same shape as you and only a bit taller," Callie said, "and there's a shop near home where she buys loads of things. The woman there makes dresses really quickly and they're fab. Totally original, kind of vintage-looking but not. If you don't find something with Katharine, maybe you could come down next weekend and see her?"

"Brilliant idea," I said. "I'll give you a shout afterwards and let you know how it goes."

Then we both closed our eyes again and let the warmth and the whale music wash over us, and I forgot all about wedding dresses for a bit.

Over lunch, I told Callie about finding Nick's blog, and the folders and folders full of wedding stuff on his computer. I didn't mention the post from 'B' saying Nick had been sent a private message, although it was niggling at the back of my mind. To my surprise, she didn't find it strange at all.

"I think it's cool that he's so excited about it all," she said. "Lots of blokes just don't care. They let the woman get on with it, and they just passively go along with whatever she decides. It's a bit feeble, I think. And it makes the day much less fun for the bride if she feels like all the pressure's on her and he isn't really involved."

I thought of Katharine's meticulous planning of her and Iain's wedding, all the care and time she'd lavished on every single detail, and all the sighing and eye-rolling he'd contributed. I wasn't being like that, was I?

"Callie," I said, "I think what Nick's doing is amazing. Really I do. And I haven't thanked you properly for all the time you've taken off work, and all the petrol you've used missioning to appointments with him, and all the emails you've sent me with dresses to look at. You've been brilliant. You're the best friend ever, and you deserve some kind of

chief bridesmaid of the millennium award. Thank you."
And I reached across the table and squeezed her shoulder
through her towelling robe.

"It's been such a pleasure, Pip," she said. "Honestly, I've
loved doing it. Nick's one of the good guys, I love spending time with him, and all the planning stuff – it's fun. I'm
just sorry you're missing out on lots of it. But don't feel bad
about me. I'm never going to have my own wedding, so I'm
getting to plan yours instead."

"You're never – Callie, you mustn't talk like that," I said.
"It's only been two years since David moved out. You're so
beautiful and clever and funny and amazing. You'll find
someone who deserves you, I know you will. And then you'll
have a perfect, wonderful wedding, if that's what you want,
and if you let me I'll be your chief bridesmaid too and I
promise nothing will be too much trouble."

Callie ate some of her superfood salad and took a sip of
her rose and pomegranate tea. I poured some into my own
cup and tried it. It smelled delicious but it didn't taste of
much, except maybe a bit of soap.

"I don't think so, Pip," she said. "I'm beginning to think
I'm not marriage material."

I looked at her, bemused. Her hair was pulled back in a
messy ponytail and because she wasn't wearing any makeup,
I could see the scattering of freckles on her pale skin, like
cinnamon over cappuccino foam. She was so beautiful and
she looked, suddenly, so sad.

"Callie, lovely, I wish you would tell me what's wrong.
It's not still David, is it? It's something else."

I've never quite understood what went wrong with Callie
and David. They met when Callie was in her final year of university and David was a trainee solicitor. They were together
for five years and I honestly thought that was it for Callie,

she'd found the love of her life and they'd get married and have kids. He was... well, he was nice. A clever, sensitive, handsome, ambitious man who didn't seem to have an unkind bone in his body and treated Callie like she was as precious and fragile as the fairy on top of a Christmas tree. And then, just when we reached the stage when our mid-twenties were threatening to turn into late twenties and our friends were beginning to get married, she dumped him. Poor David was heartbroken and Callie seemed heartbroken at first too, but she always insisted she didn't want to talk about it, and as far as I knew she hadn't had a serious boyfriend since.

"It's not David." She smiled. "I'm over David. Did you know he's married now? He did that thing of getting engaged, like, five minutes after we split up, and now he's got two little boys. I see him sometimes at court. We had coffee the other day."

"Did he... He wasn't seeing her while he was still with you, was he? Because if he was I'll go after him with a rusty spoon and when I have finished with him he will have no more children." I adopted a cod mafioso voice.

Callie laughed. "Dunno. I don't think so. I don't mind, anyway. He's a lovely man but we were never really right for each other. It was silly and selfish of me to let it carry on as long as it did. I just saw us living this perfect life, you know? And I thought that was what I wanted, but it wasn't really."

"But what do you want, Callie?" I said. "Because I just want you to be happy."

Callie finished her salad. "I want another go in the steam room," she said. "And I want to try that rainbow shower thing they were going on about, and the salt crystal cave, and then I want a cup of proper coffee instead of this worthy tea, and a piece of chocolate cake as big as my head."

And I realised she wasn't going to tell me anything more.

"Right. We need to get an itinerary nailed down for this trip." Guido, Tamar and I were sitting around the board-room table, armed with double espressos from Kaffee Klatch (and a glass of still water for Tamar). It was just over a week before Guido and I were due to fly out to South Africa for a six-day recce of the locations where we'd be filming, the restaurants we'd be collaborating with and the dishes we'd be cooking.

I'd been working with Tamar to develop an initial list of recipes for the book that would accompany *Guido's African Safari*, and we were reasonably confident that we'd got some good stuff. But I was going to be cooking in unfamiliar kitchens, with ingredients that were new to me and, worst of all, doing my own styling, with the help of a local freelancer. I was almost as excited as I was terrified.

"I've downloaded menus from forty restaurants," Tamar said. "I based that selection on the ratings from *Taste* magazine, *Restaurant Business* and Tripadvisor. It looks like there's some seriously awesome food out there, you're in for a treat, Pippa. But we also need to track down places that don't make it into the guides and magazines: the little food carts and market stalls and so on. I've got Sibongile, the stylist we'll be using out there, working on a list. She's also researching locations for us. You'll be starting off in Johannesburg, obviously, but spending most of your time in the Cape winelands, which is where most of the fine dining places are. And Zack, the producer, feels very strongly that we should include at least one episode actually out on safari, cooking and eating wild ingredients."

"Great," Guido said. "I'm meeting him tomorrow morning at nine and we'll get a provisional episode outline planned then.

It's six thirty-minute shows, with three to four recipes cooked in each one. Pippa, you and I will need to work on a long-list of dishes while we're out there, then when we're back in the office we'll get them as close to perfect as we can before we go out to start filming. Clear?"

I nodded and drank the dregs of my espresso. I knew Guido would look after me, and I knew Tamar would be waiting at the end of a phone line or on email to help me if I got stuck, but that felt about as comforting as knowing there's a safety net a hundred feet below when you're about to walk a tightrope over the Grand Canyon. This was an opportunity that could seriously boost my career – but if I fucked it up, that might be it. I'd be making supermarket ready-meals for the rest of my days, assuming Guido didn't turn nasty and sack me. There's no pretty way to say it: I was shit scared.

At the same time, though, the idea of cooking and eating in all those amazing restaurants, meeting new people, seeing a brand new part of the world and taking on a massive new challenge was thrilling. The knot in my stomach was definitely as much about excitement as nerves. In fact, I realised guiltily, I was looking forward to the next few weeks' work with rather more enthusiasm than to the wedding that lay beyond.

"All clear," I said, hoping my voice didn't betray my self-doubt.

"Good," Guido said. "We'll reconvene tomorrow with Zack." Tamar gathered up her papers and left, and I was about to do the same when Guido said, "Pippa?"

"Yes?"

"I wouldn't be asking you to do this if I didn't think you were capable of it," he said. "You're a highly talented chef. I haven't stretched and challenged you enough in the past couple of years. This is going to be good for you, and what's more we'll have a blast. Right?"

"Right. Thanks, Guido," I said. I was feeling a bit trembly inside, as if I wanted to cry, or hug him, or something. "I'll try my best."

"And you can't do better than that, sweetheart," he said, giving my shoulder a reassuring little squeeze.

All my doubt and anxiety aside, one thing was for sure: I was going to be spending six days troughing for Britain, and my wedding was just a few weeks away. This was not good. Assuming I ever found a dress, I was somehow going to have to fit into it, and ideally do so without the aid of industrial-strength control underwear. It was time, I decided, to take some pre-emptive steps.

"Eloise," I said, "I am now going to go to the gym."

"To the… Pippa, are you feeling okay? Has your body been taken over by aliens?"

I stuck my tongue out at her as I picked up my bag and left the office, but she did have a point. Since I took out my gym membership two years ago, I think I'd been once. But now I was going to need to embark on a serious exercise regimen, even if it did turn out to be too little, too late. And as I didn't actually own any gym kit, I would have to go shopping first, which just goes to show that every cloud has a silver lining.

An hour later, I was shivering in the changing rooms as I peeled off my work clothes and struggled into my brand new Lycra garments from TK Maxx. I don't know who designs sports bras, but I'd bet good money that they've never tried to put one on. I tried doing up the hooks first and then pulling it over my head, and after ten terrifying minutes thinking I would be stuck half-in, half-out of it forever, managed to escape and attempted to put it on the normal way, which was more successful, except I got hideous cramp in my shoulder and broke two of my nails. By the time I was ready to start my workout, it was almost eight o'clock and I was hot, out of breath and thinking that this really hadn't been such a good idea after all.

Clutching my towel and water bottle, I entered the holy of holies, the cardio room. I'd just cycle easily for twenty minutes on an exercise bike, I told myself. No point overdoing it the first time. And if I positioned myself in the corner at the back, I'd be suitably inconspicuous, so all the lithe, athletic girls wouldn't be subjected to the sight of my arse spilling over the saddle, and I'd be able to check them out and imagine what I'd look like when my new fitness programme had worked its magic. And, of course, I'd be able to watch the hot men.

Like that one over there, I thought, settling myself on to the bike and starting to pedal gently. He was wearing a sweat-soaked T-shirt, worn so thin it was almost transparent in places, and it clung to the lean V of his torso. I could see the muscles in his legs bunching and extending as he ran, and his tight bottom... Hold on. It was Nick. There I was, perving away like a dirty old woman over my own boyfriend.

I abandoned my exercise bike (not without a certain feeling of relief) and went over to him, just as he reduced the speed of the treadmill and slowed down to a walk.

"Blimey, Pippa," he said, his breathing only slightly harder than usual, "I didn't expect to see you here."

"Well, you know," I said, "pre-wedding fitness mission."

"Good for you," he said. "But if you're done, maybe you could reward yourself by accompanying me to the pub?"

I paused for a moment, torn. Did five minutes count as a workout? Probably not. But then, getting dressed had been exhausting. And I'd walked all the way round TK Maxx. And, of course, it was vital to keep the flame of passion alive in our relationship and that, surely, meant going to the pub together? "I'm done," I said. "Shall we go home and shower?"

But I didn't make it as far as the shower. When we got home, the first thing I saw was Spanx asleep on the sofa, blissfully cuddled up to a large, white plush rabbit.

"What the hell's this?" I said.

"It came by courier today," Erica said. "There was a card with it, but of course I haven't opened it, it must be for you and Nick." She passed me an envelope. On it was written, 'ABRACADABRA!'

I peeled open the flap and took out a card in the shape of a black top hat. On the back was printed, "Hocus pocus and shazam! Congratulations on booking The Amazing Archibald. Your event is sure to go with a bang!"

I passed the card to Nick. "Do you know what this is?" I said. "Is it meant for the neighbours? If so we'd better get their bunny back to them before it gets even more ginger fur on it." Spanx opened his amber eyes and gazed at me reproachfully, as if to say, "But this is my new friend."

"No, don't worry, Pip, it's absolutely fine," Nick said, but I couldn't help noticing that he looked a bit guilty. "It's just the entertainer guy I booked for the wedding. It's quite a cool marketing idea, don't you think?"

"But we don't need an entertainer. Why would we want an entertainer? It's not like we're having kids at the… Nick? We aren't having kids at the wedding, right?"

Erica retreated tactfully to our bedroom and closed the door.

Nick was suddenly showing great interest in the tops of his shoes. "Well, we're inviting your friends Jack and Julia," he said. "They'll bring their baby, won't they?"

"Iris is six months old," I said. "The only entertainment she needs is Julia's boobs and maybe a rattle or something.

Nick, look at me. We're not having kids at the wedding. Tell me you haven't invited kids to the wedding."

"There are a few," he muttered.

"How many is a few? And whose are they? This is about your cousins, isn't it?" My legs suddenly felt a bit shaky. I sat down and pulled the bunny on to my lap. Spanx followed, purring thunderously.

"Okay," Nick said. "We've got about thirty children on the list. Probably they won't all come. I think there'll be twenty, maybe twenty-five. And they'll need something to keep them occupied. So I booked an entertainer. He sounds really good. He does magic tricks and face-painting and plays games with the kids and makes balloon animals."

"Balloon animals. I see."

When I was working as a trainee in restaurants, I was on the receiving end of some epic temper tantrums. I won't name any names, but one celebrity chef actually used to pelt eggs at waiters who displeased him – a totally pointless exercise, because they'd have to spend ages sponging themselves down and it caused absolute carnage during a busy service. Another's speciality was a sort of icy rage, which was, if anything, more terrifying. I resolved back then that when I was running my own kitchen, I would never be like that. I would reason, calmly and quietly, with my team. I would engender respect. But I was kidding myself, because the truth is that when I get angry, I just start to cry. I could feel tears stinging my eyes now, and my nose was beginning to run.

"Are you okay, Pip?"

"No," I sniffed. "I'm not okay. I'm bloody pissed off, Nick, because I don't want children at the wedding and I thought we'd discussed you not inviting all your cousins. How many people is that? How many are on this guest list?"

"I'm not sure exactly," Nick said.

"Of course you're sure," I said. "Don't tell me you're not sure! You've planned every single stupid thing about this wedding. If I asked you how many fucking sugared almonds you'd ordered, you'd tell me, or you'd have it on a spreadsheet somewhere."

"Right," Nick said. He sat down next to me and put a placating hand on my knee. "I do know. We haven't sent the invitations out yet but there are two hundred and fifty people on the list. Of those, eighty-five are my family and as I said, thirty of them are under twelve. Three are our flower girls and our pageboy, like you agreed. Are you satisfied now?"

"No," I said. "I'm not, and I won't be until you do what you said you'd do and sort this out. I don't want loads of people at the wedding who I haven't met, and I don't want to have children there, except close friends' babies and the pageboy and flower girls, and quite honestly I'd be happy not to have them either. And if you've booked this Amazing Archibald guy, unbook him. I'm going to bed."

And I picked up Spanx and the bunny and flounced off. After a bit I heard the shower running, and then Nick and Erica went out.

When I finished shaking and crying, I fell into an uneasy sleep, but I woke up when Nick came to bed, much later. I put my arms round him and buried my head in his chest.

"I'm sorry I was such a bitch," I said.

"I'm sorry too, Pip. I love you," he said. And we had silent, surreptitious sex so Erica wouldn't hear us and then Nick went straight to sleep. Although I was relieved we weren't rowing any more, I was horribly aware that things were far from resolved. I lay awake most of the night worrying and when I eventually slept, I had a dream that I was plating up food for the cameras in South Africa and when I took the cloche off the roast springbok, it had turned into a fluffy white rabbit.

Chapter Nine

From: nick@digitaldrawingboard.com
To: housemartins@macmail.co.uk
Subject: Pre-wedding drinks

Hi Justine and Gerard

I hope you're both well and the garden is standing up to the frost! So sorry I missed you when you were in London the other day. I'm getting in touch because Mum has suggested a bit of a get-together to celebrate our engagement, and for you to get to know one another better. Although you met at Pippa's and my housewarming, that's a good few years ago now! I also thought it would be a good idea for the two sides of the family to talk about plans for the wedding – register-signing, readings, speeches and so on.

I know you're both really busy with rehearsals but please let me know if you have an evening free in the next couple of weeks, before Pippa flies off to South Africa. I'm really looking forward to catching up and so is Mum.

Love
Nick

PS – I was thinking it would be fun to make the party a surprise for Pip, so please don't mention it to her!

I t was like a particularly horrible episode of déjà vu. Here I was again, in another bridal shop with Katharine. This one aimed for more of a boudoir effect, with lots of peach chiffon draped everywhere, tasselled standard lamps, oil paintings of brides that looked like they'd been created with the aid of Photoshop effects, and the dresses concealed in white-painted armoires. But apart from that it was much the same.

The consultant this time was an older woman, who'd introduced herself as Valerie. She was Chelsea, only without the eyelash extensions and with the addition of a ruthless, headmistress-like demeanour that I suppose she'd acquired through years of persuading indecisive brides-to-be that not only were they going to buy a dress, they were going to buy one today, from her, and she was going to extract the maximum commission out of the transaction.

Katharine's manner was different, though. Although she'd met me with her usual bright smile and upbeat demeanour, I got the sense that her heart wasn't in it.

"Today's the day, Pippa!" she said. "Today, we'll find your dress. I'm feeling it!"

But I detected a hint of desperation underlying her relentless positivity.

"Now, my dear," said Valerie. "I've been matching brides with their dream dresses for almost thirty years, and I pride myself on taking a different approach to it all. Even a radical one! I think it's very easy for girls to get a bit mixed up if they try too many things. Dress fatigue, I call it! So I believe in providing a bit of firm guidance." She guided me firmly to a fitting room.

"You are a lucky, lucky young lady. You have the classic hourglass shape. Your skin is just radiant! We need to work with these qualities and enhance them. If you've been spending too much time reading wedding magazines, you may have had your head turned by trends." She wagged a scarlet-nailed finger at me. "A wedding dress should not be a trend-led purchase! It should be chosen to make the most of *you*. You should wear the dress, not the other way around. Am I right or am I right?"

I expected Katharine to bristle in the face of this hard-line approach, but she nodded meekly. I nodded meekly too.

"Let's get you out of those jeans. And if you could just help Pippa into this, dear, I'll be back in a moment with a few styles that I know will work for you." 'This' was a strapless, boned contraption that looked like it would do a pretty decent job on a construction site. "A good foundation garment is the single most important part of your wedding attire. I'll be back shortly."

Headmistress-like she may have been, but once Katharine had wrestled and hooked me into the foundation garment, I realised Valerie knew her stuff. It may have been a particularly unattractive surgical-stocking shade of beige, but the scaffolding did its work. I immediately looked taller, straighter-backed and slimmer, and there were no bulges where bulges had been before. However, I couldn't imagine being able to sit down, dance, eat or laugh, such was the garment's constraining effect on my hips and diaphragm. Even breathing was something of a challenge, and I imagined that when I took it off, it would leave fetching red welts on my skin.

"No one ever has sex on their wedding night," Katharine said, as if she'd read my mind, "so you may as well submit to the killer corsetry." I was about to remind her of her famous sex diet, which she'd promised would have us swinging from the chandeliers the second the register was signed, when Valerie bustled back through the curtains bearing an armful of dresses.

"This is just a small selection to get us started. But I suspect your dress may well be one of these. I don't have thirty years' experience for nothing!

"Now," she said, "first of all, just to make sure we're on the same page, here's an example of the sort of dress I believe you should *not* be considering."

With a flourish that would have done credit to The Amazing Archibald, she whisked a frock off the rail. It was gorgeous. The full skirt fell in a cascade of ivory tucks and folds, with extravagant silk roses holding up the gathers.

"I know what you're thinking! You're thinking, this is a fairytale dress. And it is. But it's a dress for tall, big-boned brides. Pop it on and you'll see I'm right."

And she was. I'm no delicate little sylph, but the dress swamped me. I looked like a six-year-old trying on her mother's eiderdown.

"See? Now we've got that out of the way, let's have a look at the kind of style I believe will work on you."

The next dress she produced couldn't have been more different. I felt almost disappointed looking at it. It was just simple – a straight white column with a bit of beading on the wide shoulder straps, and a little puddle of a train.

"Now don't you dismiss it until you've tried it!" Valerie manhandled me into the dress and spent a few painstaking minutes doing up the row of tiny pearl buttons down the back. I looked at Katharine to see her reaction, but she was distracted, her hair falling over her face as she tapped away at her phone.

"Let's have a little look." Valerie led me out of the fitting room towards one of the huge cheval mirrors, with Katharine following in our wake.

And she was right. It suited me. It was a good dress. I did a few turns in front of the mirror, waiting for the magic to happen. It hadn't, exactly, but it was definitely a dress I could wear. Alexa Chung, no. Me in a wedding dress, yes.

I'd noticed when Valerie had brought the dresses, that they'd all had price tags discreetly attached to them with bits of satin ribbon. But now the price was concealed somewhere next to my spine, beneath the pearl buttons.

"I don't think you mentioned how much this costs," I said to Valerie.

"Ah, now, let me see," she said. "This is one of our exclusive, limited-edition designs by Angelo Venetti – you'll have heard of him, of course – and so it's at the upper end of the range, price-wise."

And she named a figure that would have taken my breath away, had the foundation garment not done so already. It was more than Nick and I earn a month, put together. It was more than we'd spend on a holiday. But then, it was my wedding dress. Most of the women featured in *Inspired Bride* spent this much, some even more. If Katharine okayed it, I'd buy it, I decided. To hell with the cost. I'd stick it on a credit card. At least it would mean never having to try on another wedding dress.

I turned to Katharine. "What do you reckon?" But she was looking down at her phone again, and as I watched, a huge tear splatted down on to the screen.

"Just give us a moment." I hustled her back into the cubicle and closed the curtain. "Katharine! What is it? What's wrong?"

"I'm sorry," she said. "Please, don't worry. This isn't about me. We're supposed to be buying your dress."

"My dress? Fuck the dress, Katharine. I'm buying you a drink."

Valerie may have been finding perfect dresses for brides for thirty years, but I bet she'd never seen anyone get out of one as quickly as I did. I shoved my jeans, jumper, coat and boots back on, left the good-enough dress on the fitting room floor along with the punishing foundation garment, and hurried Katharine out, my arm tightly around her shoulders.

"I'll be in touch. Thanks, sorry, we have to dash," I said to Valerie, and we left her gaping like a headmistress in the process of mutating into a goldfish.

I didn't say anything more to Katharine until I'd got us ensconced in a booth in the pub across the road with two huge glasses of red wine and a stack of paper napkins. Then I said, "Tell me what's going on. It's Iain, isn't it?"

She nodded miserably and blew her nose.

"Do you want to talk about it?"

Katharine shook her head and pressed a napkin to her face. "I don't want to talk about it," she said, her voice muffled, "because that would make it real, and I can't bear for it to be real. We've only been married two months. I was going to take him to The Mortimer for our anniversary. It's paper, you know. Well, two years is, but I was thinking laterally. I was going to print out the booking and surprise him. And then," she took a big gulp of wine and almost choked, "Oh, God, it's all shit."

"Katharine, whatever's going on, there are two things you need to know. First, it's not your fault. Second, whatever it is and however awful you feel now, you'll get through it. Is he… is there someone else?"

She nodded miserably. "How did you know?"

I thought, because I've known Iain for a long time. I know he's got form for this kind of thing. He's a man of many talents but keeping his dick in his pants isn't one of them. But of course I didn't say that to her.

I said, "It kind of had to be that. You wouldn't be so shattered by a normal row. But are you sure you haven't got it wrong?"

"As sure as I can be," Katharine said miserably. "I've been so fucking stupid. It's been going on for months: suddenly needing to work late, spending the evenings when he was at home constantly texting, getting a new mobile 'for work'. I told myself it was fine, that there was no way he'd marry me if he wasn't being faithful. But it looks like I was wrong."

I poured us both some more wine. "But hold on. People do work late. When Nick and Iain started the agency they worked stupid hours. We hardly saw each other. And Guido has two phones – it's not that unusual a thing to do." I didn't tell Katharine that the real reason for Guido's second phone was so he could avoid Florence when he was at work. "So what's suddenly changed?"

"Nookie," said Katharine miserably. It took me a few seconds to remember that this was her twee term for sex. "We did the sex diet thing, remember I told you? For two months before we got married I said no nookie, so that the wedding night would be extra special. And it would have been, if Iain had been less pissed. And then on honeymoon I was so shattered, to be honest, all I wanted to do was lie in the sun all day and go to sleep straight after supper. So once we stopped doing it, we never really started again, except for a couple of times."

I thought, I knew this sex diet malarkey was a shit idea. In fact, it was beginning to sound to me as if deciding to get married had been when things began to go wrong for Iain and Katharine. "But all relationships go through dry patches," I said. "It's totally normal. It doesn't necessarily mean anything at all."

Katharine took another gulp of wine, blew her nose and said, "Pippa, I checked his credit card statement. I know it's wrong to snoop, but I did. I would have checked his phones, but it's like he's surgically attached to both the stupid things, he even takes them to the loo with him. And he's changed the password on his email, so I couldn't check that either. So I looked at his Mastercard bill. It was grim, I felt so furtive, like every single cliché of the suspicious wife. I steamed open the envelope and glued it closed afterwards, and everything."

I was uncomfortably reminded of how I felt looking at Nick's blog, as I found myself doing more and more often, and wondering again who 'B' was, with her kisses and promises of private messages in the comments. "And what did you find?"

"Oh, God. This is so pathetic, isn't it? He's spent four hundred pounds at Myla, and five hundred at Netflorist, and almost a grand at Pandora. And I haven't seen a single flower or pair of knickers and certainly not any jewellery."

"But couldn't they be Christmas presents for you?" I said.

"I've been with Iain for four years now, Pippa. The first six months, he bought me flowers every Friday. I got a Tiffany bracelet for my birthday, and on Valentine's Day he took me to Agent Provocateur and did that thing of watching through the peephole while I tried stuff on. Since we got engaged, he's given me Lakeland vouchers for every single Christmas and birthday. That stuff is not for me."

"Have you talked to him?" I asked.

"I haven't had the, 'Are you fucking someone else?' conversation, if that's what you mean," she said. "I just can't face it. I've asked him what's wrong, like, a million times, and he just says he's busy at work. And it's true, he is busy at work. But I think he's also fucking someone else."

I squeezed her hand. "I just don't know what to say. It's awful."

Katharine said, "You know what, if I could turn back the clock and not have that stupid, ridiculous, excessive fucking wedding, I'd do it in a heartbeat. Every single gold chocolate dragée and piece of organic rose-petal confetti and pair of bridesmaids' knickers – I actually bought them vintage-style silk pants to match our colour theme, Pippa, how fucking obsessed was I? – every single one of those things took chunks of my life that I'll never get back. They took time I could have spent with Iain, going to gigs with him or watching *True Blood* or sucking him off. Instead I spent it wrapping up miniature bottles of Moët for favours. There were two hundred of those stupid things left at the venue after the wedding. Two hundred. We told the waiting staff to take them."

I squeezed her hand again. We'd left our Moët miniatures behind, I remembered. I felt a bit guilty about it now.

"I put everything I had into that wedding and now it's all fucked." Then she seemed to remember who she was talking to. "It won't be like that for you and Nick, obviously. You'll be really happy, I'm sure. And your wedding's going to be lovely."

I poured the last of the bottle of wine into our glasses. "Katharine, whatever happens, I'm here. If you want to talk, or anything. Because I think it's important not to rush into anything, and to think very carefully about what you want to do."

"I want to disembowel that bastard with my eyebrow tweezers," she said. Then she started to cry again. "I love him so much."

An hour and two more glasses of red later, I finally said goodbye to Katharine at the Tube station. I'd learned a lot about her. I'd learned that there was far more to her than her fluffy, girly exterior, and that she got properly sweary when she was upset. I'd learned that she really, really did love Iain, and would probably have loved him even if he had still been the long-haired bass player from Deathly Hush and living in a

Dalston squat. I didn't know what she was going to decide to do next, and I had absolutely no idea what I was going to say to Nick about his best mate's – and our best man's – infidelity. But there was one thing I knew for sure: I'd gone right off the idea of buying that wedding dress.

The next day, while I quickly devoured my lunch at my desk (it consisted of half a bag of wine gums that I'd found in my drawer and a Diet Coke), I caught up on Nick's blog. I still, somehow, felt ashamed about reading it, because he hadn't mentioned it to me and I was sure that he would have done if he'd wanted to share it with me. But I couldn't shake off the suspicion that there were things he was choosing to share with other people, instead, and that it was vital that I kept a watching brief on what he was writing.

Hello, followers. Another update on how things are going here as the wedding planning hots up. Only 65 days to go now, and in between Pippa has two overseas trips, plus there's all the usual madness of Christmas and New Year, and I have loads of work deadlines to get out of the way too (yes, I actually have a job alongside my groom-to-be duties and rather sporadic blogging habit!).

The good news: our photographer, videographer and registrar are booked, so that's three of the big ones out of the way. Pippa's maid of honour, Callie, is having a meeting in the next couple of days with a florist, who looks ace. I've never given a toss about flowers (yes, I am guilty of having bought Pippa red roses from Tesco on Valentine's Day, when I'd forgotten to buy her anything else. She actually pretended to like them, which was one of the many things that made me realise she's the woman for me!), but Beatrice of Bea's Blooms (you can check out her website here) is bloody brilliant (see what I did there?).

A few of you have asked how Pippa's dress hunt is going, and there's still no result on that front. She's getting pretty stressed about it, and so am I if I'm honest, but I don't want her to know that, because she has so much else on her plate. I've given my mum, who's staying with us and being a total legend about helping out with all the planning stuff, strict instructions not to mention it either and she has managed to cut down to only asking Pippa about it every second day, ha ha!

It was Mum's idea to organise a bit of a get-together with Pippa's parents along with Callie and Iain, who's my best man. I haven't posted about this before because I wanted it to be a surprise for Pip, and although she doesn't read this blog... well, you never know. I'm crap at secrets and it would be absolutely typical of me to be outed by my own blog! But I managed to keep schtum and last night was a total surprise for Pip.

The big event went really well. Pip had actually been dress-shopping beforehand, and she was completely blown away when she got home and there were her parents, Callie and loads of chilled champagne. Iain arrived a few minutes late (take a yellow card, mate!) and her face when he walked in was an absolute picture. After a pretty okay dinner cooked by yours truly (well, mac and cheese with bacon, my speciality), we talked readings and vows and speeches and all the rest, and I think we've got those things pretty much nailed down now.

So, on the to-do list remains finalising our guest list. I know we've left this scarily late, but when you've got a family as big as mine, it's pretty damn complicated to try and decide who makes the cut. Watch this space!

My experience of the event wasn't quite as Nick described. By the time I got home, I'd decided that I really wanted to chat to him about what Katharine had told me. She hadn't sworn me to secrecy or anything, and I was used to telling him just about everything, and listening to (sometimes even following) his advice. But, of course, I walked in through the door and there were Mum and Dad and Callie, all going, "Surprise!" And a few minutes later Iain turned up.

Seeing him was just weird. He looked just the same as usual, with his shaven head and his goatee and his designer suit, and he greeted me with his usual affectionate hug and kiss on both cheeks. And I greeted him warmly too, once I was over the initial shock of seeing him, but all I wanted to do was shake him and demand to know what the hell he was playing at. And then everyone started asking me how the dress-shopping expedition had gone, and it was impossible to tell them without saying why the dress that I thought would do when I tried it on had turned into Not If It Was The Last One On Earth. So I lied, and waffled a bit about how I still wasn't sure, but something would turn up. I could see Nick and Callie exchanging anxious glances. Then Erica took me into the kitchen (which looked like Typhoon Haiyan had been through it, as it always does in the aftermath of Nick's cooking) for a 'little chat'.

"Nick has gone to a great deal of trouble tonight, Pippa," she said, gesturing at the carnage.

"I know he has," I said. "It's a wonderful surprise and I appreciate it so much. I'm very lucky."

"Sometimes," Erica said, "I wonder whether you in fact realise how lucky you are."

Then she gave me what I can only describe as the mother of all bollockings. Or possibly the mother-in-law of all bollockings, which would be even worse, wouldn't it? But she did it in a typically Erica-like way. She told me that she and everyone else here tonight appreciated how important my career was to me, Nick most of all, which was why he was so unstintingly supportive of me. She reminded me that my parents and Callie had also gone to a great deal of trouble to be there.

Then she said, "A wedding is a special time for any girl. But when I married Nick's father, things were very different. I was expected to defer to the wishes of my family and my future family. We didn't have the luxury of wedding planners like that nice Imogen. I bought my dress off the peg from BHS and my mother made the cake. We had our wedding breakfast in the church hall, with devilled eggs and vol-au-vents."

She paused for breath, and I thought how lovely that sounded, especially now retro food is so on trend.

"I get the impression," she said, "that brides today are encouraged to believe that the day is all about them. Pippa, this wedding is not all about you, no matter how much you would like it to be. I want you to think about that tonight."

I smarted with the injustice of it. I wanted to tell her that she was wrong, that all this was about what Nick wanted, that I was letting him get on with it because I loved him and he deserved his dream day as much as I did, and if it ended up not being my dream day, well, that was just tough. I wanted to try yet again to persuade her that I wasn't as selfish as she thought. But there was suddenly a huge lump in my throat and I found I couldn't say anything at all, so I just nodded mutely.

"Pippa, we have had our differences over the years," Erica said. "Now, my son has chosen you and I accept his choice. I hope we shall get along very well. But you've been spoiled, like so many only children, and you can be egotistical, as we both know only too well. I think it's time to get back to your guests." She made it sound as if I was the one who'd dragged her off to have a row. I followed her back into the sitting room, choking back my annoyance and the threat of tears.

She turned and hissed at me over her shoulder, "Take that sullen look off your face and smile!"

So I did. I spent the rest of the evening smiling, and chatting about the plans, and saying yes to everything everyone suggested, and writing 'fuck you' on the roof of my mouth with my tongue. It did help, a bit.

But the smile was properly wiped off my face later. I was chatting to Callie, who'd offered to stay and help with the clearing up and crash on our sofa, and noticed Mum and Dad making wanting-to-go gestures. But Erica was still in full flow, talking to Mum about co-ordinating their outfits.

"I thought turquoise," she said. "Perhaps a trouser suit – so much more modern. And a little fascinator. What did you have in mind, Justine?"

"I hadn't really thought," Mum said. "I expect I'll find something in the sales. Or failing that there's always the Westbourne Thespians' costume cupboard." I could tell from the note of mischief in her voice that she was deliberately winding Erica up. She'd seen the look on my face when Erica and I came out of the kitchen and, bless her, she was fighting my corner. "We did *The Importance of Being Earnest* last year. I played Lady Bracknell, and I wore a charming purple frock with a bustle."

"With a *what?*" said Erica.

"A bustle," Mum said serenely. "And I had a hat with a stuffed hummingbird on it, but that might be a little OTT, although it was most becoming. Now, Erica, it's been such a pleasure to see you again after so long, but we really must be off if we're not going to miss our train. Are you ready, Gerard?"

I can only think that Erica meant me to hear her, because there were only seven of us in the room and there was a bit of a lull in the conversation while Dad fussed about finding his coat. Anyway, she said quite loudly, "Of course, it doesn't signify in the grand scheme of things what anyone wears to this wedding. I can't imagine it lasting more than a year."

That was when I dropped the dish of leftover mac and cheese I was holding on to the floor with a sickening crash.

I longed to confide in Callie, and ask her if she'd heard, or if it had been some horrible hallucination brought on by stress. But, with Nick rallying around and stacking the dishwasher and Erica in the next room, presumably eavesdropping like a good 'un, I couldn't. But I resolved that I was going to prove her wrong. I loved Nick. Of course our marriage would last. And I was going to get it off to the best possible start by letting him have the wedding he wanted, and by proving to Erica that I wasn't as spoiled and selfish as she thought.

Katharine told me a while ago about a book called *The Surrendered Wife*, according to which the secret of a happy marriage is never arguing with your husband or trying to control him. I remember saying to her at the time that it sounded like a load of bollocks, and her arguing back that it worked, really it did. Obviously, if Katharine's suspicions about Iain were founded in fact, being a Surrendered Wife had done the opposite of working. But still, I decided, I'd be a Surrendered Bride. (Just until the wedding, then normal service could resume.)

If that meant wall-to-wall cousins and a million children, I would just have to live with it. And maybe one of The Amazing Archibald's magic tricks would misfire and Erica would vanish in a puff of smoke.

CHAPTER TEN

From: nick@digitaldrawingboard.com
To: pippa.martin@falconis.co.uk
Subject: First dance!

Hey Pip

Just realised we haven't got around to talking about this yet. Someone
mentioned to me that she'd had a few lessons to make sure she and her
H2B didn't make tits of themselves on the dance-floor – what do you
reckon? And I've got loads of ideas for songs.

Love you
Nxx

PS – Fancy a pint after work? Grope & Wanker at 8?

"But, Nick, you know I don't dance." I was feeling my
resolve to be a Surrendered Bride wavering peril-
ously. "I never dance, except when I'm pissed. I'm tone deaf
and clumsy. All the lessons in the world won't make me not
make a tit of myself."

It was true. It seemed to matter less now, but back when
Nick was lead singer for Deathly Hush, I found it deeply
shameful that I not only can't sing but actually don't really

care about music that much. I mean, it's perfectly nice and everything, but I've never shared Nick's passion for it. It's a bit like the way he feels about food – he loves eating, of course he does, but he doesn't get it in the same way I do. But as for dancing – let me just say that I have to be quite seriously hammered to even set foot on a dance-floor, and when I do I can be relied upon to miss the beat and attempt to twerk and then fall over, and generally make my name arse.

"But we have to have a first dance." Nick looked bemused. "Everyone has a first dance."

"Okay, I get that we might have to sort of shuffle around a bit, with everyone else," I said. "I'm cool with that. But an actual dance? Do we have to?"

Nick said, "It depends what you mean by 'have to'. It's traditional, and it makes it clear to the guests that the dancing is now, like, officially happening. If we were being really old-fashioned we'd do the thing where we'd dance the first track on our own, then Callie and Iain would join in, then your dad with Mum, and your mum with – I don't know, someone, and so on. But we don't have to do that. We can just do the first dance and then it's a free-for-all."

"Nick, seriously, I…" I began, and then I thought, no, Pippa. You're being reasonable and nice and unbratty. "Okay. I suppose I'll make less of a tit of myself with lessons than without them. How long will it take?"

"They reckon twelve hours if they choreograph a dance especially for you," Nick said. He had a slightly mad glint in his eye and I knew he'd love nothing more than to have a dance especially choreographed for us. But he added hastily, "That's bit over the top, obviously, and you don't have time. So I was thinking the standard six-lesson package, where they teach you a dance that fits your choice of song, and basically coach you through it so you're 'confident, competent and having fun'. Look here."

He took out his iPad and I could see him scrolling through a load of bookmarked wedding-related sites before he got to one called stepsoflove.com. The homepage was a picture of a couple in wedding attire, the groom sweeping the bride off her feet like something off *Strictly Come Dancing*. I cringed at the idea of us doing that.

"And look at this thing I found on YouTube," he said, and started playing a video of a couple who actually danced down the aisle together, finishing with him down on one knee and her with her foot up on his shoulder. I cringed some more (although I couldn't help admiring her shoes).

"Nick, there is no way on earth we're doing that. They just look stupid. And let's get one more thing clear. No lifting me up. You'd put your back out."

"Of course not," Nick said. "Don't worry. I won't lift you up if you don't want to be lifted up. Just a simple dance. It won't be more than five minutes long, depending on which song we choose."

"What do you mean, which song we choose?" I said. "We're having U2, *Beautiful Day*, obviously."

"Pippa," he said, "ten years ago, U2 were still cool, just. It was acceptable for us to play their covers at gigs. But now?" He shook his head. "No way. Not going to happen. Image suicide. It's Bono, you see. They could just about get away with the hats and The Edge being called The Edge and all that stuff, back in the nineties. But now Bono's gone all smug. Well, smugger. It's dad rock, Pip. We're not having it."

"But it's our song!" I said. "It's the song that was playing the first night we met, and you played it for me that night in Borderline. Don't you think of me every time you hear it?"

"To my shame," Nick said, "I do think of you when I hear it, my gorgeous fiancée, and I also feel a bit mortified that our song is by the naffest band ever, and wonder whether maybe it's time to find something else to be our song. Anyway, to be fair, there you were, looking so bloody gorgeous, I'd have played *Yellow* by Coldplay if I thought that was what it would take to get you into bed."

"Steady on! I know my taste in music is crap but it's never been that bad. But you're trying to distract me from the matter in hand," I said. "Our first dance song is going to be *Beautiful Day*. End of."

"We can think of another song," he said. "Come on, Pip. There are some awesome tracks to choose from, properly romantic. *One Day Like This* by Elbow. *Iris* by the Goo Goo Dolls. *Just Say Yes* by Snow Patrol."

"No, Nick," I said. "We're having *Beautiful Day* or we're having… I don't know. *Smack My Bitch Up* by Prodigy?"

He laughed. "*I Hate Everything About You* by Ugly Kid Joe?"

"Um… *Heaven Knows I'm Miserable Now?*"

"*I Used to Love Her But I Had to Kill Her?*"

"*I Should've Cheated?*"

"*Every Day I Love You Less And Less?*"

By this stage we were both giggling helplessly. "It's not fair," I said. "You're better than me at this game. Want another beer?"

"Go on then," Nick said.

"I'll get it. But first, you have to promise me, if I agree to do these stupid embarrassing dance classes and a stupid embarrassing first dance all on our own with everyone watching, we're doing it to *Beautiful Day*. Deal?"

"Deal," Nick said, "I'll make an appointment for our first lesson." I went and got us more drinks, and then he got another round, and then we had a burger. By closing time we'd laughed so much my cheeks ached, and we were still suggesting inappropriate first dance songs when we got home.

I was feeling considerably less chipper about the whole idea two days later, when I went to meet Nick after work at the Steps of Love studio, which was in a converted warehouse just down the road from the Falconi's HQ. I'd been cooking all day and my hands smelled of onions in spite of having been scrubbed with a special stainless steel soap thing. My feet hurt and all I wanted was to collapse on the sofa with Spanx and watch *EastEnders*. Then I remembered that Erica would be in residence, doing the insufferable thing she does of chatting over the telly, asking who all the characters were and demanding to know whether I'd found a wedding dress yet, and I decided a dance class was the lesser of two evils.

But I cheered up when Giovanna, the instructor, turned out to be absolutely lovely. She was petite and stunning, and wearing skinny jeans and legwarmers with her high-heeled shoes, and at first I was horribly intimidated by her grace and general hotness. But she quickly reassured me that almost all the people she taught were convinced they were going to be crap, and most of them managed really well in the end.

"So," she asked, "have you had any thoughts about the track you're going to be dancing to?"

"We've had a few ideas, but we'd really value your input," Nick said, at the same moment as I said, "Yes. *Beautiful Day*."

"I have a large selection of tracks…" Giovanna said.

I said, "Nick!" and gave him a hard stare.

"All right, all right. *Beautiful Day* it is."

"A very popular choice," Giovanna said. "Michael Bublé, so romantic."

Nick looked horrified.

"Er, no, U2 actually," I said.

It was Giovanna's turn to look alarmed. "That's not an easy song to dance to," she said. "Are you sure you wouldn't prefer Bublé?"

"Or maybe *Yellow*, by Coldplay?" I said.

"No!" said Nick. "No, we really have our hearts set on U2."

"Okay." I could see Giovanna's mind working furiously as she tried to decide what to do with this pair of loons who, in spite of having the dance skills of one of Spanx's toy mice, were determined to attempt a routine that would make even Bruce Forsyth struggle to be complimentary. "I'm thinking a slowed-down, dramatic tango, with lots of lifts? Very Latin, very erotic."

I said, "No lifts!"

Nick said, "Pippa, listen to Giovanna, she's the expert."

I glared at him mutinously, but I'd got my own way on the song and I knew I was beaten on the lifts.

"Don't worry," Giovanna said. "We'll start off with the basic steps, you'll master it in no time."

Half an hour later, I'd sweated oniony sweat all over Nick and trodden on his toes innumerable times. I'd fallen over twice, Nick had almost dropped me attempting a lift, and we were both in fits of laughter. Poor Giovanna was struggling to maintain her cheerful, professional demeanour.

"I think that's enough for your first lesson," she said. The poor woman looked like she needed a drink, and I knew I did.

We happily paid the extortionate fee and left.

Outside in the chilly December night, I said to Nick, "That was the best fun ever! I can't believe how shit we are."

Nick said, "Er, Pip, maybe we should think about just shuffling around a bit, along with everyone else?"

I said, "Bollocks to that! We're going to nail this sloweddown erotic tango if it's the last thing I do. When's our next class?"

Over a drink in the local curry house, we compared diaries, and I remembered with a lurch of apprehension how soon I was leaving for South Africa, and that the wedding was just a few weeks away.

I snapped a poppadom in half and dipped it halfheartedly in chutney. I wasn't feeling quite so hungry any more.

"Nick," I said, "Tonight was brilliant fun, it really was. This wedding... all the planning and stuff... are you enjoying it? Really?"

"Enjoying it?" he said. "Yeah, mostly. It's all new to me, I've never done anything like this before and it's kind of challenging, you know? Getting everything just right for you. For us. There's a lot to think about. Every time I get something crossed off the list, it seems like a whole load of new things come up and get added to it."

"Like what?" I said. "You know, I don't want you to think that just because you're doing most of the work, I don't care about it. I do." But did I, really, I wondered? I certainly didn't share Nick's passion for getting every single detail just so.

"I know you care, Pip, don't be daft," Nick said. "I know you aren't that into stuff like what the invitations look like, and that's cool. But there are loads of things you're going to need to do, when you have time."

"Great! Just tell me what they are and I'll make time to do them."

"We need to book our honeymoon," Nick said. "That's going to be so much fun and we haven't really thought about it yet. I guess with all the travel you've got coming up, you might not want to go straight away, so maybe we could think about taking a couple of weeks in March? And you'll need to apply for a new passport, obviously."

"Hold on," I said. "Planning the honeymoon sounds great. We could even go skiing if it's March, you love skiing. Or we could go somewhere with beaches, or somewhere totally different, like... I don't know. Argentina. Guido went there last year, he says it's ace and he's never eaten so much steak in his life. So maybe there. But anyway, I've got two years remaining on my passport, so I don't need to renew it, do I? I bloody hope not, because I'm leaving for South Africa the day after tomorrow and if my passport doesn't work, I'm buggered."

Nick laughed. "No, of course it's fine for the day after tomorrow. God, imagine if it wasn't? Nightmare! But I thought it would be nice for you to have a new one for the honeymoon, you know, with your new name on it."

"Right," I said. "Nick, don't think I've mentioned this before, but I'd kind of thought I'd keep my name. I like being Pippa Martin. I know it's not that exciting a name or anything, but I don't have any brothers or sisters and it feels a bit like our line would be dying out. It's silly, but you know what I mean." I didn't add that, in my opinion, Pippa Pickford just sounded stupid. Even stupider than Nick Pickford, which, while not up there with classic comedy names I've come across like Micky Moosa and Wayne King and Keith Lasagne, is a bit ridiculous. What had Erica been thinking? She could surely have selected a less alliterative name for her only son.

Nick looked absolutely stricken. "I didn't know. I'd kind of assumed... I know it's old-fashioned. But I didn't think you minded. I thought... when we weren't planning to get married, one thing that bothered me a bit was that you'd never be Mrs Pickford, and when we have kids – well, what then?"

There it was. The elephant in the room, trumpeting loudly and forcing the ostrich that was me to jerk its head out of the sand.

When Nick and I were seventeen and first started having sex, with all the associated condom-fumbling that entailed, we'd speculated about what we might do if something went wrong. I'd said that there was no way, no way on earth, that I'd want a baby. Nick had looked a bit wistful and said, "Well, not *now*, obviously." And later, of course, I'd taken myself off to the family planning clinic and gone on the Pill, and on the Pill I had remained.

Throughout our twenties, we'd had the odd totally hypothetical conversation about what we might call our children (Nick was dead set on Bernie for a brief period, when Ecclestone rescued Queen's Park Rangers' finances. Thankfully that didn't last), but they were never really serious. Nick was building up his fledgling design agency after he agreed to let Iain buy him out of Coulson Creative because he was sick of schmoozing clients and managing staff and wanted to get back to doing proper design work again, and we knew that our tiny two-bedroom flat had barely room for us, Spanx and Nick's new business, never mind a baby. I was working hard too, and even though it mostly felt like I was treading water in terms of my career, I certainly didn't want to jack it all in and trade in my chef's whites for fluffy terry nappies. So it was a conversation we never had to have, not properly, and I could never admit to Nick how relieved I was about that.

"Pippa?" Nick said. "We are going to have kids, aren't we?"

I wiped a smear of butter off my chin with my napkin and twisted it into a knot in my lap.

"Isn't it good enough to be just us?"

"Being just us is amazing," Nick smiled. "Us and Spanx, obviously. But this is a big thing for me, it's important. I thought maybe in a couple of years, we'd want to think about it properly."

And there it was – a lovely, open escape route, an opportunity to put off having the discussion for as long as possible – maybe even indefinitely.

"Of course we will!" I gushed, weak with relief. "We'll definitely think about it in a couple of years! And maybe I can do what Katharine does, and be Pippa Pickford on my passport, and Pippa Martin for work, and other stuff." For everything important, I thought. Who cared what my passport said, anyway?

CHAPTER ELEVEN

From: nick@digitaldrawingboard.com
To: pippa.martin@falconis.co.uk
Subject: Hi

Hey gorgeous

Just a quick note to say I hope you had a safe flight and you're getting a bit of free time to work on your tan! Spanx says he's missing you lots, and I am too. Remember, whatever you do, no worrying about the wedding – focus on work and on having a great time. Everything is totally under control here.

Can't wait to see you again – only three sleeps!

Your adoring husband-to-be
Nxxxx

I'd never cooked in a kitchen with a view like this before. The ground in front of me fell away into a valley, and there were distant, purple peaks of mountains beyond, with lines of lush grapevines marching up their slopes. It was all bathed in dazzling sunshine and the still air smelled faintly of ripening fruit. Unfortunately I was up to my elbows in squid ink, but that only slightly detracted from the quality of the experience.

"It's quite special, isn't it?" said Sibongile, the freelance stylist who we'd hired to help out, research locations and – this was not said but I was very conscious that it was true – compensate for my own inexperience. I'd warmed to her straight away – she was not only bubbly and permanently smiley, but also dizzyingly competent.

Since we'd arrived in Johannesburg, we'd been to what felt like dozens of restaurants, but in reality was probably about fifteen. I'd eaten so much I felt permanently on the point of exploding. I'd had the bright idea of Instagramming every single plate before I started eating, otherwise I'd never have remembered it all. It had taken five days and two internal flights, but I was finally beginning to settle into a rhythm and feel like I was actually taking things in rather than just allowing them to flood over me.

Behind me, I heard Guido's phone ring. Sibongile and I rolled our eyes in unison.

"Sì?" he snapped. "Florence, what is it now? I'm extremely busy. Yes, in Franschhoek. Yes, it's in the Cape. And tomorrow we're flying to… Florence, this is not the time to have this discussion. I've told you how I feel."

He went outside, but we could still hear him shouting. "I'm working, Florence! Working! I'm not out here for fun. I don't have time to plan a romantic holiday with you, and I certainly don't have time to listen to you when you're like this. I'll be back next Tuesday and you'd better have calmed down by then. What? Well, you've got a funny way of showing it." He ended the call and stomped back into the kitchen, muttering, "Jesus Christ," under his breath.

This had been going on since we arrived, with Florence becoming increasingly histrionic and Guido becoming more and more impatient with her. He'd had to interrupt several meetings to take her calls, and earlier that morning I'd rescued a pan of coriander, cumin and nigella seeds that he'd left toasting over a low flame seconds before they charred beyond recognition.

"Is he always like this?" Sibongile whispered.

"I'm not sure," I said. "I've never travelled with him before. Bonkers, though, isn't it?"

"One thing's for sure," she said, "if she's trying to get him to make some sort of commitment, she's not doing it right."

I thought fleetingly of Katharine, who'd waited so patiently for Iain's proposal, and wondered whether she'd told him about her suspicions, and how he'd react if she did. I wondered whether the Myla lingerie, the Pandora jewellery and all the rest were wrapped up and waiting for her under their tastefully decorated Christmas tree. I hoped so, and resolved to call her and find out how she was. Then I looked up again at the sun-washed mountains and Katharine and her problems, cold, rainy London, and most of all Nick and our wedding seemed very far away.

"So," I said to Sibongile. "Tell me about this calamari steak thing."

"You use the whole body of the squid in one piece," she said, "flatten it a bit, cook it quick-quick, and it's beautifully tender. Usually it's served with garlic butter – very retro – but I was thinking we could do something a bit different..."

And we spent the next two hours experimenting with different flavour combinations and accompaniments, and by the end of it we had a dish that was, as Sibongile put it, "To die for, doll!"

When Guido tasted it, after ending yet another angst-filled call from Florence, this time apparently apologising for her earlier rant, he did his finger-kissing schtick and said, "Pippa, sweetheart. You. Are. On. Fire."

It was true. I was cooking better than I had for years. The weather, the ingredients, the views and most of all the new challenges were inspiring me to take risks and have fun in a way I hadn't done when I was working on the Thatchell's range. I'd slipped into a bit of a rut, I realised, and I was loving being booted firmly out of it.

But, of course, it wasn't for ever. Soon we'd be back in London, I'd be back on posh ready-meal duty, and Tamar would be wanting her job back. Perhaps it was time to think about looking around for something else, once the wedding was out of the way. Now that Nick was working for himself, we might be able to co-ordinate our time a bit better.

It occurred to me as I cleaned down my bench, scrubbing away at the splatters of squid ink, that I'd pretty much shelved my ambitions in the past few years. If you'd asked me when I was twenty where I saw myself in ten years time (as Guido had done, in fact, when he interviewed me), I'd have said I wanted to run my own restaurant, or at the very least be head chef somewhere with a serious reputation. But somewhere along the way, I'd lost that hunger. I'd wanted to be with Nick more than I'd wanted anything else – no matter what Erica might think – and I'd left something important behind along the way.

"Why are you looking so gloomy, Pippa?" said Guido, snapping me out of my reverie.

"Just thinking about stuff," I said. "Nick. The wedding. Work."

Guido said, "I think we're done here for today. Let's get back to the hotel and I'll buy you a drink."

An hour later, I'd showered and changed into a summer dress, and we were sitting outside on the terrace. Flourishing magenta bougainvilleas surrounded the turquoise swimming pool, which reflected the full moon in its water. I was taking great cooling swigs of a G&T and Guido was making rapid inroads into his second beer.

We ran through our plans for the next three days and the intimidating list of things that still needed to be done, and Guido said again how happy he was with my work, making me feel all shy and pleased.

I said, "I'm having a great time. I'm really loving this – the work for Thatchell's is fascinating but this is the most fun I've had in ages."

Guido laughed. "This is the easy part. When we're out here again in January filming, there are going to be days when all you see is the inside of a makeshift kitchen in the middle of nowhere, and it's tiny even before they put the lights and camera equipment in, and you can't get from the bench to the chiller without tripping over cables. When we were filming *Guido Goes Bamboo* in Vietnam, Alex – you remember him – didn't sort some mussels properly and we were all as sick as dogs. And there was only one toilet. It's not all luxury hotels with pools."

So that was the reason for Alex's sudden and ignominious departure three years before.

As the evening wore on, Guido's stories became even more scurrilous. He told me about roping in a group of Thai ladyboys as extras in Bangkok when the models who were supposed to be playing the glamorous guests at a dinner failed to turn up. He told how he'd had a narrow escape from the paparazzi in the red light district in Amsterdam, and about the time he got sold a wrap of baking powder by a dodgy dealer in New York, and I began to understand why Florence got a bit twitchy when he was filming on location. By this stage I'd had a few drinks myself, and felt emboldened enough to ask him more about their relationship, as we ate meltingly delicious springbok carpaccio for our starter.

"Do you think you'll marry her?"

"Marry her? I doubt it, sweetheart."

I drank some wine. "Do you love her?"

"Florence is a very beautiful woman," he said. "She understands me, and she knows where the bodies are buried."

He hadn't really answered my question, I thought. Then I realised that he had.

"And what about you?" he asked. "Not long now until your wedding. Nervous?"

"Not about the wedding," I said. "Nick's got it all under control. Maybe a bit too much under control. He's gone a bit mad with it all. But it's going to be a very special day. It's what he wants."

"And afterwards?"

"I don't know," I said. "I was thinking about that today. I was wondering… when Tamar goes on maternity leave… Were you thinking of getting someone to cover for her?"

"There will be another television series, hopefully," he said. "Platinum Productions have said that if this does well, they'll pitch another to Channel 4. Maybe America next time. And if Thatchell's extend their range, there will certainly be more work there than you and I can cope with. So we'll need to get either another Tamar or," he paused, "another you, if you'd like to do more of the television work."

"Guido, I'd love to," I said. "I'm in my element here."

"Good," he said. "It's yours if you want it, Pippa."

I was thanking him with embarrassing gushiness when my phone rang, and it was Callie to talk about the hen night. When I had finished chatting to her and returned to our table, Guido had ordered grilled pineapple with mint gremolata, and the mood had reverted to businesslike. We made plans for the next day's work and drank coffee and after a bit I started to yawn uncontrollably, and made my excuses and went to my room.

Even though I was alone, I felt a bit furtive when I opened Nick's blog on my phone. Checking it had become a bit of a habit, a compulsion, like biting my nails. He posted something on it just about every day, and he'd built up a little community of followers who laughed at his posts, gave him advice and shared their experiences with one another. And even though he and I had spoken on the phone almost every night – well, three out of five nights – I was conscious that our conversations had mostly been about me, my work, the exciting new world that was opening up to me. When Nick talked about the wedding, he talked to other people. It made me feel uneasy, jealous even, of the relationships he was building up with these online strangers.

Today's post was about the wedding photography.

So, today I met up with Eliza, who's going to be recording the big day for posterity. This is the only aspect of the day that I'm dreading. Obviously we're going to have photographs of the wedding, and I'm sure they'll be great, but... I look like a chud in photos. I know what you're thinking, but it's true. Even when I was a kid, I was always the one at the back of the class photo caught with my face all scrunched up, about to sneeze. And as an adult, I always look like my head is too big - like, way bigger than everyone else's head. When I try to smile I look like I'm gurning, and when I don't I look like someone's died. So Eliza is going to need some serious Photoshop skillz to sort me out!

How did your wedding pics turn out? Are there any you really rate or hate, and why?

There were loads of responses, many of them with photos attached. I scrolled down through them: men in morning suits with top hats like Iain had worn; men in dinner jackets and ordinary-looking suits with any number of different-coloured ties and waistcoats and buttonholes. A couple in skiing gear at the top of a mountain, looking happy enough to fly back down it. Arty images of brides in wedding dresses, flatteringly posed and lit. It was one of those that made me pause, scroll back a bit, and zoom in. Nick hadn't commented on all the photos, but he had on that one. He'd written, "Blimey! You look gorgeous, although to be fair the photographer did have pretty good raw material to work with."

The woman was wearing a dress so plain and perfectly fitting it had to have cost a fortune. She was standing in a stone archway, half-turned away from the camera, looking down at the simple bouquet of lilies in her hands. Her tousled blonde hair concealed her face, but I could see from the curve of her forehead and cheek how beautiful she was – and how familiar.

"This is my favourite wedding photo. I hate the camera too, as you know – I didn't even realise the tog was taking this one, which is probs why it's my favourite! It turned out a lot better than my marriage did, rofl. B x." And then I understood.

The first time I saw Bethany, I didn't really see her, if you see what I mean, because of Nick. There were loads of people in Borderline that night ten years ago, a hundred at least, but he was the only one that mattered. Bethany was there, though. She was there because her band, an all-woman post-punk outfit called 'Grrl, Banned' had played the first set, and she'd stayed because she was Nick's girlfriend.

I like to think that if I had known about her, I'd have said no when Nick rang me a few days later and asked to meet for a drink. But he didn't tell me, when their set finished and we had a shouted conversation over the music about how amazing it was to see each other and what we were doing now, and I gave him my new number and told him he must call me, he must promise he would.

He did call, and we met up on Sunday, my day off work, at a riverside pub. It was late summer, the leaves just beginning to turn golden, but still warm enough to sit outside with our jackets on, collars turned up against the breeze, sipping lager and telling each other about our lives.

I described my shitty room in the house I shared with three other chefs and a girl who was trying to break into modelling, and made him laugh with my accounts of how we were all permanently skint, but still managed to find enough spare change for cheap red wine on our nights off, even if it meant not buying food or even loo paper. He told me that Deathly Hush was doing okay, they had loads of gigs lined up but the longed-for record deal was proving elusive, and Iain was thinking about trying something different, like starting a design agency, which was after all what they'd both trained to do.

Then there was a bit of a pause in the conversation, and Nick said, "So, are you seeing anyone?"

I blushed. The truth was, I hadn't actually had a boyfriend since him. I'd had a long succession of one- and two-night stands, but I'd stayed resolutely single, determined not to have my heart broken again.

"Not right now," I said. "You?" I was confident that his answer would be no too, because otherwise why were we here? Surely he could feel the same, incredibly powerful sense of connection I felt, the sense of coming home?

But he said, "It's kind of complicated." And then he told me about Bethany. Bethany, who played in a band and loved football and sounded like the coolest of cool girls.

They'd been going out for about a year, he said, on and off. The on was because he really liked her – he didn't have to say it, I could tell by the look on his face when he talked about her, a kind of hurt that made me twist inside with jealousy, and at the same time wrap my arms around him and make it all better. And the off was because Bethany was, as he put it, a free spirit. It didn't take much questioning to learn that this meant she was chronically unfaithful.

"Why do you put up with it?" I asked.

"I don't," he said. "I tell her it's over, but then she comes back and tells me she loves me and she's sorry, and I end up forgiving her." He shrugged. "What a mug."

"So, like, right now, is it on or is it off?" I said, emboldened by three pints of Stella. "Because, Nick, the thing is, when I saw you the other night, I felt…"

"I know," he said. "I felt it too. And as of now, it's off. The other night, when I saw you, I ended it."

He wasn't lying – Nick's never lied to me, as far as I know, in all the time we've been together. So we started seeing each other again, just casually, testing the water, seeing whether what we'd had when we were teenagers could be made to work again, in our new, grown-up lives. We met up for drinks a couple more times, we saw a movie and afterwards he came back to my shared hovel and had coffee, but he didn't stay the night. And I believed him when he told me that Bethany had come back yet again, wanting to be taken back, and he'd said that this time it wasn't going to happen, because he'd met someone else. I believed him because when he told me about it, he also told me he'd slept with her.

"I'm so sorry, Pippa," he said. "I'll totally understand if you want to call it off. It was a shitty, stupid thing to do. It's inexcusable."

He'd called me at work, asking to see me about something important, and I'd met him during my break from work in a branch of Caffè Nero on the Strand. The table where we sat was so tiny our knees were touching, and the room was so crowded I couldn't move them away, so I stood up, leaving my coffee unfinished.

"You're right," I said. "It's inexcusable. Now I'm going to go back to work."

And I did. Nick didn't contact me, apart from a text saying again that he was sorry. But I couldn't stop thinking about him. We hadn't actually been going out, I reasoned. He hadn't cheated on me, as such. And I missed him. Those few meetings, dates, whatever they'd been, had brought back such a torrent of longing for him, a tap that, once opened, couldn't be turned off. I waited a week, then another, to see if I'd stop thinking about him, stop missing him, stop longing for his touch and his smell. But I didn't, so I gave in and called him.

"Okay," I said. "Let's give this a go, if you still want to."

I spent that night at Nick's flat, and never really left. For the first couple of months we were together, I was on high alert all the time, constantly worried that she was going to invade our life like some tousle-haired, Converse-wearing Visigoth and steal Nick back again. I combed the flat obsessively for reminders of her, and found a handful of photographs, a demo CD for her band, and a stash of her Calvin Klein toiletries in the bathroom, and threw them all in the bin as soon as they came to light.

And I snooped. Looking back, I can remember the shame I when I accessed Nick's email to see if she'd contacted him, picked up his phone if a text message arrived when he wasn't in the room, to see who it was from. But she never did contact him, and as the months went by I began to feel more secure, more confident that I was the one Nick wanted to be with, and eventually, I reached the point where I simply stopped worrying about her.

There were a few moments, like when we were packing to move to our new home, and I found a gorgeous silk scarf crumpled up at the back of a drawer, still bearing a hint of scent, and realised it must have been hers (and consigned it to the charity shop bag without a backward glance). When Iain told us he'd heard that Bethany had moved up to Edinburgh, and Nick said, "Oh, really?", and I wondered if he was just pretending to be indifferent or really was. And when her wedding photos appeared on a mutual friend's Facebook feed and I couldn't resist looking at them and spending a few minutes torturing myself with her effortless, cool beauty. But apart from that, I barely thought of her, and I had no reason to believe that Nick thought of her either, until now.

The next couple of days passed in a blur of sunshine, cooking and frantic note-taking. I was learning all the time, I loved the new people I was meeting and the new ingredients I was tasting and experimenting with. Even Florence appeared to have calmed down and was restricting her calls to two or three per day – or perhaps Guido was just limiting the number he answered. I was busy and stressed, I'd broken four fingernails and was sporting a sunburned nose from a lunchtime spent playing truant in the swimming pool. And I'd managed to put my worries about Nick to the back of my mind.

We landed back in Johannesburg on another brilliantly sunny morning, and Guido announced that we'd have the day off before our flight home in the evening. He was going to meet an old friend for lunch, he said, so I was on my own.

"Go shopping, Pippa," he suggested. "You deserve a treat, you've been working very hard. We need to be at the airport for six o'clock. I'll meet you there."

This suddenly seemed like an excellent idea. I entrusted Guido and our driver with my luggage and got in a taxi.

"Take me to the good shops," I said.

"Sandton City," said the cabbie. "That's where all the ladies go to shop till they drop."

He wasn't joking. I hadn't seen very much of South Africa beyond the inside of restaurants, but I had seen heartbreaking glimpses of the poverty in which many people lived: shanty-towns sprawling for miles alongside motorways, manual labourers carefully counting their coins before buying roast corn on the cob for their lunch, and women with babies begging for spare change at traffic lights. Sibongile had told me without a trace of self-pity that she was putting her three younger sisters and two brothers through school on her freelance wages.

But Sandton City was all about wealth. It was a vast mall, glittering with Christmas decorations and housing just about every high-end designer store I'd ever heard of, along with a few I hadn't. Everyone was immaculately dressed and there was just the same air of controlled frenzy you get on Bond Street on a Saturday. I mentally flexed my credit card and entered the fray.

Two hours later, I was buckling under the weight of packets of biltong for Nick, a book of South African poetry for Mum, wine for Dad, scent for Callie, gorgeous tigers-eye necklaces for Tamar and Eloise, a biography of Nelson Mandela for Erica, a giraffe on a stick for Spanx and two pairs of shoes for me. I just had time for a late lunch and a final browse before getting the train to the airport.

I was heading for the nearest coffee shop in the manner of a weary traveller struggling through the desert towards a distant clump of palm trees that might be an oasis or might be a mirage, when I saw the dress.

It was as if the bright lights of the mall had been dimmed and the chattering of the crowd stilled. It was as if there was nothing in the world but me and the dress. It was as if sweet music started to play... Okay, it was just a dress. But it was seriously cool. It was the only thing in the window of a little boutique, styled to look like a winter wonderland with sparkly icicles and frosted fir trees, and the dress itself looked like it was made of snow – not the horrid icy, sludgy kind but the soft pillowy kind you want to lie down and make angels in.

I stopped noticing my aching feet and hurried towards the shop as fast as I could. It was only a few yards away, but what if someone else got there first? I was quite out of breath by the time I burst through the door, grabbed the nearest assistant and gasped, "That dress in the window! I have to try it!"

"But, madam," he looked bemused, "That dress is left over from our winter collection. It's only in the window for display purposes, it's not actually for sale."

"Please!" I said. "It's so beautiful, and I'm flying back to London tonight and I'm getting married in February and I don't have a dress, and if you don't let me try it, I'll... I'll cry. And you don't want to make me cry, do you?"

He looked understandably alarmed at the mad English woman who had invaded his store. I could see him wondering whether to call security.

"Please," I said again, a bit more calmly.

He shook his head. "I'm going to have to call my manager."

It took him three goes to get through, while I paced up and down, looking longingly at the dress.

"Yes," he said. "The one in the window, the Trina Joubert. The lady really wants to try it on." He lowered his voice and I didn't catch what he said next. I suspect it may have been something along the lines of, "And I'm worried that if I don't let her, she'll tear my head off with her bare hands and then go after my family." But after a bit more persuasion, he said, "Okay. Yes, of course I will. Okay. Cheers."

"She says yes," he said.

"Thank you!" I said, "Thank you so, so much. You're the kindest person I've ever met."

It took him ages to make his way through the faux forest and get the dress off the mannequin, while I stood shifting from foot to foot and looking at my watch. I was going to have to get into the frock in record time and make the fastest decision ever, or I'd be horribly late to meet Guido. Eventually it was liberated.

And it was perfect, far better than the last one I'd tried with Katharine. It wasn't even particularly weddingy, just a lovely column of plain white silk that clung in all the right places and slid forgivingly over all the other bits. It had a low back that was just high enough for my bra not to show. It had sparkly straps almost exactly the same as the ones on my shoes, and it came with a little faux fur wrap that covered my shoulders and would stop me freezing to death. I couldn't stop smiling as I emerged from the fitting room to give the assistant, who'd told me his name was Valli, a quick twirl.

"Look!" I said. "I've found my wedding dress! And it's all thanks to you!"

"Aww, that's just beautiful," he said. "It's like it's made for you, hey? And you won't believe this. My boss called again while you were trying it on, and she said that because it's old stock, it's been reduced by seventy five percent. And – this is seriously amazing – Trina Joubert has emigrated to

New Zealand and she's not making wedding dresses any more. So it's not just a bargain, it's a one-off!"

By the time I'd paid for the dress, Valli and I were best mates. He told me that he and his boyfriend were getting married next year too. I promised to friend him on Facebook, and gave him one of the bottles of wine I'd bought for Dad. I even told him that if he happened to be in London in February, he must come to our wedding. Then I legged it to the station and flung myself and my legion of shopping bags into a carriage just as the sliding doors were closing.

"Good shopping?" Guido asked, when we finally located each other at the airport.

"Amazing!" I said. "Look at the stunning jewellery I bought for the girls in the office, and the shoes I found. And you won't believe it, but I've finally bought a wedding dress. It was such a bargain and it's gorgeous. I'll show you."

But I couldn't. The books were there, and the shoes and the wine and all the rest, but not the dress. I'd left it behind, somewhere in the mall or on the train.

When I told Nick about it, I cried. As soon as I got home, he ran me a hot bath with some aromatherapy oil in it, brought me a cup of tea and perched on the lid of the loo.

"So," he said, "tell me all about the trip. How did it go?"

And instead of recounting all my adventures and waxing lyrical about the scenery and the amazing food and the challenge of it all, instead of telling him I'd read the blog and asking him if he was back in touch with Bethany, I said, "I found a wedding dress. But I lost it." And I let out a huge, gulping sob, and soon I was having a good old howl on his shoulder, drenching his shirt with jasmine-scented water.

"My lovely Pippa, don't cry," he soothed. "We'll get it back, surely? Someone will have found it and handed it in?"

"They won't," I sniffed. "There are so many poor people there, Nick. If they found a dress that cost a month's wages, they'd keep it. Of course they would. Or sell it. And I wouldn't blame them at all. It's my fault for being such a stupid idiot."

"You'll find another dress," Nick said. "I know you will. You know what kind you want now, get Callie to help you look on Google. And anyway, you're so beautiful, you could get married in your nightie and still look stunning, and I'd still love you."

I managed a feeble laugh. My nightie is an ancient sweatshirt of Nick's with a picture of Robert Plant on it and a big hole under the left armpit, and I wouldn't let anyone but him see me in it.

"Anyway," I said, "how's the rest of it going? The wedding stuff?"

"Great!" he said. "Mum and I have done all the invitations, they're ready to post. I printed some extra ones for you to see, they look awesome. Mum thinks we should send them in batches, in case there's some sort of terrorist action and our local post box gets blown up. I can't decide if that's bonkers or actually quite sensible. And I've emailed Royal Mail to ask whether they do first-class stamps in silver, because they'll tone in so much better with the colour scheme. And then we've got our menu tasting at Brocklebury Manor next week. Mum's going to come along to that, she's got loads of good ideas about catering for the kids. And Callie says everything's sorted for your hen night – having it on New Year's Eve is going to be brilliant, don't you think? And I asked your mum to make a list of suggested readings for the ceremony, so when you've got a second, have a look and tell me whether you like them…"

He carried on, saying something about the flowers he and Callie had chosen and something about the plans Iain was making for his stag night. I closed my eyes and lay back in the hot water. He wasn't going to mention Bethany, and I couldn't summon up the courage to, either. I suddenly felt very, very tired and the excitement of the past few days had evaporated along with the last whiff of jasmine.

"Oh, and I bought you a present," he said. "Hold on, I'll go and find it."

I heard the door of our wardrobe open and close, then a few drawers opening and closing too, and then Nick came back.

"Look!" he said proudly. "I ordered it online. Mum found the website, she's gone a bit online-shopping crazy."

He held up a black cotton T-shirt. In large, squirly foil letters across the front was printed 'Mrs Pickford'.

I'd been wondering when to talk to Nick about what Guido had said about work, and now I was faced with another conversation I really didn't want to have. Mrs Pickford was Erica, not me. I was Pippa Martin, and I had no intention of changing that, no matter what it would say on my passport.

I pulled the plug out of the bath and wrapped myself in my towel.

"I'd better unpack and get to work," I said. "I told Guido I'd try and be in by lunchtime."

CHAPTER TWELVE

From: nick@digitaldrawingboard.com
To: imogen@brockleburymanor.co.uk
Subject: Numbers

Hi Imogen

I hope you're well. You'll be relieved to hear that we have finalised our guest list at last, and the invitations have been sent out. As it's been such short notice, we're expecting a relatively high attrition rate, so I expect there will be about 150 guests. As soon as we have RSVPs I'll be able to confirm the exact numbers. Obviously this will affect the menu to some extent, but we'd like to go ahead with the tasting on Friday anyway, as discussed with Hugh.

Hope that's all okay, and thanks again for your patience. Look forward to seeing you then.

Nick

"Well, this is very nice, isn't it?" said Erica, as the taxi's headlights illuminated the stone façade of Brocklebury Manor. "What an attractive building. When was it built?"

Nick launched into a potted history of the place, which I realised he must know off by heart by now. I had to admit that it did look gorgeous – the huge hall was dwarfed by a giant Christmas tree, festooned with twinkling white lights and tasteful gold and silver decorations, not at all like the tatty multicoloured ones that Nick and I have on our tree at home. There was a gorgeous smell of pine needles and mulled wine hanging in the air.

Imogen greeted us at the not-a-reception-desk.

"Hello, Nick, hello, Pippa, how lovely to see you again. You do look well, have you been somewhere hot? And you must be Mrs Pickford, how nice to meet you." She kissed us and shook Erica's hand. "Now, if you'd like to come through to the dining room, Hugh is waiting to meet you."

Hugh Jameson was hard to miss. He made the solid dining chair he sat in look like something out of a doll's house, and when he stood up to greet us he towered over Nick, who's six foot two, and I almost had to reach up to shake his hand. Restaurant kitchens aren't renowned for their spaciousness, and I decided that Hugh must have serious talent to make up for what was a quite significant physical disadvantage. I remembered Nick's joke about him being called Huge Amazon, and caught his eye and realised he'd remembered it too. We only just managed not to giggle.

"Now," said Imogen, "You've got your work cut out here, Hugh, because Pippa's a chef too and she's extremely hard to please! I'll get a bottle of champagne sent out for you and leave you all to it."

"Where is it you work then, Pippa?" Hugh asked as we sat down.

I told him about Guido and Thatchell's and the television shows, and then said, "But Imogen mentioned that you used to work for Marcus Wareing. Amazing! Is he as scary as he seems on telly?"

But just as Hugh opened his mouth to tell me, Erica said, "Now, Pippa, you know it's rude to talk shop," as if I was about six years old. I felt myself flushing with annoyance, Hugh shut up and there was a bit of an awkward silence while the champagne was opened.

"Er… This is a sparkling wine from the Loire region," Hugh said. "It's a very popular choice with our wedding couples but of course there are many other options on the list at a range of price points, if you'd like to have a look."

Nick said, "Do you have any with silver labels, rather than gold?"

"Nick!" I said, "Shouldn't we be tasting the wine, not doing a design crit on the label?"

Poor Hugh. I could see him thinking that this was going to be a long afternoon.

"I have three menus to show you," he said, "Of course we're completely flexible and can accommodate just about anything, within reason, but these are just a few of the choices that have proved popular at the weddings we've hosted recently."

He handed us each a little sheaf of printed cards.

"This looks fab," I said. "I really like the selection of canapés on this one, and I love the idea of serving venison. And cheese toasties at midnight sound great. But then so does this one, with the monkfish. It all looks gorgeous, it's going to be so hard to decide! I'm so glad you don't do boring, horrible menus like something out of the seventies, with melon then supremes of chicken. I'm really looking forward to it."

Hugh said something about how it was an honour as well as a challenge to be catering for a fellow cook, and I glowed a bit with pride, especially as he was way out of my league professionally.

Nick said, "I could have some personalised sticky labels printed to go with the design of the invitations. I'd have to do them slightly larger, so they'd cover the gold labels, or we could just soak them off, I suppose. It wouldn't take long."

A look of alarm crossed Hugh's face at the idea of his hard-pressed waiting staff spending hours peeling labels off wine bottles, but he said diplomatically that he was sure the front-of-house manager would be happy to discuss whatever thoughts Nick had about serving the wine.

Then Erica said, "Now, there are a few people who have dietary preferences that we'll have to bear in mind. I've made a little list." She took a sheet of A4 paper, covered in dense print, out of her bag and smoothed it out. "My niece Deirdre has a severe nut allergy, so that rules out anything with chocolate, as well as the cherry tomato and pesto canapés and the lavender and almond-crusted lamb. My niece Alison and her husband recently converted to Islam, and understandably they object to anything containing pork being prepared at the same time as their meals. So we won't be able to serve the Iberico ham croquettes or the monkfish, because I see that is wrapped in pancetta. But that wouldn't be an option anyway, because my brother David has never been able to eat fish. Andrew and his wife Barbara dislike foreign food, and will only eat well-done meat, so I must ask that if we do serve venison, it's cooked through. Although Patricia has a moral objection to eating game anyway, she feels it's elitist and I'm inclined to agree. And of course we have quite a few children attending, and I always believe it's wiser to keep things simple for them. It's so important that the little ones eat a good meal at all-day events or they can get a bit fractious. And of course I'm a vegan and prefer to eat locally produced, organic food, but apart from that I'm not fussy at all."

I gazed at her in horror. Was the menu at my wedding going to be dictated entirely by the innumerable cousins and their horrible offspring? If parents were worried about their kids slipping into hypoglycaemic comas because they were too fussy to eat perfectly normal food, why the hell couldn't they just stop off at MacDonald's on the way or bring bags of crisps in their handbags? Erica's idea of locally produced food seemed to include tinned tomato soup from our corner shop. And Alison was one of the few of Nick's cousins who I had actually met, when we'd been to her wedding just a few months ago, and they'd served a hog roast, so I took this Damascene conversion story with a pinch of salt.

As if reading my mind, Erica went on, "And of course, as a healthcare professional, I have grave concerns about the level of salt in modern diets, so I think it's important that we keep that to a minimum across all the dishes, and don't serve it on the tables unless it's a low-sodium alternative."

I drank some champagne and said mutinously, "But salt in cooking is important. I'd never serve food to a diner that wasn't properly seasoned and the low-sodium stuff just tastes of chlorine. Don't you agree, Hugh?"

Erica said, "It's just a question of educating one's palate. I find fresh herbs and lemon juice are all the seasoning I need."

No you bloody don't, I thought, you put mountains of raw chilli on every single thing I cook.

In spite of his height, Hugh seemed to have shrunk slightly in his chair. "We've won many awards for our food here at Brocklebury," he said, "but that doesn't mean it always has to be fancy. We can keep things very simple if you'd prefer, and we can cater for just about any dietary restriction, although it does increase the cost if we're preparing lots of special dishes. I would recommend that, purely for practical purposes, we keep the number of off-menu choices to a minimum and focus on choosing a meal that all your guests will be able to enjoy."

I said, "But I really liked the sound of the monkfish."

Erica said, "Monkfish is extremely vulnerable to overfishing. I would have thought that as a chef, Pippa, you would pay more attention to choosing sustainable ingredients."

Nick looked up from his iPad and said, "You know me, I'll eat anything, so long as it's not parsnips. So don't worry about me. Look, I've done a rough design for the wine labels."

I said, "Okay, fine. Venison then. But I'm not having it well done."

Erica said, "Pippa agrees with me that the most important thing about a wedding is the bringing together of friends and family, and the sharing of a joyful day. I know you aren't going to be selfish or unreasonable about this, and anyway you'll be far too excited to eat much on the day, as well as watching your weight for the honeymoon."

Hugh said, "Excuse me a moment, I'm just going to see how things are going in the kitchen," and legged it.

I didn't speak to Nick or Erica all the way home. I bought a copy of *Heat* at the station and read it from cover to cover, silently fuming. Nick asked if he could borrow my phone because his iPad battery was flat, and spent the journey tapping away on it. Erica closed her eyes and breathed deeply, apparently catching up on her evening meditation.

When we got home I went to bed, and opened Nick's blog on my phone. I'd guessed right – he had been composing a post on the train, and as guilty as it made me feel, I couldn't not see what he'd said.

So here it is, followers – the great menu reveal! It's quite tricky because there are loads of fussy eaters in my family, which I hadn't had a clue about until Mum told me – just as well, otherwise we would have had a load of starving guests! But because Pippa's so creative with food, she's suggested a menu that I reckon should go down well with all of them, and I'm sure will be delicious too. I'll mostly be getting pissed and feeling too sick with nerves about my speech to eat, anyway! (Speaking of which, I've had a brilliant idea for the wine – I'm going to get some custom-designed labels printed that will fit with our colour and font choices. I've posted an initial layout below, and I'm really pleased with it.) But back to the food. What do you reckon to this?

Canapés:
Raw vegetable crudités with olive oil and lemon dressing
Smoked tofu in filo pastry
Home-made beetroot crisps with fresh herbs and chilli

Starters:
Tomato soup
or
Fresh melon balls

Main course:
Supreme of chicken with steamed potatoes, carrots and peas
or
Soy bean roast with steamed potatoes, carrots and peas

Dessert:
Meringues with berry coulis
or
Fresh fruit salad

Late-night nibbles:
Mixed bean and vegetable chilli tortillas

That sounds like it's going keep everyone happy, doesn't it?

As had become my habit, I scrolled quickly through the comments, looking for one name. There it was, about the seven posts down. "Sounds totes mezzin! Wish I could be there. YHM, btw ;) B xx."

That night, I had a dream that I was walking down the aisle on my wedding day, holding Dad's arm. My hands were clutched tightly around my bouquet, but when I looked down at it, I realised I was holding a bunch of carrots, and I had no clothes on, only my strappy silver shoes. And when I looked up towards the table where the registrar was waiting, I realised that Bethany had got there first, and she was waiting in my place next to Nick. I tried to make Dad hurry up, to get to the end of the seemingly endless aisle so I could tell the registrar that there'd been a mistake, and I was here, but there seemed to be a forest of thorns in my way, and when I tried to push through them they pierced my naked skin agonisingly.

My eyes snapped open and I realised Spanx was lying on my chest, kneading me with his needle-sharp claws.

"Hello, you," I mumbled sleepily. "That's no way to wake your humans up on a Saturday morning, is it? Is it?" Spanx narrowed his eyes at me and cranked up the volume of his purrs. I gave him a scratch behind the ears. "And where's Nick? What's he doing up so early? And more to the point, where's my morning coffee in bed?"

Spanx didn't know, but there was a look of steely determination in his amber eyes that told me I wasn't going to be allowed to get up for a good long time, not while I was required for duty as heated cat furniture. We rolled over and I pulled his warm furry back against my tummy and covered us both with the duvet. Spanx purred even louder, and I strained to listen for any sounds from the rest of the flat. Then I heard Nick's voice.

"Here you go, Mum, green tea and a bowl of that worthy granola stuff you like, with oat milk."

"Thank you, darling," Erica said. "Now, what's on the agenda for today?"

"Well, I thought I'd get cracking with designing the menu and order of service cards, as soon as Pippa wakes up," he said.

"And there are the table centrepieces to do," said Erica. "That helpful man I rang at the garden centre in Hendon had so much good advice on how to grow snowdrops in pots, I thought I might get the Tube up there later and buy some bulbs, and we can order the pots online and get them planted up before Christmas."

"Speaking of which," Nick said, "I need to go into town and do a bit of shopping. I'm not looking forward to braving Bond Street but it's got to be done. And while I'm there I thought I might have a look at that shop you found that does the antique silver cake stands."

"That's marvellous," Erica said. "And if I do have a spare second, I might as well pop into Selfridges and have a look at hats. Justine still hasn't confirmed what she's going to be wearing so I think I shall probably stick to taupe, that's safest, isn't it?"

"I can't really advise on the hat front, Mum," said Nick. "Maybe drop Callie a line if you're not sure? But that reminds me, I need to pick up the ushers' ties at some point. If I don't have time this weekend I'll make a plan to get to Saville Row at some point next week. Typical that there's only one shop in bloody London that does the right shade of grey!"

"Why don't I put that on my list?" Erica said. "What was the name of the shop again?"

"That would be brilliant, thanks Mum. If you're able to go that, then I can finish off the playlist I've been putting

together for the band, and do the labels for the vodka miniatures – we did decide Grey Goose for the favours, didn't
we? Let me write down that address for you."

I pulled the pillow over my head, but it didn't help – I
could still hear them.

"It's no good," I said to Spanx, "We can't lie here lazing
about when they've been up doing Wedmin for shagging
hours already. Come on, get your fluffy orange arse out of
bed." I pushed him gently away and he stalked off in high dud-
geon, his stripy tail curved like an affronted question mark.

I showered and dressed and sloped through to the
kitchen, feeling both useless and guilty.

"Morning, sleeping beauty," Nick said. "I was going to
bring you a coffee earlier but you were out like a light. I
think you're still jet lagged, you know."

I switched on the kettle, and said rather testily that you
don't get jet lag on overnight flights when the time difference is only two hours.

"Well, I'm delighted you had a good sleep, anyway,"
Erica said pointedly, "because you've got a busy day ahead
of you, if your to-do list is anything like as long as Nick's."

Did I? Actually, I'd been thinking it would be rather nice
to wander down to Maltby Street and pick up some coffee
and custard doughnuts, then spend the afternoon on the
sofa with Spanx and the duvet, catching up on *EastEnders*
until it was time to open a bottle of wine and watch *The X
Factor*. But something told me Erica would take a dim view
of that plan.

"Er… yes," I said. "I've actually got an appointment to try
on dresses at…" I racked my brains, "Liberty! I've not been
there and they've apparently got a really good selection."

Erica nodded approvingly. "Well, I'll be heading into
town later so why don't I come along and have a look too?

I'm beginning to think your expectations must be unrealistic, Pippa, because it's quite absurd that you haven't found anything suitable yet. A bit of firm guidance…"

"No!" I said. "No, thank you, Erica. I've agreed to meet Katharine. We're going to have lunch first and then she wanted to go shopping for… er… vibrators. So really, I must be off."

Blushing furiously (I've never been a convincing liar), I stuffed my purse, phone and keys into my bag, put my coat on and hurried out.

Once I emerged into the street, I'd rather run out of steam. What the hell was I going to do? I'd effectively exiled myself from the flat for the rest of the day, and I had no intention of embarking on another soul-destroying wedding dress-shopping session, even if there was any chance I'd be able to get a last-minute appointment, which there wasn't. I thought of getting the train to Hampshire and going to visit Mum and Dad or Callie and Phoebe, but I couldn't face more wedding talk. I could go and see a film, but there wasn't anything on that I wanted to watch.

So I went to Borough Market and bought three kilos of springbok steak, and then got the Tube to work and spent the afternoon in the kitchen, happily experimenting with recipes for the rather tastelessly named 'More Bang for your Buck' episode of *Guido's African Safari* until I had them nailed.

It was after eight that evening when I got home. I felt so buoyed up by my successful day that I think I might have actually been singing when I opened the front door, and I called out a cheery "Hello!" to Nick and Erica, who were sitting in the kitchen with a bottle of red and a takeaway from the Vietnamese place.

"Hey Pip," Nick said. "We ordered you some meatball pho, is that okay?" He paused, his chopsticks halfway up to his mouth. "Pip? You look... You've done it, haven't you? You've found a dress!" And he pushed back his chair and swept me up in a massive hug and spun me round. "I could tell as soon as you walked in! Look at you, you're grinning like a loon! Is it cool? No, don't tell me, I want it to be a surprise!"

Christmas with Nick has always been my absolute favourite time of the year. With Erica abroad and my parents choosing to spend most of their Christmasses travelling to exotic destinations together ("The south coast of England in December!" Mum always laments, "Could anything, anywhere be more depressing?" This year they were off to Vienna to watch operas and eat sachertorte), we've never had any family obligations, and although one year we hosted Christmas lunch for a few of our similarly unencumbered friends, mostly we loved just being alone together.

We had various little rituals and traditions that were just ours. On Christmas Eve we'd order a curry and watch *Love, Actually* on Netflix. We made Christmas stockings for each other, filled with random, silly gifts (and one for Spanx with new toy mice, Dreamies and a tin of corned beef, which is his favourite thing in the world) and opened them in bed as soon as we woke up. Nick made bacon sandwiches for breakfast and we ate them with a glass of his lethal bloody Mary, then went for a walk along the river, laughing about how tasteful everyone else's Christmas trees were compared to ours. After we got home I'd change into the beautiful new underwear Nick always put in my stocking and one of my less saggy jumper dresses, we'd open the first of several bottles of prosecco and start cooking together.

By the end of the day we'd be smug and sated, congratulating ourselves on our good food and good fortune, before dancing badly together to the cheesiest of our favourite songs and falling into bed long after midnight.

Like I say, perfect. But somehow this year I wasn't looking forward to it as much as I usually did. I'd even felt a bit let down, instead of delighted like I would have expected to feel, when Erica announced that she was off to spend a few days with Andrew and Barbara in Halifax, no doubt feasting on Aunt Bessie's roast spuds and sprouts that had been in the pressure cooker since the clocks went back.

When Erica was around, especially when she was being her most insufferable, she successfully distracted me from the fact that I was constantly annoyed with Nick – a low-grade, niggling annoyance that threatened to spill over into anger at any second. Her presence made it difficult for the horrible tension between us to escalate into an actual argument, and I was afraid, once we started a row, of exactly how and where it would end.

Nick must have sensed my mood, because he was carefully solicitous of me. When I said, "Shall I ring the Ivory Arch, then?" Nick said, "No, don't worry, Pip, I'll do it. Why don't we have lamb rogan josh, I know you like it better than vindaloo?" even though vindaloo was what we had every year. He pressed pause on the remote control when I got up to put the kettle on, even though we'd seen the film so many times I could practically recite it in my sleep. He kept asking me if I was okay and not too tired and having a nice time. And the more solicitous he was, the more irritable I became.

Even the contents of my stocking were more lavish than usual. Instead of the usual panic-buy from Debenhams, he'd splashed out and bought me a beautiful silk bra and French knickers from La Perla. There were chocolates from L'Artisan instead of the usual family pack of wine gums, and a gorgeous cashmere cardigan, and even a pair of real pearl earrings.

"I thought maybe you'd want to wear them for the wedding," he said, looking all pleased and shy.

I was appalled by how much it all must have cost, and dreadful that I'd bought all his presents in one hasty Amazon order, and my guilt made me feel even crosser.

"Shall we head out for a stroll?" Nick said, once the stockings were opened, the bloody Mary drunk and Spanx happily mauling his catnip giraffe.

But when we opened the front door, it was pissing with rain.

"Let's not bother," I said.

"Go on, Pip!" said Nick. "We'll wear wellies and take an umbrella. It'll be fun. I'll run you a hot bath when we get back, with some of that whatsit Provence stuff I put in your stocking."

I said, "No, I don't really feel like it."

So Nick went for a run on his own and I put the oven on to cook our dinner and started to peel chestnuts in a resentful sort of way, and thought how ungrateful and petulant I was being, and how I really needed to snap out of it. But I couldn't.

"Pippa," Nick said later, once we were sitting at the table with our first glass of fizz, the flat beginning to fill with the smell of roasting goose, "we need to talk."

"Do we?" I said.

"I think we do," he said. "Something's wrong, and you're not telling me what it is. I know it's been hard for us to have time together, with Mum staying. You've been so good to her, and she really appreciates it. And I know it's been crazy for you, and with your hen night coming up next week, and then your trip to South Africa, and then obviously the wedding… There's so much going on, and I think you're worrying about stuff. I wish you'd talk to me."

Spanx jumped on to my lap and I scratched his bristly chin. I could feel a flood of words building up in my chest – about the wedding, about Bethany's reappearance on Nick's blog and in his life, and about the other thing, the one we never spoke about. But I had no idea how to begin to get them out. "I'm just a bit stressed, I guess. Work, you know."

"Pip, I don't think that's what it is. Come on. You're loving work at the moment. It's hectic and everything, but when you talk about it... That's the only time you seem really happy."

"Nick, I am happy!" I protested. "You know I am, and I love you. I'm just a bit worried about the wedding." I took a gulp of prosecco and a deep, slightly trembly breath.

"Pip. You don't need to worry about the wedding," Nick said. "Now you've found your dress – and I can't tell you how happy I am for you about that – there's nothing more for you to worry about. Mum, Callie and I are on the case. Everything's booked and sorted and all the deposits are paid. And you mustn't feel bad about me having done more of that than you. Are you worried things won't be right? I know you want everything to be perfect but we've done our best to make it be the kind of day you'd want. Shall we have a look at the USB Stick of All Knowledge? It's all on there. If there's anything you really want to change I'm sure it won't be too late, you must just say."

God, how I wished it was just a question of telling him I wanted pink peonies rather than snowdrops, or for Callie's dress to be Cadbury purple rather than the silvery grey she'd chosen, which I only knew about because I'd seen a picture of it on Nick's blog.

"It's not that," I said. "You've all been amazing, I appreciate it so much. But I just feel kind of like... Brocklebury

Manor, you know? The whole thing. It's got so huge and it's not what I imagined we'd have, really, ever."

"God, I know what you mean!" Nick said. "I didn't, either. Mum's been so generous. I never thought, when we went to Iain's wedding and it was all so fabulous, that we'd ever have anything like it. But we are. It's kind of daunting, isn't it?"

I wanted to scream with frustration. How could I tell him that I didn't bloody want an identikit stylish wedding in a country house hotel with hundreds of his relatives there and flower girls and pageboys and the most boring menu known to man? How the hell could I possibly tell him I'd lied about the dress? And if I couldn't talk about those things, how could I talk about the stuff that actually mattered?

"I'm just going to baste that goose." I opened the oven and over the sound of sizzling fat, I said, "It's too late to change things now, anyway. We've only got a month and a bit."

"It's not too late! Pippa, all that matters is that you're happy. Is it the food? I can email Hugh, and we can make a plan for you to go down there and see him again and change anything you want to change. Bollocks to the cousins, it's your wedding and if you want truffled foie gras and roast nightingale, that's what you must have."

He stood up and put his arms round me from behind. I turned round in his embrace, my hands still in the oven gloves, and looked up at him. I could feel tears starting to pour down my face, which was hot and scarlet from the heat of the oven.

"I don't care about the food," I said, "Well, I do, obviously. But that's such a small thing. I'm more…"

"Here," Nick said, "sit down. I'll top up your glass. Spanx wants to know what's wrong, and so do I. Come on, tell us."

"When you say it isn't too late to change things..." I began.

But then there was a knock at the door.

"Leave it," Nick said. "It'll be Jehovah's Witnesses, or something."

"No, I'll get it." I blew my nose on a piece of kitchen roll and went to the door, just as the knock came again and a familiar voice called, "Nick? Pippa? Are you there?"

It was Iain. He had the beginnings of a spectacular black eye, and there was blood all over his white shirt.

"I'm sorry I didn't ring first," he said. "I couldn't. Katharine chucked my mobile in the fishtank."

Once we'd got him changed into a jumper of Nick's and given him a stiff whisky, and reassured him that it was totally fine, he hadn't interrupted anything at all, it was only Christmas dinner after all, and Iain had stopped shaking quite so much, Nick said, "Surely Katharine didn't do that to you, did she?"

"Katharine? God, no," Iain said. "It was some bloke I've never seen before. I know who he is now, obviously, but until today I didn't have a fucking clue he even existed. Because Ludmilla never fucking said."

I had a pretty good idea what he was on about, of course, but Nick didn't. So I turned my back to them and started cutting crosses in sprouts, and listened in silence while Iain spilled the beans.

"I'm a total shit, I know," he said. "I feel like the world's biggest cunt. But you know how it is. Ludmilla's only twenty-two. She made it so easy. She was so, like, grateful for everything. She admired me. And Katharine... nothing I do is good enough for her. Because she deserves everything to be the best, obviously. And I let her down. And I deserve this, totally." He gestured at his rapidly swelling nose.

"Are you sure we shouldn't go to A&E?" said Nick.

"Nah," Iain said. "It's not broken. I've been twatted in the face before and lived to tell the tale. God, he was a big bastard, though. A fucking brickie, or something, by the looks of it."

"Peelers?" said Nick.

Iain shook his head. "I'm not going to report it. I'd have done the same thing, in his shoes. Sneaky fucker, though! He was waiting outside our flat when Katharine and I left this morning to go to bloody church. He said, 'Are you Iain Coulson?' And like a total dick I said yes, and he said, 'You've been fucking my woman, now I am going to fuck you up.' And it would have been a lot worse, only Katharine kicked him in the bollocks and we managed to get back inside the door."

"Bloody Nora, mate," said Nick.

"Yeah," said Iain. "And then she went completely mental. Not that I blame her. So she drowned both my mobiles – the main one and the other, the one I'd been using to… you know. It turns out she knew, she's known for a while. She was just waiting to see whether some of the stuff I'd bought on a credit card that she knew about was presents for her or not, but it wasn't, obviously. I got her a Lakeland voucher, same as usual. I thought that was what she wanted. And she's told me to fuck off out of her life and never come back. So I hailed a cab and, like, here I am."

It was undeniably true. There he was, at our kitchen table, with Spanx on his knee, a glass of our Jack Daniels in his hand and the flat filling up with smoke from his Marlboro Lights.

"Stay as long as you like," Nick said.

CHAPTER THIRTEEN

From: nick@digitaldrawingboard.com
To: caroline.travis@khanclarkegardner.co.uk
Subject: Begurk

That's how you spell the noise hens make, right?

Just wanted to say thanks for organising tomorrow night, and have a great time.

Nx

Want to know what's a bad idea? Having your hen night on New Year's Eve, the day before you leave to spend two weeks working abroad. And what's an even worse idea? Having the estranged husband of one of your hens being your self-invited house guest when you're getting ready to go on said hen night. Honestly, it was seriously awkward. There I was trying to put my make-up on, craning my neck because the only mirror in Nick's office is really high up on the wall, tiny and poorly lit, when Iain came and hovered in the doorway. I could just see a corner of his head in the mirror.

"Er… Pippa?" he said.

"Uhhh," I said, because I was putting on mascara and as everyone knows, it's essential to have your mouth open while doing this.

"I just wanted to say, um, I really appreciate you letting me use your sofa, and everything."

I hoped that this would be the prelude to him saying he'd found a hotel to move to, but it wasn't.

"Especially at such a busy time, with the wedding and all that."

"It's no bother," I lied, putting the cap back on my mascara and starting to apply lipliner.

"Pip. Is Katharine... you're going to be seeing her tonight, right?"

My hand jerked a bit and my lipliner skidded southwards over my chin. "Shit! Yes, as far as I know she's going to be there. But I haven't spoken to her. I left a voicemail for her the other day asking whether she was okay but she hasn't come back to me."

"If she's there, Pip, please could you tell her I'd love it if she would call me? And that I miss her, and I'm sorry."

"Iain! Seriously, that's mental. It's my hen night, if Katharine does turn up – and I wouldn't be a bit surprised if she doesn't, she must be devastated and I'm actually quite worried about her – the last thing she'll want is for me to stage some sort of intervention on your behalf. I don't want to give you the idea that you aren't welcome here, because of course you are, but it's just... It's weird, you know? It puts me in a bit of an awkward position where Katharine's concerned." I squirted mousse into my hand and turned upside down to scrunch it through my hair. It felt horribly inappropriate being watched while I did this stuff, by someone who wasn't Nick.

"I do understand, honestly I do," Iain said, looking a bit sheepish. His black eye was fading, I noticed; it was getting to the point where it was nothing a bit of Touche Éclat couldn't handle. "But if you were to have a moment, when you were, like, confiding, or whatever girls do on hen nights, maybe you could talk to her?"

I didn't say that what girls do on hen nights was, in my case, going to be some mystery activity organised by Callie – for which I'd been instructed to dress warmly – followed by drinking enough cocktails to sink a fleet of battleships, then going on for dinner and eating until our spines stuck out at the back, and then possibly going on somewhere to dance. Not a trace of confiding in sight.

"Iain, I promise that if Katharine comes tonight and if there's a moment when it seems appropriate to talk to her, and if my female intuition says there's a chance that wouldn't totally ruin her evening, then I'll think about it. And that's the best I can do. Now I need to get changed." And I gave him a look that I hoped said as eloquently as possible, 'So get out of my makeshift bedroom, you adulterous toad.'

In the event, Katharine was the first of my hens to arrive at the designated meeting point at Waterloo. I'm sure she'd been doing her fair share of crying, but I guess she'd been at the Touche Éclat too, because it didn't show one bit. She'd had her hair cut into a really short, sexy pixie cut, she was wearing super-skinny jeans and gold boots and a squashy faux fur coat, and she looked absolutely knockout stunning. I gave her a hug and told her so.

"And I'm so glad you came," I said, "It's wonderful to see you, it really is."

For a second her lower lip wobbled. "I'm sorry I didn't return your calls," she said. "It's been a bit shit, really. Actually, it's been a lot shit. I still don't know what I'm going to do, but I got sick of sitting at home counting the walls and crying and deleting Iain's messages, so I thought I'd better come out and get pissed. Do the others know?"

I assured her that I hadn't said anything to Callie. "I'll tell her if you want, but I thought you'd rather do it, or not mention it at all."

"Not mention it at all, definitely," she said. "I expect I'll show myself up horribly later by pouring my heart out and crying, but for now I'm going to have a good time and celebrate with you. Speaking of which, have you found a dress yet?"

But before I could update her, Callie and Phoebe arrived, shortly followed by Eloise and Tamar, Julia and my old mate Tom who I trained with, who'd insisted he was an honorary girl and should be allowed.

"So, here we all are then," I said to Callie. "Come on, let's have the big reveal."

"Right, follow me," she said. "It's just across the river."

Callie's idea of booking ice-skating at Somerset House proved to be inspired. I felt as if I'd wandered into a Christmas card – apart from the fact that my arse was soaking wet, obviously. I'd fallen over more times than I could count, and I couldn't stop laughing. I'd attempted to skate backwards, with some degree of success, holding the edge of the rink with one hand and Katharine with the other. Callie and Phoebe had braved the middle of the ice, fallen over, and found it impossible to get back on their feet, and the harder they tried the more they laughed. Tom had not unexpectedly put us all to shame by proving to be really good at skating, and was doing all sorts of fancy one-legged manoeuvres in between zooming around at top speed. Tamar had wisely decided that she wasn't risking falling over in her condition, thanks, and was sipping mulled apple juice in the bar, and Eloise and Julia had taken a break and joined her.

It felt like about five minutes since we'd first glided – or rather precariously slid – on to the ice, that our session was over and it was, as Callie succinctly put it, "Time to fall face-first into a vat of cocktails."

So that's what we did. We went to The Savoy, where they have a fabulous martini trolley that gets wheeled over to you by a charming and patient mixologist who doesn't mind when you ask for the fourth time what the other kind of bitters was, not the rhubarb or the chocolate but the other one? There were handsome waiters who kept bringing us more bowls of smoked almonds, cheese straws and olives without us having to ask. There were totally fabulous loos with ankle-deep carpets, marble tiles, rose hand cream and mirrors that made me look like I'd lost a stone.

After a bit we went on to a so-hip-it-hurts burger bar, and I have no idea what Callie had had to do, probably promise them the blood of her first-born child or something, but instead of having to queue outside in the cold like everyone else, we got whisked straight in to a table, and we ate fat- and salt-laden junk food washed down with bottles of lager and followed by ice-cream sundaes for those who had room. It was over the pudding that Katharine finally did start to cry, but it was only to say what a great time she was having, how much she loved us all, how glad she was that she'd come, and how Tom was the best ice-skater in the world, easily, and should enter the Winter Olympics.

Then we went on to a club and danced, and Eloise was absolutely sure she saw Harry Styles and Kendall Jenner, but Tamar said that was impossible, because she never sees any celebs, ever, but then she saw Daniel Radcliffe and had to admit that she was wrong. By this stage both she and Julia were starting to feel the pace, and said they wouldn't come with us to see the fireworks, but would head home early and go to bed instead, which I chalked up to my growing list of reasons why motherhood is clearly a bad idea.

And that's where it all gets a bit fuzzy, to be honest. We walked back to the river, fighting to stay together through the crowds of tourists. It was absolutely mad – there were people everywhere, tides of them all appearing to be trying to move in different directions. I was almost pushed off my feet several times, and when we eventually got to fireworks viewing point, Eloise said she thought she'd go home as well, before the Tube got too rammed. The rest of us agreed that if we got separated, we'd just head home too.

So I waited with Tom, Callie and Phoebe for midnight to come and the fireworks to start. And it was amazing, it really was – everyone counting down, then the chimes of Big Ben echoing over the noise of the crowd, and everyone kissing everyone else and wishing them happy new year, and then all going, "Oooh," in unison at each spectacular explosion and shower of white, green, golden or violet sparks. The display seemed to take ages and I stood, happily transfixed, even forgetting about my sore feet, until it was over. Then when I looked around me I realised I'd lost everyone else.

I checked my phone, but there were no messages and I realised they probably wouldn't get through anyway, because all around me tourists were frantically sending texts to their relatives in New Zealand and Nigeria and Nicaragua. So I decided to wander in the general direction of home, and if I found them that would be great, but if not I'd just walk back to the flat or get a bus.

It wasn't long before I spotted Callie and Phoebe in the crowd ahead of me, but there was no way I could get to them – there were just too many people. I started to feel a bit panicky, pushing against a wall of humanity, trying not to let Callie's blonde head and Phoebe's fur-hatted one disappear from view. After a while they paused, leaning against the balustrade and looking out over the dark river, and I hurried towards them.

But then I stopped, because they kissed each other. It wasn't the kind of celebratory, suddenly-we're-all-friends kiss everyone had been exchanging on the stroke of midnight. It wasn't the sort of cheesy snog some girls always seem to do with their mates when the DJ plays Katy Perry and they want to impress blokes. I wasn't very close to them, but I was close enough to see that this was the real thing, the way two people kiss who love each other.

Callie's fingers were buried in Phoebe's tangle of red hair, keeping warm against her skin under her fur hat. Phoebe's arms fitted snugly, familiarly around Callie's slim waist. As I watched, she reached a hand up and stroked Callie's cheek, and Callie broke off the kiss to brush her lips against Phoebe's fingers. I knew I was intruding on a moment that was, in spite of the throngs of strangers surrounding them, intensely private. I knew I wasn't supposed to have seen them, so I turned away and went home, the picture of the two of them together mixing with the martinis and champagne and lager and shaking my brain into a cocktail of confusion.

I didn't know whether I was going to say anything to Callie about what I'd seen. I had no way of telling when things between her and Phoebe had changed. I felt hollow with hurt that she hadn't felt able to tell me something so important. But still, a lot of things had begun to make sense.

Here's another thing that's a seriously poor idea: packing for a two-week trip abroad with only two hours to go before you absolutely have to leave, and a stinking hangover that's kept you confined to bed for most of the day.

Nick tried several times to wake me up, but I just hid under the duvet and said, "Leave me alone, please, I'm dying." So he put a can of Diet Coke next to the bed and went out somewhere with Iain, leaving me to spend the day wallowing in my own filth, cuddling Spanx, trying to sleep and worrying about Callie.

If she hadn't told me about her and Phoebe, she wouldn't have told anyone. And that was weird, because honestly, I wouldn't have cared in the slightest, and she knows that – Tom's been out ever since I've known him and he's one of my best mates. And besides, this is England in the twenty-first century, not Victorian times or Uganda or something. Only a reactionary idiot would react to Callie and Phoebe having a relationship with anything other than delight that they'd found something that made them happy.

Only a reactionary idiot like Phoebe's dad. Over the last couple of years I'd heard a few stories about him, some from Phoebe herself, who tried to make light of his behaviour, and some second-hand from Callie, who didn't. And given how protective Phoebe was of him, I guessed there were many, many other things that only she and her mum knew about.

I remembered when we'd been chatting about holidays, and Callie and I reminisced about the epic Club 18-30 binge to Ibiza we'd been on together a few years before. Phoebe had looked all wistful and told us that she'd planned something similar with her mates, only a couple of days before they were due to leave her mum had come down with absolutely awful flu and hadn't been able to do all the heavy lifting and stuff for Vernon, Phoebe's dad. Which would normally have been fine, because although Vernon's mobility was limited, he was capable of getting himself to the shower and sticking something in the microwave, or whatever. But then his back suddenly locked into terrible spasms, Phoebe said, leaving him unable to stand, and that was the end of her holiday.

It must have taken a huge amount of courage for Phoebe to leave home at all. I remembered when Phoebe first moved in with Callie, shortly after Callie and David had split up. I'd got the train to Southampton to see her and do a brief stint on drunken text prevention duty, but soon realised that no drunken text prevention would be needed. Callie had looked all happy and shiny, somehow, like she'd been dipped in glitter, even though she was wearing her normal sombre dark lawyer's trouser suit.

"How are things?" I'd said gently, as you do to the recently bereaved or newly single.

"Great!" Callie said. "God, it's just such a relief that it's all over. Such a weight off my mind! Poor David, I feel shit for hurting him, but I so made the right decision."

I sat down and poured myself a glass of wine, and Callie went on, "You know, the last few months, we've been arguing quite a bit and it's been horrible. All the time, this atmosphere in the flat, because either we'd just had a row or we were about to have one. And now he's moved out and it's, like, bliss. I've bought new curtains and new bedding with hummingbirds on, and it's tack-tastic but so pretty. And I let David take the fridge so I could buy a new pink Smeg. You know how David always wanted everything to be beige?"

I said, "God, fridge envy! I'd kill for a pink Smeg but Nick would never let me. Maybe I should dump him so I can have one too."

Callie laughed. "I'll let you come and visit mine," she said. "It's a fridge of beauty. And you can sit on my new gold chesterfield."

"Gold chesterfield! I could cry with jealousy! How fabulous, I'm so pleased you're happy, Cal."

"Yes," she said. "I am. Only I'm also a bit skint. Gold chesterfields don't come cheap, you know. So I put an ad on Gumtree for a flatmate and I've found someone."

When Callie decides to do something, she doesn't hang about. "Cool! What's she like?"

"Her name's Phoebe. She's the same age as us, and she's a teaching assistant and she's got mad ginger hair. She's really pretty. She seems like good fun, too. You'll meet her soon, I expect."

"When does she move in?"

"It was meant to be the day before yesterday," said Callie, "But there was a bit of a drama with her dad."

And then she'd told me a bit more about Phoebe's situation, and how she got the sense that Phoebe was absolutely desperate to leave home, partly because she was twenty-six, after all, and partly because her dad was a total tyrant.

So it wasn't hard to imagine why, just as much as Callie would be confident of her friends' and family's reaction if she told them she was in love with another girl, Phoebe would dread her father's. And that the other option, the nuclear one of just walking away, wouldn't be an option for Phoebe, because her mother would be left behind to cope with him alone.

I turned all this over in my mind, until eventually I fell asleep again, only to be jerked awake by my phone about half an hour later. Nick had set the alarm for me so I had enough time to pack.

I dragged myself out of bed and immediately Spanx appeared and started twining himself around my ankles and yowling, so I topped up his food bowl before having a shower and doing my face, aiming for the 'jet-setting celeb chef' look, but ending up with 'murder victim pulled from sewer after three weeks'. Then I went into our bedroom to unearth some summer clothes.

Although Erica was still away, the room felt like it was hers. It smelled of the herbal skincare stuff she used, and more faintly of the green tea she drank every morning. The curtains and the window were closed and the heating turned up high, so the room was stuffy and hot. It had been like this for ages, I thought angrily. Our gas bill was going to be astronomical.

I dragged my suitcase out from under the bed and opened the wardrobe, releasing a fresh blast of the Erica miasma. For a second I stood, frozen. Where the hell were all my clothes? It had all been normal when I'd packed for my first trip, now everything had been moved. What the fuck was going on?

"Nick?" I yelled, then remembered he was out, and reached for my phone. His number went straight to voice-mail. Where was he? And what had happened to my stuff?

I returned to the wardrobe and tried to assess its contents in a calmer frame of mind. The hanging rail was full of the drapey linen tunics and trousers Erica wears, in various shades of cream, stone and oatmeal. On the shelves were folded scarves, knitted jumpers and shawls. She hadn't had this much stuff when she arrived – clearly she had been shopping and run out of space. I looked up and saw, on the top shelf, an unfamiliar row of bin liners. I hefted one of them down, dropped it on the bed and ripped it open. Sure enough, out spilled my summer clothes.

There was my violet silk Monsoon dress, tangled up with the vest tops I'd bought at Selfridges in the sale and not worn yet. There was the swishy knife-pleat skirt I'd lusted after on Net-a-Porter for weeks before Nick bought it for my birthday, except its pleats weren't so knife-like after being rolled up in a ball. There was the yellow hat I'd worn to Iain and Katharine's wedding, squashed beyond recognition. And everything stank of mothballs.

I picked up my phone again, stabbing inaccurately at the screen until I managed to dial Nick's number. This time he answered.

"Hey, Pip! I'm right outside the…" and then I heard his key in the lock and his digital and real voices saying together, "door."

I ended the call and threw my phone on to the bed. "Could you come here a second?"

"What's up?" Nick said, sticking his head round the door.

"Look at this," I said. "Just look. What the fuck has your mother done with all my stuff?"

"Er… packed it away, I guess," he said. "She mentioned that she could do with a bit of extra space, and I said it was fine for her to shift a few of our things."

"Except she hasn't shifted 'our' things, has she? She's shifted *my* things. And crammed them into bags and now they're unwearable, and I have…" I looked at my watch, "about twenty-five minutes in which to pack for two weeks away in thirty degree heat. Why the hell did you tell her it was okay? You knew I was going away."

"Pippa, I didn't realise she was going to… I was distracted, okay?"

"Distracted doing what? Looking online for table napkins in the right shade of white?"

Nick flinched as if I'd tried to slap him. "Yeah, probably I was doing something to do with planning our wedding, Pippa."

"You know what, Nick?" I tried to speak calmly. "It really is beginning to feel to me like absolutely everything in my life has been taken over by this bloody wedding and your fu- your mother."

We stood and glared at each other from opposite sides of the bed. I had a horrible feeling that this row wasn't going to end quickly and easily, with one of us saying sorry. Nor could it end in raw, angry making-up sex, because there simply wasn't time. What there was time for was for us to goad each other into causing maximum hurt. And it had already gone too far for me to back down, apologise and try to defuse what I'd said.

"Pippa, this 'bloody wedding' is what you wanted, in case you've forgotten. Do you think I like poncing around florists and cake designers on my own, trying to second-guess whether you'd prefer fondant or buttercream? Do you think I like having to cram all my real work into about four hours a day and turn down invitations to pitch for new business because they clash with my meeting with the videographer? Do you think I like having to reassure my mother constantly that she's welcome in my home when you treat her like a leper?"

"What the hell do you mean, I wanted it? Nick, I didn't want any of this shite. I didn't want three hundred of your distant relatives who I've never met turning up and getting pissed at our expense. I didn't want the dance classes and the conjuror and the tomato fucking soup. It was all your idea."

"Don't be ridiculous," he spat. "You came home the day after we got engaged with about ten glossy wedding magazines. You've not said a word about wanting anything different, just yes Nick, no Nick, three bags full Nick, as long as I'm doing the work and Mum's picking up the tab. And then you can't even be bothered to be civil to her. This wedding is meant to be a celebration of our love for each other, Pippa, but right now I don't even like you very much."

And then he stormed out of the room, slamming the door behind him. Although part of me wanted to go rushing after him and carry on with the row, there was a small, sensible part that was extremely glad he'd gone, because I honestly don't know what I would have said if he'd stayed.

I sorted quickly through the bags of clothes and extracted some of the less mangled and noxious-smelling things, packed them in my suitcase and left the overflowing bin liners on the bed. They'd been Erica's idea in the first place – let her sort them out when she got back from Yorkshire. Then I went back into the living room, where Nick was sitting slumped on the sofa, almost horizontal, his chin on his chest, watching the football.

"I'm going now," I said.

"Right. Have a good trip."

"Yeah. I'll call you, okay?"

"Okay."

I carried my bags down the stairs and started walking to the Tube. Then I thought, what if the plane crashed? What if I got malaria and died, or Nick got stabbed to death by some random nutter, and I hadn't even kissed him goodbye? Abandoning my heavy suitcase outside the corner shop, I sprinted back towards the flat, and when I was halfway up the first flight of stairs, I met Nick, running down. We squeezed each other in a huge hug, and Nick said, "Come home safe, Pip."

I said, "I'll try." Then I said, "Nick, have you been in touch with Bethany?"

"I don't know what you're talking about," he said.

Nick didn't lie – he never lied. But now he was. I knew it, but I didn't know why.

I turned away, ran back to where I'd left my bag, got on the Tube and sobbed all the way to Heathrow. One sweet woman asked me if I was okay, and a couple of creepy blokes said, "Cheer up, love, it may never happen," but mostly people just ignored me, and I was glad they did.

By the time I'd checked in and got through passport control and security, I'd managed to stop crying, and I had time to wash my face and put on some makeup, and buy supplies of wine gums, water and glossy magazines for the flight, before rendezvousing with Guido at the departure gate as we'd arranged.

When I got there, he was on the phone. "No, I'm not doing this just to hurt you. Please, Florence. You're making it worse for yourself. I'm sorry, but we can't go on the way things have been. I meant what I said last night, I'm not going to change my mind. And I really can't listen to this now, Florence, I'm about to get on a plane. You'll be okay. Call your mother." He disconnected.

"Evening, Pippa. Excited? Good. That's our boarding call now."

We walked up the stairs and into the chilly aircraft. Guido went one way, to the luxury of first class, and I went the other, to the relative squalor of business. *Guido's African Safari*, I reflected as I fastened my seatbelt, might be the best thing that ever happened to the world of food, but it looked like having a horrible tendency to put the kiss of death on relationships.

CHAPTER FOURTEEN

From: nick@digitaldrawingboard.com
To: info@okayontheday.co.uk
Subject: Wedding insurance policy number 489X435NG1A

To whom it may concern

I purchased the above policy from you in November last year. I'm getting in touch to clarify your T&Cs on cancellation – I've tried to get through to you on your Freephone number without success, so I'd be grateful if your representative could call me on the number below to talk through what exactly is and isn't covered in the terms of the policy.

Thanks and kind regards
Nick Pickford

I was standing with Sibongile under a shadecloth awning by the side of a road. The awning kept the sun off us, but it didn't protect us from the fierce heat reflecting off the tarmac and radiating from the red-hot coals that filled the barbeque a few inches from my face. I pushed my hair up under my baseball cap and watched as a minibus taxi pulled up in a haze of dust. About twenty people spilled out – women laden with shopping, children with school bags and scooters, men in suits and, finally, Guido.

"I'm here in Soweto," he told the rolling cameras, "where Vusi Mbeki has made a name for himself and his fantastic street food. Vusi's food cart" – he gestured, and the cameras panned to the van next to us, where a tall young man in a Lacoste polo shirt and low-slung jeans was turning sausages and burgers on the grill, grinning cheerfully, bantering with his diners and seemingly impervious to the heat – "pulls in hundreds of customers every day, and I've come here to find out why.

"What first attracted me to Vusi's food is not only that it's so iconically African, but that it spoke to me of my childhood. Really? Street food in Soweto, reminding me of the cuisine of Italy? It may seem unlikely, but it's true."

One of the crew passed him a paper plate laden with sausage, maize porridge, rich red sauce and a vast white bun. It looked delicious – just the kind of thing you'd want to eat at the end of a night out, if you were somewhere very cold. Guido took a big, squelchy bite.

"Good," the director said.

That was Sibongile's and my cue to spring into action. We passed up trays of the sausage we'd made earlier, vats of braised onion and marinara sauce, a large bowl of polenta and a platter of sourdough rolls. Guido took his place in the van next to Vusi.

"Okay?" said Guido.

"Okay," said the director.

"You see, the rustic food people queue to eat here on Chris Hani Road made me think of Italian peasant food. So I've prepared my take on Vusi's specialities, and we're going to see what his hungry customers make of it. South African boerewors is not that different from the luganiga sausage my nonna used to make when we slaughtered a pig every autumn – a wonderful ritual that was as much a part of my childhood as herding goats in the hills and hunting for truffles on my way to school. Her sweet sausage was seasoned with fennel, garlic, rosemary, thyme and sage, and I've brought these flavours into a beef sausage – a boerewors – along with the traditional South African spicing of coriander and a hit of chilli. The maize porridge – 'pap' – which is a staple food here, loved by rich and poor alike, is the African version of the polenta I adored as a boy – and still do! But I have to watch my figure now, not like you young men." He gave Vusi a matey dig in the ribs, and Vusi laughed obligingly.

I don't know whether our Italian/South African sausage hybrid went down well with the crowd, some of whom were Vusi's regular customers, some paid extras, and some random members of the public who'd turned up with the unerring instinct people all over the world have when there's free food going. But soon, whether out of politeness or hunger, people were tucking into Guido's boereworsimmo rolls and polenta pap with every appearance of enthusiasm. It was a wrap.

"Bravo!" Guido clapped Vusi on the back and they exchanged the complicated handshakes that seemed to be de rigeur here – I'd asked Sibongile to demonstrate the right way to do them several times, and still not got the hang of it. "Now, back to the hotel for a shower. We're filming the fine dining scene this evening."

God, I thought, this was only our first day, and I was dead on my feet. The long flight, on which I hadn't managed to sleep at all, the heat and the gnawing anxiety about Nick, about Bethany, about Katharine and Iain, which I couldn't manage to shake off, had left me feeling flat and unfocussed.

"Get some rest this afternoon, Pippa," Guido said as we climbed into the wonderful chill of our air-conditioned car,

"And you too, sweetheart." I saw Sibongile bristle. "It's been a busy morning, and we've got a long evening's work ahead."

He wasn't kidding. It seemed I'd barely closed my eyes after sinking with relief on to the gorgeously comfortable bed in my mercifully cool bedroom, when my alarm jerked me awake and it was time to get in yet another taxi, this time to the five-star Sandton Heights hotel.

"I was surprised and delighted," I could hear Guido telling the cameras as I carefully pipetted drops of butternut squash purée into a calcium bath, "when I found high-end restaurants here in South Africa as good as anything in Milan, Paris or London. Here at Kaya, flagship restaurant of the new Sandton Heights hotel, Alice de Jong and her team have melded uniquely African flavours with the sophisticated molecular techniques found in top restaurants all around the world. The dish that put Alice on the map is Knysna oysters served with spheres of…" I tuned him out, forcing my hands to keep steady as I painstakingly squeezed out blob after identically sized orange blob. Next to me, Sibongile was doing the same thing, only her blobs were green.

"Excuse me," a voice behind me broke my concentration, and my hand jerked, sending an amoeba-like orange ooze into the water. "Could you tell me where I can find Mr Falconi?"

I turned around, ready to administer a bollocking for interrupting us when we were preparing for service, and point out that Guido was in front of the cameras, and interrupting him would be an even worse idea. But I was silenced by a dazzling smile from the most beautiful man I've ever seen.

I mean, seriously. You know how some people are so stunning, it's like they belong to some sort of superior master race? Like they're a higher level of Thetan, or whatever the bullshit theory is that Scientologists have? That's what I thought when I saw him. He wasn't very tall, not nearly as tall as Nick, and he had a sort of sculpted leanness, broad shoulders tapering to a narrow waist under his grey and white striped shirt, and long, elegant legs in tailored charcoal trousers. His hair was dark blond and artfully messy. His eyes were the most amazing colour – almost golden – and his teeth were dazzlingly white and straight. He looked like some mad scientist had taken Orlando Bloom, Michael Fassbender and Chris Hemsworth, mixed them together and made a new man using only the best bits. Such was his overpowering glamour that I didn't even particularly care that my hair was a state, I wasn't wearing any makeup and my chef's whites were smeared with butternut squash. Even if I'd spent three weeks being starved at a health farm and then several days being given the full treatment by Gok Wan and a team of celebrity stylists, and left looking so good that none of my friends recognised me, he would have been out of my league, and I knew it.

Fortunately, while I'd been standing there gawping like a fool, Sibongile had put down her pipette and turned around too.

"Sibo!" the man said. "I wasn't expecting to see you! How are you, my darling? You're looking amazing as always."

"Well, hello, trouble," she said, but the two of them hugged each other warmly. "What are you doing here?"

He rolled his remarkable eyes. "The usual. I'm being a fake friend for tonight's shoot. Turn up, eat food, laugh lots, pretend I'm one of Guido Falconi's best buddies and try not to get too pissed until afterwards. And not even then, because I'm hoping they'll book me for another episode. You?"

"The usual, too," Sibongile said. "Spending three hours on plates of food that the chef pretends to make in ten minutes. But I'm in luck this time, because I'm working with lovely Pippa, who's here from London. Pippa Martin, Gabriel Meyer."

I desperately tried to remember how the complicated handshake worked, but I didn't need to, because Gabriel leaned in and kissed me on both cheeks. He didn't just go 'mwah, mwah' at the air next to my face, but nor, thankfully, did he slobber. I just felt his warm, dry lips touch my skin, once, then again. He smelled of honey and pine forests and leather. I felt myself blushing like a schoolgirl.

"Come on, then," Sibongile said. "I'll show you where to go. You shouldn't have come into the kitchen in the first place, you know that. I expect you were looking for food to scrounge again, weren't you? It's like having a street kid hanging around." She aimed a swat at his hand and they both laughed.

"Lovely to meet you, Pippa," Gabriel said. "I hope I'll see you again soon." And the two of them disappeared into the restaurant, where a faux chef's table had been set up for filming.

"So how do you know Gabriel?" I asked Sibongile when she returned to her watercress spheres.

She gave me a sideways glance and grinned. "Don't tell me the Meyer magic is doing its work on you! That boy has more spells up his sleeve than Harry Potter, and a much bigger wand. I went out with him for a bit. We worked together on a similar job to this a year or so ago, and saw each other for a few months afterwards, on and off. He's an actor. He's quite good, he was in Fugard's *Hello and Goodbye* at the Grahamstown festival last year. But there aren't enough parts out there to go around, and no one wants him for modelling work because he's such a short-arse. So he does gigs like this and works as a waiter, because of the free food."

"What's he like?" I asked. I was blushing again.

"He hasn't got a mean bone in his body," she said. "Sweet, sweet boy. But as a boyfriend? Disaster. He's never had to learn responsibility, because everyone just looks at him and loves him. So he's full of shit. Turns up late, or not at all. Forgets my birthday. Forgets we're going out, and disappears off to Mauritius for a week because his friend's got a job on a yacht. That kind of thing. So I kicked him to the kerb, and I don't regret it, but I couldn't stay pissed off with him for very long, you know? No one can."

Before she could tell me anything more, Guido came over to see how we were doing, and told us the camera crew was ready and we could start plating up. From the pass, I watched the staged dinner guests talking and laughing together, and couldn't help noticing that Gabriel ate the bread rolls off both his neighbour's plates as well as his own, and then tore through all eight courses, not leaving so much as a smear of springbok jus behind. But when at last the director gave the command to cut and Sibongile asked me if I fancied a drink in the bar, I said I was too tired. I didn't say that for someone who was getting married in five weeks, becoming better acquainted with a beautiful, sweet boy who was trouble was clearly the shittest idea ever.

But later, in bed, I found sleep wouldn't come. I longed to talk to Callie but when I rang her, her phone went to voicemail, so I left a message asking her to let me know when we could have a proper chat on Skype.

Then I brought Nick's blog up on my phone to see if he'd posted anything new. He had.

The loneliness of a long-distance wedding planner

That makes me sound like a sad bastard, doesn't it? And lonely is definitely too strong a word – Mum's here and Iain, my best man, is crashing on our sofa for a bit, so we've got a houseful. But Pippa is away with work again, and it's not the same without her around.

Still, the wedmin list is getting shorter as the day approaches and it feels as if all the big stuff is pretty much under control. Lots of our guests have been in touch asking about presents, but when you've been together as long as Pip and I have, it's hard to think of anything we actually need. Mum insisted on a trip to John Lewis the other day, and the place was packed with couples going round with those little barcode scanner things, marking plates and vases and stuff. But we've got stuff! (All the stuff we need, anyway. As far as I'm concerned no one needs guest towels or poultry shears.)

So apparently some people ask for cash, instead. Sometimes they even ask in the form of a poem, like this work of genius:

Thanks for sending your RSVP
And for asking our gift list to see.
But we've got a home full of cushions and things
A wok and a toaster and a kettle that sings.

We don't need more glasses, pots or pans
But we've got some exciting honeymoon plans.
To help with our holiday by the sea
Please make a transfer to HSBC.

Cringy, right? So we're not going for that, either, and the gift list is going to remain a work in progress for now, at least until I have a chance to chat to Pippa about it. As usual, any ideas are welcome in the comments.

I scrolled quickly down through the comments, some of which had included their own embarrassingly awful poems. Soon I found what I was looking for.

"Hey you! I'm no poet (and don't you know it?!) so can't advise. But re the other thing… Have inboxed you. Bxx"

Inboxed? What the fuck? I stared at the screen in frustration. What the hell were all these messages Bethany was sending Nick? I didn't even know you could do that on blogs. Then I noticed the little envelope icon at the top of the page. I was sure it hadn't always been there, but I clicked on it anyway, and I was in. There was a whole list of messages – from someone called Matt about The Amazing Archibald, from various florists and car hire companies offering their services, and, right at the top, one from Bethany.

I'm not effortlessly competent with modern technology, like Nick is – I've never had a blog or even a Twitter account. It's all I can do to programme the Sky box to record *EastEnders* when I'm working late. Put me in front of a blast chiller or a sous-vide machine and I'll figure out how it works in seconds, but with most other things, I'm a total numpty. So it took me a few seconds to work out what must have happened. At some point – and I remembered now, it had been when we were on the train back from Brocklebury Manor with Erica, and I'd been too busy sulking about the wedding menu to pay much heed – Nick had used my phone to write a blog post. It must have remembered the password, and I was now logged in as if I were Nick.

I didn't even stop to think about whether it was right or wrong to snoop. I just clicked on Bethany's message, and read it.

Hello love bug (I know I shouldn't be calling you that any more. But, old habits...)

God, I know what you mean about wedding stress! It's a tough time, it messes with your head and with your relationship. But listen, if you're really having doubts, don't go ahead with it. Better to cancel now than split up down the track. Trust me, I know. Call me if you want to talk. I care about you, you know. Been thinking about you a lot these last few months.

Beff xxx

And she'd posted her mobile number. Nick hadn't replied to the message – I didn't even know whether he'd seen it. But I did know that if he hadn't, he'd see that it had been read. Before I could properly think what I was doing, I deleted it, and immediately felt horribly guilty and ashamed. I resolved that the next time I spoke to Nick, I'd admit what I'd done, and tell him how I felt about Bethany's new presence in his life, but I never got around to it. Even as I was lying in the strange silence of my hotel room, missing the sound of Nick's breathing, Spanx's snuffly snores, the rain drumming on the plastic lids of the wheelie bins below our window and all the other noises of home, things were in the process of going utterly tits up.

I jerked awake the next morning about two hours too early, and lay in the dark for a bit hoping I'd be able to go back to sleep. But as soon as I opened my eyes, anxiety clawed at me. Had Nick seen Bethany's message? Had he actually met her? Were Iain and Katharine still not speaking to each other? It was no good, I was awake and I might as well check Facebook on my phone and try and get some sense of connection to home. But as soon as I swiped the screen to life, I saw I had a new voicemail.

"Hi Pippa, it's Eloise. Listen, I'm really sorry to call you so late, but I guess you're asleep so it won't matter. I wanted to give you a heads-up on what's happening. You need to read tomorrow's *Sun on Sunday*, okay. Guido knows, because Lauren emailed him late last night. She's on her way there now, with Toby from Marshams. Their flight lands just before eight tomorrow, so they should be there by ten. You need to cancel this morning's filming until everything's sorted out. I'll talk to the people at Platinum in London as soon as I get to the office, but you'll have to handle it at your end. Tell them there's been an emergency. They'll find out soon enough what it is. Okay... er... call me when you can. Hope you and Guido are okay. Cheers."

Lauren from the PR company and Toby the solicitor were on their way? Actually flying out to Johannesburg? What the fuck was going on? I navigated with desperate haste to the *Sun on Sunday* website, then realised I would have to subscribe and had forgotten my Paypal password. It seemed to take forever to input my credit card details and create a new account, but at last, I was in. I scrolled down past stories about Kate Middleton wearing a frock for the third time, some woman I'd never heard of off *Geordie Shore* falling out of a nightclub pissed, the Tories' tough new stance on crime and the influx of Romanian immigrants, before I saw a picture of Guido. It was a particularly unflattering one, showing him about to eat a huge forkful of what looked like linguine carbonara. The headline under it said:

GUIDO FAKE-ONI
Celeb chef's secret past exposed!

- TV chef cashed in on Italian background – but it's all LIES
- "Tuscan peasant" father is a GEOGRAPHY TEACHER from Berkshire
- "NOT SO HOT in the bedroom" – ex-lover speaks out

I tapped the link. It took me three tries, because my finger was trembling.

He's found fame and made his fortune through a chain of swanky restaurants. He's travelled the globe for his TV series, and his books sell in the millions. But we can reveal that celeb chef Guido, who boasts about his humble upbringing and the peasant tradition behind dishes like the £65 white truffle risotto served at Osteria Falconi, is living a lie. And that's not all.

Then there was a photo of the risotto, with a caption underneath that said: "Posh nosh? But celeb chef Guido is all hot air."

The Sun on Sunday can exclusively reveal that the man we know as Guido Falconi was born Guy Fallon. Far from being raised by humble subsistence farmers in rural Tuscany, Fallon grew up in a leafy village near Newbury. Dad Brian taught geography at £18,000-a-year St Francis's school, where pupils included the sons of cabinet ministers and minor royalty. Mum Lucia was the daughter of a well-off banker from Milan, and it's thought that Guy may have acquired a taste for Italian food on family holidays to the region.

There was another photo, this one of a thatched cottage on a pretty, unmistakably English village street. The caption was, "Rural Tuscany or Ramston-on-Thames? You decide." I felt sick, but I couldn't stop reading.

Young Guy attended the Queen Elizabeth II grammar school, where he was known more for his skills on the cricket pitch and going after girls than sautéeing steak.

"He was always a bit of a dish," remembers former classmate Susie Norman. "He had those big brown eyes, and he was just charming, you know? All of us wanted to go out with Guy. When I first saw him on telly, I went, 'Now isn't he the very spit of Guy Fallon?' But you don't think anything of it, do you?"

I scrolled past the inevitable photo of Susie Norman, who was wearing a Barbour and walking a labrador.

It was shortly after leaving school with just one O-Level that young Guy dropped off the radar, Mrs Newman remembers. "There were rumours that he'd gone off to Italy to be a ski instructor, or that he'd moved to London and become involved with East End gangsters, but no one really knew," she told our reporter.

It is not known at what point Fallon assumed his new identity, but by 1986 he had taken on the name Guido Falconi, remembers Maurizio Mauro. It was he who gave Falconi his big break at the flash Enoteca Mauro, a favourite haunt of rock stars and politicians like Adam Ant and Margaret Thatcher.

"Guido was young, but he had talent. I never questioned his background. His Italian was perfect," says Mr Mauro.

Maurizio clearly wasn't important enough to warrant a photo, but Florence certainly was. The next two pictures were of her. In the first, she was wearing a black dress and looking sombre. "'Italian stallion' betrayed my trust, says glamour-model ex", said the caption. In the next picture, she was posing in a see-through leopard-print peignoir, apparently remembering, "How not-so-tasty Guido was no Latin lover".

I couldn't bear to read what she had to say, so I skipped to the end of the article.

Guido is currently soaking up the sun in South Africa, filming his latest bogus blockbuster *Guido's African Safari*. Will the cheating chef be blacking up to add authenticity to the show? He could not be reached for comment.

Dry-mouthed, I turned off the screen. The only way this could be worse was if the website had allowed comments on the piece, but they hadn't – presumably because they were worried about being sued. Then I realised that this meant they were confident that what they had printed wasn't libellous, so it must all be true. And it could only have come from Florence.

Over the past seven years, I'd seen Guido lose his temper countless times. I'd seen him hollow-eyed with exhaustion when he'd arrived at the office after finishing service at one of the restaurants three hours before. I'd seen him get through a tasting with Thatchell's when he had norovirus, and only just manage not to throw up until the client had left. But I'd never seen his self-belief so much as dented.

He was my mentor, my champion – but he wasn't what I thought he was. As I straightened my hair and trowelled on what I hoped was a glossy, professional veneer courtesy of Laura Mercier, I tried to identify moments when Guido had seemed insincere or artificial, but I couldn't. And, I realised, it was because he wasn't. Whatever fiction he'd created about his start in life, he was still the person who'd taken me into his kitchen when I was a hapless, overconfident junior chef and taught me all he could about food, about how to inspire people, about how to build a brand.

As I was putting on my shoes, my phone rang. It was an unfamiliar UK mobile number.

"Hello?"

"Pippa Martin?"

"Yes."

"Hello, Pippa," it was a woman's voice, unctuous and confiding. "My name's Anna, I'm calling from the *Daily Star*. I wonder if you..."

"No comment," I said. My phone almost slid out of my hand, my palm was so sweaty. If the press were already ringing me, they'd be hounding Guido. I turned off my phone and stuffed it into my bag, along with a notepad and pen, my room key and a huge wodge of tissues from the box in the bathroom. Then I went along the corridor to the palatial suite where Guido was billeted, and knocked on the door.

"It's only me," I said. "I think we should order a couple of cappuccinos."

An hour later, we were seated around the meeting table in Guido's suite. Lauren had her laptop open in front of her, and Toby had a stack of files that I guessed must contain our contracts with Platinum Productions. Guido had a bottle of water. There were deep furrows in his cheeks and his designer stubble looked a lot greyer than it had the previous night.

"So," Toby said. "Clearly we have a situation here. First off, is the story true?"

"Of course it's true," said Guido.

"All of it?"

"Sure," Guido said.

"And... the rest? I'm sorry to ask this, I know it isn't easy. But what you had written in your autobiography, in *Searing Ambition*, about your career?"

"True too. Apart from the beginning. I went to Italy when I was seventeen, after my mother died. I learned to speak Italian, I worked in restaurants. It was all I'd ever wanted to do. But I had to leave my background behind, and to do that I needed a new story. So I made one up, and it was a good story."

"Okay," Lauren said. "This is a PR disaster. But we can turn it into a PR triumph, because that's what we're good at. First off, Florence. I take it this has come from her?"

Guido nodded. "We split up, just before I left London, and she said I'd regret it. She has known about all this for a while. She found my birth certificate and some pictures I'd kept of my father – stupid. She held it over me for a while, threatening to go public, otherwise we wouldn't have stayed together for as long. But in the end I couldn't stand any more of her. This has come as a shock to me, of course, but it's not as surprising as you might think."

"Right," Lauren said. "So, first thing, we discredit her. She was a lingerie model, right? Anything there? Sleeping her way to the top, that kind of thing? And what about her daughter, Tanith, is it? Who's the father?"

Guido shook his head. "No, Lauren. Remember, I was a father to Tanith for five years. This is going to be hard enough for her. I'm not having her mother dragged through the gutter press too."

Lauren said, "But…" then stopped herself.

Toby said, "I've looked over the contract you signed with Platinum. They could can the series, but I don't think they will. They'll take the view that this will do the ratings no harm, and I think that's correct. I've been in contact with their legal team this morning and I'm waiting for confirmation, but we can take that as read for now."

"So what we need to do is turn this into good publicity for you," Lauren said. "You'll need to issue a statement apologising and explaining why you did it."

"That's easy," Guido said wearily. "You know what the London restaurant scene was like back then. Or maybe you don't. No offence, Lauren, but you're, what, thirty-five? It was all Marco Pierre White and Gordon Ramsay and egos and twenty-hour days and bankers snorting coke in the bogs. It was all about personality. No one would have been interested in a boy from Berkshire who could cook a bit. As I said, I needed a story. And the important parts are true. I scrubbed mussels in restaurants in Rome and was so skint I slept on the kitchen floor. And everything I've ever said I feel about food and cooking is true too. Everything I teach the young chefs coming through my kitchen is real, isn't it, Pippa?" He looked at me, almost imploringly, for validation.

"It's true," I said.

"So we need to put together a proposal that's going to shift the focus of this show away from you, the celebrity, and towards you, the mentor," Lauren said. "The man who cares about young people and good causes. I've researched some schools, homeless shelters and conservation charities we can approach. It will mean some personal financial commitment from you, and it will mean giving others more exposure in the filming. The actor you worked with in last night's show – I watched the unedited footage on our way over, and he's gold. The camera loves him. We'll book him for more hours, do a thing where you teach him to cook. Go out to schools and hospitals in deprived areas – we need to make people love you like they love Jamie Oliver."

"Fat-tongued mockney c…" Guido began, but Lauren silenced him with a glare.

"And Pippa – you've worked with Guido for a long time. Would you be prepared to take a more prominent role in this?"

I felt like I was on a roller coaster. You know, like at Alton Towers or somewhere, when you've been slowly, slowly edging upwards, and suddenly you reach the top. The view is dizzying, the knowledge that you're going to plunge downwards is terrifying, and you wish you'd got off while you were at the bottom, when there was still the option of being a coward and going for a beer and a burger instead.

"I don't know," I quavered.

Then Guido's phone rang. "Eloise? Right. From Bryn? That was to be expected. I'll let Toby and Lauren know. Not to worry, sweetheart. Ciao."

He put his phone carefully down on the table, but it still rattled against the polished wood.

"Thatchell's have pulled the plug," he said.

CHAPTER FIFTEEN

From: nick@digitaldrawingboard.com
To: iain.coulson@coulsoncreative.com
Subject: RE: Fw: Termination of contract

Shit, mate, that's not great news. You've had the Top Travel business for, what, nine years? Can't believe they're doing this. And you've won loads of awards for them too. Bastards. Anyway, I'm happy to give you a hand with some creative for the pitch next week. I'd say we can brainstorm some thoughts tomorrow night but we'll be too busy getting off our heads on my stag – so that's something to look forward to, anyway! And good luck tonight with K. Hope you guys can sort things out.

Onwards and upwards, right?

N

By the end of that day, I knew every ripple in the grain of the walnut meeting-room table by heart. I'd drunk so much coffee my head ached and my stomach was churning. We'd redrafted the shooting schedule, had it ripped up by the production company, and redrafted it again. Lauren had fielded hundreds of calls from the media, telling everyone to wait for a statement from Guido, and eventually it was recorded and released. Guido had chewed his way through three packs of Nicorette gum and shredded two of the hotel's notepads into tiny, even strips, which were scattered all over the table and the surrounding carpet. Toby was hoarse from negotiating with the Platinum lawyers.

At last, there was nothing to do but wait and see what the reaction was on that night's news and in the next day's papers.

"Does anyone want any dinner?" Guido asked.

I could tell that all he wanted was to be left alone, and Toby and Lauren looked as hollow-eyed and exhausted as I felt.

"I think I'll just order something from room service and get an early night," I said. The others agreed, and we all shuffled off, drained and zombie-like.

An hour later, I'd had a bath and demolished a plate of smoked salmon sandwiches and most of a bottle of wine. I was curled up on my bed talking to Callie on Skype, my phone propped up on the pillows so she could see me.

"So that's the story," I said. "It's carnage. I don't know how long I'm going to have a job for. Without the Thatchell's partnership… Fuck knows what Guido's going to do. I don't think he's even thought that far ahead."

Callie shook her head. She was lying on her gorgeous gold leather chesterfield at home, her hair spilling over a peacock-blue cushion, and she was drinking rosé. "I was going to have a dry January," she said, taking a sip, "But then I thought, fuck that. Poor Guido. It just goes to show, you can fool all of the people some of the time, or some of the people all of the time. Or something. I'm trying to be profound and failing, aren't I?"

It wasn't the perfect opening for me, but it was an opening. "Callie, is Phoebe there?"

"No, she's round at her parents' place. Again."

"Good, because there's something I want to ask you. I've been wanting to ask since New Year's. Callie, lovely, is… what's going on with you and Phoebe? I don't mind, but I wish you'd tell me."

Her face went very still for a bit. I could see her trying to decide whether to tell me anything, and if she did, how much. "I'm not sure what you mean," she said.

"Callie! Look, it's okay, you don't have to talk about it if you don't want to. But you need to know I'm here… well, not there, obviously, but here. And I love you, and if you're happy that's all that matters to me."

Her face crumpled, and she pulled the pillow from behind her head and pressed it to her eyes. The movement obviously made her laptop slide off the sofa, and I heard a crash and then all I could see on my phone's tiny screen was polished floorboards. I started to laugh, and after a bit I heard Callie laughing too.

And between her laughter and her tears, the story came spilling out. How, when she was still with David, she'd known there was something that wasn't right, and how relieved she'd felt when she'd ended it with him and was ready to take the first steps towards being her true self. How when Phoebe had moved in, although it hadn't quite been love at first sight, it hadn't been long before they'd realised they were mad about each other. And how Phoebe had dropped the bombshell that they couldn't tell anyone, it must be a secret, because her fear of her father was too powerful.

"I love her so fucking much." By this stage Callie had righted the laptop, and I could see her tear-stained, happy face. "She makes me laugh every day. She's so sweet and funny – well, you know that. And she's so fucking sexy. I'm so proud she's chosen me, she could have anyone. My girl."

I was weeping a bit too. "I'm so glad. Being in love is just the best. But you're going to tell people, aren't you? Soon?"

"I want to. I want to tell everyone how happy I am, and why. I hate being all furtive about it. The other day I was holding her hand in the supermarket, not really thinking about it, and we almost bumped into your mum. Phoebs dropped me like I was radioactive. She absolutely refuses to tell anyone. She's known she's gay for longer than me, and she's more used to knowing and not telling, I guess. She says we have to wait, but I don't know what the hell we're waiting for. I asked if she meant wait for her dad to die, but that just made her cry. She feels so guilty, still. He's made her feel guilty. Rotten old bastard, sometimes I wish he would bloody die but he's as strong as a tank."

"Callie!"

"Okay, I don't really wish he'd die. Just sometimes, a bit. He's only in his fifties, we could be stuck like this for another thirty years. And we can't go and live somewhere else, because she won't leave him and her mum."

"You poor love. It must be so hard."

"You know what, Pip, it's not all that bad. There's a lot to be said for having a secret. In some ways it's amazing. Just the two of us, in our own little bubble. That's the good part."

"I wish you'd told me, Callie. And you've done all that work planning our wedding. I feel awful, making you do that for me."

"It was fine," Callie laughed. "It's been fun. And it's going to be so amazing! Nick and I went to see Imogen the other day, and she's got the light canopy sorted, it's going to look so awesome. The plan is for the lights to come on – there are more than a thousand bulbs – just after you say your vows, when it's almost dark. Even if it rains, it will be beautiful, like fairyland.

And the florist emailed to confirm the final order and she sent through photos of all the individual flowers – it's going to be so stunning. She's found these things that look like cotton wool – I can't remember what they're called but they're some sort of seed pod. And Nick's booked a string quartet to play when you come in, and while you guys sign the register and stuff. And he told me about the menu – I know you think I'm the world's biggest dullard, Pippa, but I fucking love retro food like that. Chicken supremes – lusherama. You're going to have the best day."

I closed my eyes. I could see it all: the canopy of fairy lights reflecting in the mirrors on the tables, the tubs of snowdrops, the named – or possibly numbered – tables. The only thing about the day I couldn't picture was me.

"Oh my God, Pippa, I totally forgot to ask about the dress! Nick told me you've finally found one. Go on, spill!"

I looked at her small, excited face on the screen. She'd just told me the most important secret about herself, and I couldn't tell her I'd lied to my boyfriend about a frock.

"Yes!" I said. "It's amazing. It's… er… white. And simple." I wanted to describe the dream dress, the one I'd lost last time I was in South Africa. I'd hoped to go and find Valli and his shop and ask if there was any way at all he could get me another one like it, but we were leaving the next morning to go to a remote village in the Eastern Cape and film at a school. I'd be on a flight long before the shops opened. And now, trying to describe to Callie the dress I didn't have, the dress I'd lost, I found I couldn't quite remember what it had looked like.

"You'll see it when I get back," I said.

"Great," Callie said. "And Pip, you know, thanks. Thanks for being so amazing and kind. And I'm sorry I didn't tell you. I hated you not knowing, and I'm so glad you do."

I felt a bit teary again. "It's cool. Honestly, it is. I'm so happy for you."

"Got to go – Phoebs is home. I'm going to tell her I told you, okay?"

"Course. Love you both."

I put down my phone, stretched my stiff neck and drained the last of the wine. My head was buzzing with alcohol and tension. I remembered what Callie had said about her and Phoebe in their private little bubble of love, and I realised that that was how it had been for Nick and me, for so long. But it didn't feel like that anymore. Our bubble had been burst, our world invaded – by Erica, by Iain, by the tasteful invitations landing in the letterboxes of cousin after cousin, and most of all by the wedding I hadn't wanted. And now, thanks to the wedding, Bethany was back in Nick's life. I felt the same sick hollowness in my stomach I'd felt that morning, the sense of being harnessed into a rollercoaster that was going to plummet downwards at any moment, taking me with it whether I liked it or not.

I called Nick's mobile again, and this time I left a message.

"Hi, it's me. I have to be up in five hours so my phone's going to be off. But I want to talk – I need to talk to you about the wedding. I'll try again tomorrow. I hope you're having a good evening."

Hearing his voice, I tried to imagine him next to me, what he'd say if I told him how I was feeling. But the image of his face in my mind was as hazy as my memory of the white dress, the dress that had made me feel like a bride. And I realised it was no good – our wedding was going to happen, just weeks from now, unless something drastic happened to stop it.

"See that over there?" I muttered to Sibingile.

"What?" She stared in the general direction of my pointing finger, past the tin-roofed concrete schoolhouse, the immaculately tidy flowerbeds where bright pink Michaelmas daisies and lush aloes grew, to the parched grey-green hills that stretched beyond.

"There," I said, "just disappearing on the sand road in a cloud of dust. That's not a lorry, it's my comfort zone."

Sibongile laughed. "Come on, Pippa, you'll be fine."

I was so not fine. I was standing behind a table laden with meat, eggs, herbs and tomatoes. I'd had to abandon the safety of my chef's whites, and I was wearing shorts and a pink T-shirt, my hair scraped back in a ponytail. Guido was in the background, subjecting the schoolteacher to the full force of his charm. She was a large, motherly woman in her fifties, and I suspected it had been many years since anyone had flirted with her. Every now and then I heard her squeal with delighted laughter.

But I wasn't looking at her, I was looking at the sea of expectant faces in front of me. About twenty six-year-olds, all in old but spotlessly clean white collared shirts, were waiting to be shown the wonders of Italian cooking through the medium of meatballs. And I was going to have to show them, and be filmed doing it.

I heard Guido begin his spiel to camera.

"We're here in the Eastern Cape at the Adelaide Tambo primary school," he said. "Four hundred pupils come here every day, some walking several miles from home to school and back. I am in awe of the commitment and determination these little ones and their families show to the vital goal of obtaining an education – but we all know children can't learn on empty stomachs! So with me is Pippa, who is one of the most talented young chefs I ever took on at Osteria Falconi. She's going to prepare a nourishing lunch and demonstrate some basic skills, and perhaps we'll discover some cooking talent right here!"

Reluctantly, I left the safety of my table and ventured into the midst of the children. Forty eyes were staring at me, grave and expectant. One little girl started to giggle, then put her hands over her face.

"What's your name?" I said, squatting down next to her.

"Gladness," she whispered.

"How would you like to come and help me work the mincing machine, Gladness? It's a job for a big, strong girl, and you look like a good choice."

Her eyes widened and she burst into a flood of giggles. Sibongile brought a stool for her to stand on, and I showed her how to turn the handle of the mincer, making sure she kept her small fingers well out of harm's way. It wasn't long before her arm got tired and I had to enlist a second child to take over, a boy called Pakiso, who announced that he was the best at football and extremely strong. After a few minutes, though, his bravado faded and it was time for a new assistant. By the time we'd ground two kilos of lamb, all the kids had had a go, except one little boy, who just looked at the floor and shook his head when I talked to him.

"That's Solomon," said the teacher. "He's a very shy boy."

"Well, maybe he's too shy to cook but I'm sure he won't be too shy to eat," I said. I broke a couple of eggs into the meat. "Now, here's the fun part. You've all got clean hands, right?"

"Yes!" chorused all the children, except Solomon.

The kids crowded round the big bowl of seasoned meat and I showed them how to shape it, trying to encourage them to make nice round balls and discourage them from eating it raw. Soon they were all chattering away to me and each other, and the director had to ask their teacher to tell them to be quiet, because I could hardly make myself heard over their excited voices.

I showed them how to make a simple tomato sauce, giving them little tastes of the fresh herbs and garlic. They'd absolutely reek of it tonight, I realised, but that was their mothers' problem, not mine. Eventually – and it took ages, working with a brigade of six-year-olds was far harder than getting even the most hungover commis chef to keep his mind on the job – we had a heap of cooked meatballs, a vat of sauce and a huge pan of pasta ready to go.

"Right, you lot," I said. "I think you've earned your lunch. Who's first?"

"Me!" said Pakiso.

Sibongile helped me dish up twenty enamel plates piled with food, and the children sat under a tree to eat. I found a spot next to Solomon.

"Hello," I said. "My name's Pippa. And yours is Solomon, isn't it?"

He nodded silently. I noticed that, while all the other children were tucking into their food, his plate was untouched.

"Did you get dud meatballs?" I asked. "Why don't you have some of mine? I put extra pepper on them, so they're very special."

He stared up at me, wide-eyed.

"Go on," I said, "try a bit." I loaded up a fork with food and passed it to him. He ate, and his eyes widened some more.

"Like it?"

He nodded.

"Have a bit more then."

Together, we finished the food.

"How was that?" I said.

"It was delicious, thank you," said Solomon in perfect, unaccented English.

I laughed and gave him a hug. His little body felt warm and skinny and strong, and for just a moment, he squashed his face against me. "When you're grown up, you must come and see me in England and then you'll make it for me."

"Cut," said the director. "Outstanding work, Pippa. We'll edit in more commentary but there's definitely enough usable footage for an episode there. Thanks all."

I was hot and knackered and grubby, and there was a big smear of tomato sauce on my shoulder from Solomon's mouth, but I didn't care – I felt as if I'd conquered Everest.

"It's been so amazing," I told Nick, "but absolutely hectic. We've been up at, like, five every morning to get wherever we're going, and we haven't finished shooting most days until after nine. Thank God for Sibongile, she's a star, and Gabriel's working incredibly hard too. He can't cook at all, it's hilarious, he literally can't chop an onion, but because of the way he is in front of the camera they've roped him in to pretend to be this gifted young chef pursuing a dream. And in reality the only thing he's pursuing is his next meal. I don't know how he stays so thin, he literally eats all the time."

There was a pause, then Nick said, very casually – too casually, "Who is Gabriel?"

I was glad we weren't on Skype, because I could feel a hot blush creeping up my neck.

"He's... just some guy. An actor. He came on set in Jo'burg and we've booked him to do more scenes because apparently the camera loves him. He's going out with Sibongile." Which he wasn't, of course. I'm not quite sure why I felt the need to stretch the truth, but I did.

Not that anything was happening with me and Gabriel, or ever would. Partly because he was so far out of my league it would be ridiculous, and mostly because I was going home in two days' time, and two weeks after that, I was going to marry Nick. It was all going to be fine – I was going to put my doubts behind me and eat the tomato soup and be nice to the cousins, and after that Erica would leave and everything would be back to normal with Nick and me. I'd thought about it and that's what I'd decided.

But in the meantime, what harm was there in a bit of flirtation with a handsome man? I know just how mad this sounds, but I felt as if Gabriel was a sort of insurance policy – a guarantee that as long as I behaved myself and resisted temptation, nothing would happen between Bethany and Nick.

And Sibongile was right, Gabriel was an absolute sweetheart. The previous day, we'd been filming in the Drakensberg near the top of a mountain. Lauren had tracked down a conservation group who were working to preserve the fragile ecosystem and maintain the purity of water in the area, and the idea was that we'd film Guido fishing for trout in a mountain stream, and then Gabriel and I would cook it for the hungry ecologists.

Except the fragility of the ecosystem meant that we had to leave our vehicle at the bottom of the mountain and then walk about six miles up a vertical slope – at least that's what it felt like – with all our cooking equipment as well as the cameras. Gabriel insisted on carrying all my stuff, and then when we got to the top he'd expertly repaired my makeup, which was ravaged by sun and sweat, before the cameras saw me. And then he carried it all down again, and helped me over the rocky bits when my totally unsuitable shoes couldn't handle the terrain and I was scared of falling over and looking stupid.

I won't say that I was developing a bit of a crush, but... Yes, I was definitely developing a bit of a crush. But it didn't matter, because soon I'd be home and I could forget all about Gabriel. I wouldn't see the flecks of green and gold in his eyes, admire the perfect, even whiteness of his teeth and hear the husky crack in his voice when he laughed, or feel the warmth of his hand when he helped me over the...

"Are you still there, Pip?"

"Yes, of course, sorry. I was just thinking... telling you about Gabriel, wasn't I?"

"Good. I thought I'd lost you for a moment."

"No, still here. So tomorrow's our last day filming. We're right in the bush, it's amazing, at a game lodge. I wish you could see it, Nick. I've got a beautiful little thatched cottage to myself – it's almost as big as our flat. I'm sitting outside now, and even though the sun set a couple of hours ago, it's still really warm. There's a lake just down the hill and you can see animals drinking there. This morning there were three giraffes. One of them was just a baby and it was so cute. You must tell Spanx it was just like his toy giraffe and he so would have taken it if he'd seen it."

Nick laughed. "Spanx says he misses you, and so do I. I've been kind of bored, now all the wedding stuff is more or less done."

"Aren't you out on the piss every night with Iain?"

"Not exactly," Nick said. "We've been out a few times, and tomorrow's the stag do, so he's organised that. But he's having a hectic time at work. They've lost a couple of big clients, and I think he's realising that he expanded the agency too fast. He's talking about having to make people redundant. And tonight he's seeing Katharine, she finally agreed to meet up. I hope it means they're going to sort things out."

"I'm glad," I said. But I wasn't sure I was, really. It seemed unlike Katharine to just accept what Iain had done, and carry on as before. Nick and I have always agreed that infidelity would be a deal-breaker for us, and I'd assumed that everyone else would feel the same. But then, once you're married, perhaps it's different. Perhaps the commitment you've made is more significant than the pain you're feeling. Perhaps love is stronger than anger? But I was pretty sure that if I were Katharine, I'd want Iain to be alone and miserable for the rest of his life and never have sex again, and for his dying words to be, "If only I hadn't fucked the Czech work experience girl."

Okay, maybe not that. But I'd want him to pay for what he'd done in harder currency than a couple of weeks sleeping on his best mate's sofa.

"Nick, do you think we'll be different once we're married? Like, together, I mean?"

"Do you mean, will our relationship change?"

"Yes, I suppose."

"It might," he said. "I expect it will. When we have kids it definitely will."

There it was again, the thing I never wanted to talk about. Now, looking out into the black night, hearing the sounds of Africa magnified by the silence, with Nick thousands of miles away, I felt compelled to talk about it.

It was pretty stupid timing, I'll grant you that. The time to have this conversation was probably over a bottle of wine or a pot of tea, maybe over one of those coupley lunches people seem to have in glossy magazines, sitting outside a pavement café in some European city, with me wearing a simple yet elegant shift dress and Nick with his Armani shades pushed up on top of his head, and both of us being terribly adult. Oh, and ideally we'd have got it all out of the way about five years earlier.

"Nick, I don't want to have children."

"Obviously not now!" he said. "God, Pippa, did you think I was going to flush your Pills down the toilet as soon as I had a wedding ring on your finger? Don't worry, I mean when eventually we have them."

"Yes, okay, thanks for that. But I don't think I want them ever, Nick. I'm not the maternal type."

"Yes you are! Look how you are with Spanx. You look after him much better than I do. You always notice if he's feeling poorly, and remember his birthday and stuff."

"Nick, Spanx is a cat. I didn't say I didn't want a cat, I said I didn't want a baby."

"But you'd love our baby if we had one," Nick said, sounding just like Mum. "Of course you would. Look how Suze was before she had the twins, she couldn't have cared less about kids. And then once they started trying and it didn't happen straight away, she says she just wanted them more and more until she thought she couldn't ever be happy otherwise. And she loves being a mum now."

"I'm sure she does, and good for her. But I'm not your sister, I'm me. And I'm not just some ticking biological clock with an alarm that's going to go off any minute. I've thought about this a lot, and I'm pretty certain about how I feel."

"I see. So you've been doing all this thinking, but it never occurred to you to talk to me about how you felt, until just before I make a promise to be with you forever."

"Hold on. How is it my responsibility to tell you I don't want kids? It's not like you've sat me down and had long heart-to-heart talks about how you do want them."

"No, because what I want is the standard, default option, Pippa. People get married, then after a bit they have babies. Or they have babies and then after a bit they get married. That's normal. It's what you do."

"It's not what I want to do. That's what I'm trying to tell you, but you're not listening."

"I am listening. What I'm not doing is just agreeing with what you say and going, 'Okay, fine, no kids. We'll do what Pippa wants and fuck what Nick wants.'"

"But you knew!" My voice was raised and I could hear how petulant I sounded. "You've always known I'm not interested in babies. And I'm the one who'd have to feel sick and get fat and then push something the size of a suckling pig out of my chuff."

"Other women seem to manage it."

"I'm not other women."

There was a pause. I imagined our words, laden with misunderstanding and hurt, beaming up to some satellite in space and then ricocheting down again, like something fired from a gun in a computer game. And it was a game at which we were both proving to be pretty good, every shot on target, maximum damage inflicted.

It was Nick who called the truce.

"Pippa, it's ridiculous to talk about this now." He still sounded angry, but now he sounded weary too.

"When do you want to talk about it? The night before our wedding? The night after?"

"I'm trying to be sensible about this, so stop scoring cheap points." I wondered if he'd been thinking about computer games, too. "You're in the middle of fucking Africa, it must be nearly midnight there. You'll be home on Monday, we'll talk about it then, and we'll talk properly, not have a massive row about it."

"I don't want to have a row, Nick, I really don't," I said. "It's just... what we had – have – is fine. Why change it, when there's nothing wrong? I feel like since we decided to get married, we're just fucking everything up."

"Maybe 'fine' isn't good enough, Pippa," he said. "I thought getting married would make things better, move things forward. Nothing was wrong, exactly, but lots of things weren't right. And so I tried to change it in a good way, in the right way, by reminding us we love each other. I don't know about you, but I really need reminding of that at the moment. But this isn't the time to talk about it. Get some sleep."

So we said a sad, distant good night and I went and lay awake in the dark, listening to the frogs croaking and the cicadas chirping, until gradually the sounds changed to the first song of unfamiliar birds. Slowly, imperceptibly, the black sky lightened, then it blazed abruptly to life and my alarm clock went off.

CHAPTER SIXTEEN

From: nick@digitaldrawingboard.com
To: imogen@brockleburymanor.co.uk
Subject: Pickford/Martin wedding

Hi Imogen

I hope you're well. I'm getting in touch to let you know there's been a change to our plans. Please accept my apologies for the late notice once again. I will be in touch by phone shortly to discuss this in more detail, but in the meantime I wanted to give you a brief run-down of where things are at my end.

First of all, I

Oh fuck. I'm going to have to call her, aren't I?

[Draft saved]

Throughout the next day, I was scratchy-eyed and distracted. Guido was back in the spotlight, cooking venison and expounding the benefits of eating meat that is entirely free-range and hence has the highest welfare standards. It didn't matter very much what he said, because most of his script was being put together by the copywriter back in London, and was going to be recorded afterwards as a voiceover to make sure it was all on message. I cooked on autopilot, confident that these recipes, which had all been tested and developed weeks before, would work with minimal effort on my part.

"Are you okay, Pippa?" Sibongile asked. "You're too quiet today."

"I'm fine," I lied. "Just tired. I was up late talking to Nick, and then I couldn't sleep."

"Ah, pre-wedding nerves! You must be looking forward to getting back to him."

"I am. But I guess I'm also sad that this is almost over. It's been amazing. I've got that last day of the summer holiday feeling. Apparently it hasn't stopped pissing with rain in London since I left."

"Everyone always feels like that on the last day of filming," she said. "It's why wrap parties are such a big thing. Tonight should be fun."

There had been murmurs all week about the approaching blow-out, and speculation about who would be spending the last night on location in bed with whom. One of the camera guys had even opened a book on it – I'd noted with amusement that Guido and me were at five to one; Gabriel and Sibongile were evens, although it had been argued that they didn't count, having previously been an item.

"They shouldn't waste their money," Sibongile said. "There's no way I'd ever sleep with him again. Madness!"

For once, the day's shooting went without a hitch, and by mid-afternoon the director had called, "Cut!" for the last time. We cleaned our makeshift kitchen and packed up the leftover food to be given to the staff at the lodge. There was a move by some of the crew to head out for a drive and see the sunset, Sibongile announced that she was going to spend the rest of the afternoon in the spa having a massage, and Guido said there was just enough light left for a couple of hours on the golf course.

"What about you, Pippa?" he asked.

I decided that the spa sounded like a winner. My hair was a mess and my skin needed some serious attention, as I'd been too tired the last few nights to do much more than wave a cleansing wipe in the general direction of my face. And besides, I needed something to stop me obsessively looking for messages from Bethany on Nick's blog. So I spent the rest of the afternoon being exfoliated, steamed, extracted, waxed and plucked to within an inch of my life, then went back to my room, painted my nails, did my make-up properly for the first time in ages, put on a floaty red dress over my bikini, and went to find the party.

Two huge barbeques were filled with glowing coals, and the air smelled deliciously of charring meat. Someone had brought portable speakers and the dulcet tones of Robin Thicke were competing with the sounds of the African night. Clearly I was a bit behind on the drinking. I fetched a G&T and went to join Jan and Chris, two of the camera crew, by the fire.

Chris was chattering excitedly about their drive, on which they'd apparently seen a leopard and her cubs. Jan was topping the story with one of his own, about how he'd spent two weeks filming in Kenya and seen more leopards than you could shake a stick at. Sibongile joined us and we compared notes about our spa treatments. Guido was holding court and opening bottle after bottle of champagne. There was no sign of Gabriel.

I finished my drink, and accepted another, then another, then had a couple of glasses of champagne, and somehow forgot to have any food. After a while things started to go a bit fuzzy around the edges. I remember dancing with Sibongile, treating Chris to a long and, I thought, hilarious account of the excesses of my wedding plans, and making an impassioned speech to Guido about what an honour it was to work with him, and how I loved him like a father.

It was after that that I decided I'd probably better back off before I made more of a fool of myself, so I topped up my glass and took it and my phone down to the swimming pool.

I longed to talk to Nick. But our home number rang and rang, and went to voicemail – the impersonal, professional message Nick had recorded years before thanking me for getting in touch with Digital Drawing Board, but regretting that Nick Pickford wasn't available right now. I tried his mobile but he didn't answer that either. Then I remembered – of course, it was Saturday night. It was Nick's stag night. When I'd asked him about it, he'd said he had no idea what Iain was planning, and I'd been cool with that. But suddenly I felt very far away, and terribly insecure. Sitting on the edge of the pool, my feet and ankles in the lukewarm water, I opened his blog on my phone.

Staggering

So tonight's the night. I've got no idea what Iain has up his sleeve for me but I'm sure it's going to get messy. I'm trusting that the worst that will happen is the mother of all hangovers tomorrow – my mates won't clingfilm me naked to a lamppost and tip tins of beans over my head like something out of Loaded magazine circa 1995, will they? Will they?

See you on the other side. I hope.

I scrolled down through the comments. There were lots of good luck posts from Nick's usual followers, and a couple of stag night horror stories. Then I clicked on the 'view private messages' button, and what I saw made me feel like I'd been kicked in the stomach.

Nick and Bethany had been messaging each other all day.

At 8am she'd posted, "Morning lovebug," and he'd replied straight away, "Hey Beff," and they'd been at it ever since. I scrolled down through the messages.

"Just heading off to Loftus Road now," Nick had written at two o'clock in the afternoon. "Reminds me of going to games with you – good times!"

"Don't you take Pippa to football then?"

"Nah, she's not that interested. Gotta go now – will touch base later."

"Can't possibly be the girl for you then! Where you heading after?"

"Don't know, will ask Iain. Why – want to come?"

"Naaaaah, I can't crash your stag do… can I?"

"Only if you're wearing Hoops strip."

"Hmmm, I seem to remember you quite liking that, back in the day. Except then I wasn't wearing anything under it…"

My eyes were burning, and I realised I'd been staring so fixedly at the messages on the screen, I'd forgotten to blink. When I did, I felt tears course down my cheeks. I carried on reading. Throughout the afternoon, the messages had been going back and forth between the two of them. Every goal scored meant a joint celebration. He'd updated her throughout the evening, from the first pint, and she'd responded to every message within seconds. As the messages continued, I could see Nick's typing getting more erratic, until the final thing he had written.

"Ohgod Beff I don't knowif I'm donig the right thing here. Dos everyone feel likethis on stga night?"

And she'd replied, "I'm coming to get you."

That was it – there were no more messages since that one, sent half an hour before. It would be after one in the morning in London, and I had no way of knowing where Nick was or who was with him.

I was furious, baffled and absolutely gutted. I wanted to speak to Nick and ask him what was going on. I wanted to feel his arms around me and hear him tell me it was okay, there was nothing to worry about. But at the same time, I wanted to hurt him as badly as I was hurting. I wanted it all to stop.

For a bit I just sat on the edge of the pool, my feet dangling in the water. Then I pulled off my dress and lowered myself gently in, walked to the centre and floated, letting my body drift and wishing my thoughts could be washed away.

I lay on my back, the water as warm as the night air that surrounded it, moving my legs and arms slowly to keep myself afloat. The sky was dense with stars, thousands of them, spinning in unfamiliar constellations. I could see the glow of the dying fires and hear the distant hum of voices from the party and the occasional shout of laughter, but I felt quite remote from it all, as if I'd been alone in this moment for a long, long time and would never be able to leave it.

Then I heard a gentle splash, the water rippled underneath me and I realised I wasn't alone any more. Gabriel was swimming towards me.

"I came to check you hadn't drowned," he said.

"Still afloat, last time I checked," I said.

"Just as well. I thought you might have gone all Ophelia on us. 'Her garments, heavy with their drink, pulled the poor wretch from her melodious lay to muddy death'," he quoted.

I attempted a laugh. It came out sounding all shaky and wrong, half laugh, half sob. "I might be heavy with drink, but my garments aren't. If Ophelia had been wearing a bikini she would've been grand. I was just looking at the stars. They're so different here."

"There's the Southern Cross, obviously," he pointed. "And Orion, and the Great Bear. It's a good night for stargazing, because there's no moon."

"How beautiful," I said. But I didn't mean the night sky, I meant him. His face suddenly seemed like the answer to everything.

He kicked his legs up and floated on his back, and after a while I joined him. It might have been the copious amount of gin and wine I'd shipped – in fact it almost certainly was – but I felt entirely weightless. The water holding me up and the sky above me seemed to meld together, and I was conscious of the time slowing, the stars circling, my head spinning. I dipped below the surface of the water and came back up to my feet, spluttering.

"You look like a mermaid," Gabriel said. "A very cold mermaid in a bikini."

I realised I was shivering, although I didn't feel cold.

Gabriel put his arms around me, and I could feel the heat coming from beneath his cool skin. His kiss, when it came, was unexpected but also entirely unsurprising. I closed my eyes, unresisting, and let myself be kissed. Here it was: my out, and my revenge.

When Gabriel lifted me out of the water, took my hand and guided me to my room, I didn't resist either. As the door closed behind us, I'm sure I heard Chris shout, "Yes! My fifteen to one shot!"

Gabriel said, "Come on, let's get you out of those wet things."

I said, "Wait. Hold on, I don't think I can…"

But then I flopped bonelessly on the bed, and the room started to spin around me much faster than the stars had done.

I was woken by bright sunlight stabbing my head like a Global knife. My hair was still damp and smelled of chlorine. I was naked under the duvet, and Gabriel wasn't there.

You know how sometimes you wake up with a hangover and lie, twitching with horror, trying to piece together what happened the night before. Just when you think you've got it all, the final pieces of the puzzle of how embarrassingly you behaved, a new piece of information surfaces through the haze, leaving you squirming with renewed mortification? This wasn't like that. I could remember every detail of the evening. Reading the exchange of messages between Nick and Bethany, and how it had made me feel. My conversation with Gabriel, the stars, the way his body had felt, so much slighter and lither than Nick's, the way his mouth had tasted of swimming pool and beer and he'd smelled of sunblock. Right until that last moment, every detail was clear. But afterwards, it was blackness, like when you set the digital TV box to record a film and when you play it back, it's cut off the end.

I stood by the door of my room for a long time before I was brave enough to face the world. Hiding behind sunglasses and a baseball cap, I crept past the swimming pool and on to the main lodge, where I could see people standing around drinking coffee, someone frying bacon, others rushing around loading equipment into trailers. Chris, Jan and some of the other camera crew were in the breakfast-cooking detail. I could hear their bursts of laughter over the sound of spitting fat as I approached, then, suddenly, they all fell silent. Their eyes turned to look at me, and stayed on me as I approached.

"Good morning," I said, ultra-casually.

"Morning," a couple of them muttered back.

"Never mind 'good morning', it's your good night we want to hear all about," said Chris.

"Aren't you going to offer Pippa commission on your winnings, dude?" said Jan, and they all laughed.

I forced a laugh too, totally unable to hide a flaming blush of mortification, and went to find Sibongile. She was sitting at one of the wooden tables drinking coffee and tapping busily away on her phone, but when she saw me approaching, she stood up, gave me a long, still gaze and walked away, leaving her almost full mug behind.

I spent the rest of that day swamped by a blanket of shame. Gabriel had left a few hours before, Guido told me, checking out early to start the eight-hour drive home. The knowledge that I would never see him again was a faint relief. Guido was quiet too – no longer having to put up a front, he was sunk in gloom. I was sure he, too, was dreading what was waiting for him back in London, though for reasons very different from mine.

We didn't speak apart from exchanging essential details about the plan for the day – the short flight back to Johannesburg, the long wait at the airport, then the longer flight home, the week's holiday I'd arranged to take. Throughout the long journey, I kept my headphones on, even though I didn't have any music on. I wouldn't have heard it anyway, over the soundtrack of guilt that was playing on a constant loop in my head.

Of course, I knew that Nick need never find out. I could go home, carry on as if nothing had happened, get married. I could spend the rest of my life knowing that I'd been betrayed, and committed a far worse betrayal myself. But how, then, could I ever respect Nick again, or myself? He'd always be the man I'd cheated on and duped. And I'd be depriving him of the right to make a choice about how to respond to my behaviour. Or I could confess everything, but let him decide what to do – abdicate responsibility, let him be the one who'd have to end it, tell the florist and the videographer and all the army of people who were set to descend on our wedding like a swarm of worker bees hungry for honey, that it was all off.

I couldn't do either of those things, I decided, at some point during the interminable night flight up Africa. The only way that I could salvage some courage and self-respect out of this whole mess was to be brave and do it the hard way.

So when the taxi deposited me outside our front door, I asked the driver to wait. I went upstairs, tipped the contents of my bag into the washing basket and repacked it with winter clothes, and I told Nick I couldn't marry him, because I'd slept with someone else. I was quite calm. I said I was going to stay with my parents, I was leaving, it was all off. I told him I was sorry.

CHAPTER SEVENTEEN

From: nick@digitaldrawingboard.com
To: nick@digitaldrawingboard.com
Bcc:
Subject: Pickford/Martin wedding

Dear friends

I'm writing with great regret to let you know that the wedding planned between Pippa and me will not now take place.

I know many of you have made travel plans and other arrangements, and we are both deeply sorry for your trouble. Some of you have also sent generous gifts, for which we were very grateful. These will be returned as soon as possible.

Thanks for your friendship and understanding.

Warm regards
Nick

Mum took one look at me, standing on her doorstep dripping with tears and rain (I'd decided to walk from the station, and it had started pissing it down when I was halfway there, but, masochistically, I'd carried on instead of phoning and asking for a lift), and realised what had happened.

"Oh, darling," she said, enveloping me in a fragrant hug. "My poor little Pippa."

"It's all my fault," I sobbed into her shoulder.

She shushed me, told me I could talk about it when I was ready, ushered me inside, made me tea and a hot bath and put me to bed as if I was six and had been sent home from school after throwing up in assembly.

And that's where I remained, in my childhood bedroom, long since stripped of the Spice Girls posters and Pony Club rosettes that had adorned it when I was a teenager, for the next three days. As if I were an invalid, Mum plied me with poached eggs on toast (the toast burnt and the egg whites undercooked and mucusy), endless cups of tea and a huge stack of Agatha Christie novels, which I devoured mindlessly (unlike the eggs, which I choked down so as not to hurt Mum's feelings). Occasionally I heard her and Dad having worried, whispered conversations outside my door, but they didn't ask me about what had happened, beyond establishing that the wedding was off, and I didn't tell.

It was just the same as it had been the first time Nick and I split up, except that I was twelve years older and not pregnant.

It was the end of the long, hot summer after I'd finished A-levels, and my friends were beginning to drift away into their new, adult lives. I was both terrified and triumphant about having got a coveted place at college to learn to be a chef, having passed several terrifying and intense rounds of interviews and tests. Callie had left to begin her year out teaching English in a primary school in Peru. Suze was Interrailing around Europe with a friend. Nick had finished his first year at art school, and when I wasn't at my part-time waitressing job, he and I spent almost every minute together, lying in the garden in the sun, going to gigs and making love. I couldn't possibly say which of the many, many condoms we'd got through had failed us, but clearly one of them did, because a week before I was due to leave for London and start my training, I realised my period was late.

I've never known such blind panic. I didn't want to tell Nick – I felt stupidly ashamed, and was sure he'd think it was my fault. Callie could only check her email intermittently at an internet café. I couldn't face making an appointment with our family GP, a grandfatherly old codger who'd given me my measles vaccine when I was a baby and set my broken wrist after I fell off my pony when I was twelve. And I still believed Mum didn't know Nick and I were sleeping together.

Besides, I was as sure as I've ever been about anything that I couldn't have a baby. I'd seen girls from school who'd 'got themselves pregnant', as people said, as if some sort of immaculate conception had taken place or they'd wilfully lain around in a bath of sperm. Cerys Brown had moved into a council flat with her boyfriend, but it wasn't long before he pushed off and whenever I saw her in the street with her baby it was screaming and she looked exhausted and defeated. Lisa Henderson was still living with her parents and back at school, brightly positive about her future, but when I imagined that life for myself, it just seemed bleak and frightening.

I'd have to give up my place on the course, or try to defer it, and perhaps never be able to get it back. I'd have to stay at home with Mum and Dad, and because they were both at work all day, there would be no one to look after my baby except me. Everyone else would have moved on and I'd be left behind.

And Nick? I'd got it all planned: he and I would carry on seeing each other, even though I'd be in London. We were in love, we were going to be together forever – what did a couple of hundred miles matter? But if being with me meant a tiny flat somewhere with a baby and no money, would he still want me? I didn't think he would. But I didn't know what to do or where to turn.

So I told Erica. We were friends, she was a nurse, she'd know what to do, I reasoned.

I chose a time when I knew Nick would be at band practice, and went round to their house. Erica was in the kitchen making one of her worthy vegetarian dinners, and the smell of boiling chickpeas made me feel sick (it still does, to this day). She welcomed me warmly, as she always did back then.

"Nick's off gallivanting somewhere," she said.

"I know," I said. "I came to see you, actually."

"Well, what a nice surprise!" She made tea and produced a plate of dry flapjack and we sat down at the kitchen table, and I spilled out my sorry little story.

"And I thought maybe you'd know if there was something I could take… some herbal thing, like a natural remedy, to bring on my period?"

I'd been looking down at the scrubbed table top, pushing a few crumbs around with my finger, but now I looked up at Erica. Her face was white.

"But that's abortion!" she said.

I realised that it was, of course. Erica wasn't some modern-day white witch who could make it all disappear by magic or with some homeopathic drops in a glass of water.

"I know," I said in a small voice. "But I don't think there's anything else I can do."

"Pippa, I think you're making a dreadful mistake. I know you think you're grown up, but you're not. You're rushing into something I know you will come to regret very, very deeply. This is not just an inconvenience, a stumbling block to your ambition. It's a human life. It's your baby, Nick's baby, my grandchild. What you're suggesting is… it's wicked."

I was appalled. I'd always thought of Erica as laid-back and liberal in her views, but now I remembered her ten brothers and sisters and realised that there was more to her background than I'd considered. I would have done anything to take back my words, but I couldn't.

"I have thought about it, Erica. I'm not rushing into anything. I can't have a baby. I don't want to. I'm frightened."

"Of course you are, my dear! Any girl would be. Even when a baby is longed for, strived for, it's a frightening time. Being a mother is the most important job any woman can do. It's a wonderful, precious opportunity. And we can make it work, Pippa. You'll have my complete support, and of course that of your parents, when you tell them."

I thought, no, I'll only have your support if I do what you want.

"I'm sorry, Erica," I said. "But I can't. I'm going to London, I'm going to be a chef. There were hardly any places on my course, and I got one. I was so proud of myself. I can't give it up and have a baby."

"There are other ways, Pippa," she said gently. "Have you thought how many childless couples there are, so full of love, who would give anything – anything! – for the life you're carrying? Surely the mature, generous thing to do is to wait a little while to pursue your ambitions? You're so young, you have your entire life ahead of you. This need only interrupt your plans for a year."

"No!" I said. "I don't care about those other people. I don't know them. I'm not going to go through this just so some random people I've never met can have my baby. And working in a kitchen all day – it's hard, physically hard. It's so competitive. I don't think I could manage it if I was being sick and stuff."

Besides, I'd heard what Lisa had said about the overwhelming love she had for her child, how she didn't regret having Callum for a moment and wouldn't change a thing. How she couldn't understand how anyone could ever bear to give their baby away. The prospect of that happening to me was the most frightening thing of all.

Erica stood up. "I don't think there's anything left for me to say, Pippa. You can only examine your conscience and choose whether to do the right thing or the other, the selfish, sinful thing. And please know that if you go through with this abhorrent act, you will no longer be welcome in my home."

And then she quite literally showed me the door. If she could have thrown me out bodily, I'm sure she would have done.

I went home and sat in my room in the dark, alone and terrified, until Nick came over. I had decided that I would talk to him about it, and we could make the decision together. But I didn't in the end, because he had something important to tell me, and it was that he didn't think a long-distance relationship could possibly work, that I needed my freedom, and that since I wasn't going to end our relationship, he was.

So the final week of that summer I spent in bed, in tears, being brought tea and detective stories by Mum. There wasn't any choice to make any more, there was just me, alone and afraid, with only one option open to me. As soon as I got to London, I phoned a number I got off a poster on the Tube and a few days later, I wasn't pregnant any more.

Erica was wrong – I've never regretted my decision, not for a second. But the sense of shame she left me with has never quite faded, and that's why I've never told anyone else what I did. Not Mum, not Callie, not Nick. Especially not Nick. And now that it was over and we weren't going to get married, I'd never tell him. At least Erica would be pleased about that.

In my rush to unpack my suitcase, pack it again, say what I had to say to Nick and walk out of our life together, I'd somehow neglected to pack my mobile phone charger. I could picture where I'd left it, on the packing box that had been serving as our bedside table, next to the beautiful ring I'd never wear again. I stared at the steadily emptying battery icon on my phone's screen. Seven missed calls and messages from Nick and five from Callie were taking their toll. But Callie's concern and Nick's recriminations would have to wait – I had important plans for the precious fifteen percent of battery life that remained.

I called up my email and started a new message to erica@visionforliberia.org – although she wasn't at work, I knew she'd still been using that address.

"Dear Erica," I wrote.

So, you've got what you wanted. I'm not going to marry Nick, and you never need to see me again. More importantly, I need never see you. That feels pretty good right now. I hope you feel good, too.

I looked at the words on the screen, bitter and untrue. Then I put my finger on the delete button and watched them disappear, first one letter at a time, then one word at a time, then all the rest of the message at once. I pressed the compose button again.

Dear Erica

I expect Nick has told you what's happened, and you're delighted with the news. I can't change the way you feel about me, but there's something I wanted to explain. I know you think I made the choice not to have a baby lightly and selfishly, but I didn't. It was one of the hardest things I've ever done. For a long time, I cried about it every day. Even now, I sometimes wonder whether I did the right thing.

Nick always wanted to have children, but whenever I think about it, I feel as afraid as I did when I was eighteen. If I'd had someone to support me, someone I trusted, it might have been different. But we can't change that now. I have to live with what I did, and so do you.

I read it through, then deleted almost all of it, and tried again.

Dear Erica

I expect Nick has told you what's happened. Please take care of him. I'm so worried about him, but I'm really glad you're there.

I'm sorry I made such a mess of things.

Pippa

This time I pressed send, quickly, before I could change my mind, and watched anxiously as the progress bar inched forward. I think it reached the end before my phone gave a final pathetic bleep and died. That was it – until I got hold of a new charger, all I could do was lie in my bed and hide myself in endless words about Venetian paperknives, lace handkerchiefs dropped on the library floor and sleepy villages rocked by murder most foul. As soon as I stopped reading, I'd find myself thinking of Nick again. What was he doing? Had he made all the calls and sent all the emails he'd need to, to call everything off? Was he missing me? Was Spanx? I was missing them, with a hunger that was almost physical.

But, as I'd learned back when I was eighteen, you can only lie in bed and cry for so long. After a while, my bedroom began to feel more like a prison than a refuge. When I looked in the bathroom mirror I realised that my hair hadn't been blow-dried since I left South Africa. My bed was becoming increasingly scratchy with toast crumbs. I needed to man the fuck up and face what I had done.

So on the third day, so to speak, I rose again. I had a shower and dressed properly and even put on some makeup, and went downstairs to find Mum and Dad in the kitchen surrounded by seed catalogues.

"Hello," I said.

Dad said, "Morning, Pippa. I was telling your mother that neon calendulas would be just the thing to brighten up that dark corner next to the weeping pear, but she insists that orange flowers are vulgar. What do you think?"

Of course, I couldn't care less about gardening, but I was grateful to spend a few minutes focussing on something that wasn't Nick, my wedding, or whether the butler or the vicar had done it. So I joined in the debate, taking Dad's side because if orange is a good colour for cats, it must surely be good for flowers too.

After a bit Mum admitted defeat and said, "All right, order them then, Gerard, but if we get trounced by the Alcocks in the parish garden awards again, I shall blame you.

"Pippa, Callie rang up again. She says she completely understands if you don't feel like talking, but she's at home all weekend, and she said do pop round if you're able to. I think perhaps…"

I realised it was Saturday. Two weeks to go until the wedding that wasn't going to happen. "You're right, Mum. Of course I'll go and see her. Do you mind if I borrow the car?"

Dad said, "I'll drive you over, and you can ring if you need a lift back, or get a taxi. I know what you girls are like when you get together."

It was official. I was eighteen again. "Can we go to Carphone Warehouse on the way?" I said.

Dad might treat me a bit like I'm still at school, but there's no denying that he knows what he's talking about when it comes to Callie and me. She opened the door holding a cocktail shaker, and ten minutes later we were ensconced on her gold leather chesterfield with cosmopolitans and a massive bowl of popcorn.

"You really should talk to Nick, Pip," she said. "I know you don't want to, but you'll have to at some stage."

"I know," I said, looking down at my newly charged phone. There were now twelve new voice messages on it, and five new texts. It felt like a grenade with the pin out. "I know I have to. Just not now. Have you spoken to him?"

She nodded. "He's okay. Not good, but okay. He says he's leaving it a few days before he cancels everything, because it won't make any difference to not getting the deposits back for stuff. But I think it just hasn't sunk in properly yet. When I spoke to him he sounded like he was in shock."

I squeezed my eyes shut to keep the tears back. "He needn't worry about the money. I'll pay Erica back. I've got some savings and Guido's giving me a fat bonus for the South Africa trip."

"He got savaged in the press at first, poor bloke," Callie said, tactfully changing the subject. "But there's been some really supportive stuff in the last few days. People love him, they reckon he's won the PR war over that cow Florence. *The Guardian* had a piece yesterday comparing them to Nigella and Charles Saatchi. With Guido as Nigella, obviously."

"He'll be pleased about that," I said. "But God knows what we'll do now the Thatchell's thing isn't happening any more. I've still got a job for now, but long-term, I don't know. I think I'm going to have to start looking around for something else. Maybe go back to working in a restaurant, since I'm free and single again." I swallowed hard, realising that I'd gone and changed the subject straight back.

"Pippa, we don't have to talk about it if you don't want to," Callie said. "But there are a few things I want to say, and after that I'll shut up, I promise."

I knew if I tried to talk I'd just start to cry again, so I nodded mutely.

"Nick loves you," she said. "All this stuff with the wedding – I was there, remember. I saw him planning and deciding about everything. All the time, he was like, 'Will Pippa like this? Is this what Pippa wants? Is this good enough for Pippa?' He was doing what he thought was right. And it wasn't, but that's not really his fault, because you never told him."

"I thought it was what he wanted," I said miserably. "I thought I could just go along with it and let him have his perfect day, even though it wasn't mine. But it's ended up exposing loads of other stuff that I don't even want to think about. I thought we were great together, you know? I thought everything was fine and I didn't need to worry, and we'd just carry on as we were forever. But you can't just stay in one place, can you? And the wedding made me realise that everything wasn't perfect, and now I've fucked it all up completely, and there's no going back."

Callie poured more of the pink drink into our glasses. "What happened in South Africa?" she asked.

I told her about the messages between Nick and Bethany, how I'd felt, and what I'd done.

"Yep, that's bad," she said. "I'm not going to say it isn't. But it's not unsalvageable, you know. And you don't even know anything happened with Bethany. It was his stag night, you were both pissed, you were miles away from each other and missing each other. If you were to ask him to forgive you, you could move on from it. People do."

I thought of Iain and Katharine. "I know they do," I said. "But I can't do it. I don't deserve him to forgive me, and I don't want to spend the rest of my life feeling like I have to make up for what I did."

Callie opened her mouth to say something else, but then we heard a key in the door and Phoebe burst in.

"I told them," she said, and sank down on the floor and buried her head in Callie's lap. Her shoulders were shaking and she was making high-pitched sort of squeaking sounds. I couldn't tell whether she was laughing or crying.

Callie stroked her hair, and we waited until she'd stopped.

"Are those cosmopolitans?" Phoebe said. "Gimme."

Callie poured her a glassful. Phoebe necked about half in one gulp.

"So you told your mum and dad?" I said, absolutely agog to hear the details, and relieved that we were talking about someone else's problems.

Phoebe nodded. "God, I could do with a fag," she said.

"Really?" said Callie. "I can go and get some if you want."

"No," Phoebe said. "I needed all my lung capacity when he chased me down the street. I'm not risking not being able to get away if it happens again."

"He chased…" Callie and I said together.

"Start at the beginning," I said. "What happened?"

Phoebe finished her drink and held her glass out for a refill.

"I told Mum first," she said. "She was cool. Bless her, she said if she was going to have a daughter-in-law, she couldn't think of anyone she'd rather have than you, Callie. And then she said we should tell Dad together. So we did. I sat down and did the whole thing, like, 'Dad, I'm gay, and Callie and I are in love.' And he jumped out of his chair like it was red hot, and started shouting at me. It was terrifying. I've never seen him so angry."

"Oh, Phoebs," Callie put her arm round Phoebe's shoulders and I passed her the box of tissues I'd been using.

"And I was like, 'Dad, stop shouting. I'm not going to be spoken to like that.' I was shit-scared but I didn't want him to know."

"Good for you," I said.

"And he goes, 'You'll be spoken to however I choose to speak to you, or you'll get out of my house.' So I said, fine, I'd go, and I started to leave, but he came after me. He chased me all the way to my car. He was like Usain fucking Bolt." Phoebe started half-laughing, half-crying again.

"And your Mum?" asked Callie.

"She's gone to my aunt Linda's. Don't you see, there's no way he could have run like that if it was true about his back? He's been waited on hand and foot by me and Mum all this time and there's nothing wrong with him."

Callie and I looked at each other, and then we started to laugh too.

"It's not funny," I said. "It's not a bit funny. All those years. All the money he's had in benefits. It's awful, it's fraud."

But we couldn't stop laughing, even though we were crying as well.

"We can tell everyone now," Callie said. "We can get married."

I said, "You know what? I've got an idea."

The church hall at St Boniface's was absolutely freezing, in spite of being packed to the rafters with the great and good of Westbourne parish. I could feel my toes going numb in my Uggs, and I was glad of my decision to leave my wristwarmers, woolly hat and Dad's Barbour jacket on. I was perched on a narrow wooden chair that felt like the sort of thing that backchatting Victorian schoolchildren or nuns caught sneaking out of the convent for a burger on a Friday might have been ordered to sit on by way of punishment, and my arse was going numb too.

I glanced at my watch. We were twenty-five minutes into the second half, and by my reckoning there was at least two hours of this torture still to be endured. In spite of my discomfort, I felt extremely sleepy. The elderly man sitting next to me had already succumbed to ennui and the warm Bristol Cream sherry we'd been served in the interval, and occasionally a guttural snore rent the air. Although most of Mum's scenes were done, I needed to stay awake so I could think of nice things to say about Dad's performance as the second gravedigger.

What Mum had said about Dominic Baker's talent was true – he was giving the performance his all, and not one line appeared to have been cut. Unfortunately he was only convincing in the role if you were able to suspend disbelief enough to accept a Prince of Denmark who was as thin on top as the Prince of Wales. The grey head of the man next to me slumped on to my shoulder and I gave him a gentle dig in the ribs. He started awake and said loudly, "Pass me my nine-iron!" before lapsing back into silence. I dug my nails into my palms to stay awake.

At last the ordeal was over. For a Westbourne Thespians production it hadn't gone too badly, apart from the bit where Dominic dropped Yorick's skull and it rolled off the stage and into the lap of a lady in the front row who, judging by her startled yelp, had also nodded off. With much scraping of chairs, everyone stood up. I resisted the urge to rub my bum to restore circulation, and filed back through to the vestibule with the rest of the audience, all of whom fell upon the sherry, dry madeira cake and platters of egg sandwiches as if they hadn't seen food for a week. I armed myself with a glass and went and stood in a corner waiting for Mum and Dad to appear, hoping that none of their friends would come over and talk to me and ask me how Nick was.

But, inevitably, it wasn't long before someone did. As I hovered in my corner, I could see a tall woman in a hijab approaching me, and felt rising panic. Not only was I going to have to deal with an awkward conversation about my relationship status, but I hadn't got a clue who she was. I rooted desperately through my memory of Mum and Dad's friends. She was too young to be one of their contemporaries. A former colleague from the university? A gardening person? Shit, I was going to have to make polite conversation with someone I didn't know from a bar of soap.

"Hello, Pippa! How lovely to see you here, and how unexpected. Are you visiting your parents?" She kissed me.

"Er… hello," I said. "Lovely to see you too. Yes, I came to support Mum and Dad in the play."

"Oooh, were they in the cast? You must be so proud. Let me see if I can guess who they were." So, not a friend of Mum and Dad's then. Who the hell was she? "The lady who was Gertrude, she looked just like you. That must have been your mum."

I smiled politely. "That's right, yes, good spot. And Dad was the second gravedigger, I don't look as much like him, especially not with the smears of mud all over his face."

"They were both excellent. Yes, I think I can see the resemblance to your dad too. Did you enjoy the performance?"

If I'd known the woman, I could have had a long, enjoyable bitch about the freezing room and the hard chairs, but I couldn't risk it.

"Very much," I said. "It was very comprehensive. Not too short."

She gave me what I thought might have been a wink. "No, it certainly wasn't too short! But I would have thought that you'd be on honeymoon, getting away from this horrible weather. Oh, but I've messed up my dates, haven't I? The wedding isn't until February."

Okay, so whoever she was, she hadn't been invited. So not one of the handful of Mum and Dad's close friends who they'd said they wanted to be there, and who had now been informed that it was all off. I cursed myself for not fessing up in the beginning and saying I'd forgotten her name. That window of opportunity was now well and truly closed, and I was just going to have to brazen it out.

But I really didn't want to pour out my relationship woes to this stranger, so I said, "It's next Saturday, actually." Which was kind of true, in a sense.

"How lovely! And how amazing that you could still manage to be here to support your parents, it's such a busy time. We must arrange to get together afterwards, once you're back from honeymoon."

Fuck. I gulped. "Yes, yes we must. We haven't seen you for... um... ages."

"Not since our wedding," she said. "I really do envy you and Nick, deciding to keep it small and not invite all and sundry. We did, and although it was a lovely day, I sometimes wish we'd limited it to close family, like you have, and not invited all the cousins and their little ones."

Finally, light dawned. Thank God. It was Nick's cousin Alison, the one who'd recently converted to Islam. No wonder I hadn't recognised her – I'd never seen her in a headscarf before. I felt dizzy with embarrassed relief.

"But it was such a great day anyway," I burbled, "so nice to get to meet all the family. Thanks for being so understanding about... you know..."

"Don't give it another thought! Nick explained why it wasn't possible to invite us. But do give me a ring soon, Nick's got my number. I must be off now, early start for salat al fajr tomorrow." And she kissed me again and bustled off.

My head was spinning, and it wasn't from the warm sherry. What the hell was going on? Alison and Darren hadn't been invited to our wedding. From what she'd said, none of the cousins had. But what about The Amazing Archibald and the halal chicken and the pile of invitations I'd seen? What had Nick done?

But of course none of it mattered now. Poor Alison, she'd have to find out sooner or later, and she'd think I was barking mad, but that was okay, because I'd never see her again.

On the other side of the room, I could see Mum and Dad, still in their stage makeup, surrounded by their admiring public. I fought through the crowd towards them, collecting two glasses of sherry for them on the way.

"Congratulations!" I said. "You were both brilliant, I was so proud. Dad, the way you turned the thing with the skull into comedy stage business was just inspired."

"You are kind, Pippa," said Mum. "I fluffed my lines in scene one, did you notice? I don't think anyone else did."

I assured her that I hadn't, then my peripheral vision alerted me to the approach of Dominic Baker. I remembered his bottom-pinching ways from previous opening nights, and decided it was time to exit stage left.

"I'd better head off now," I said, "I'll walk home, you stay and enjoy the party. And, Mum, I think tomorrow I'll go back to London. I'm back in the office on Monday and there are things I need to sort out."

Mum said, "Yes, darling, I'm sure there are."

CHAPTER EIGHTEEN

From: nick@digitaldrawingboard.com
To: susannahburgess@webmail.com
Subject: tomorrow

Hey sis

I suppose you'll see this email when you're in a transit lounge in Dubai. Thanks so much for making the effort to come over, and I really wish it hadn't ended up being so shit. But there you go – it is what it is. Really looking forward to seeing you and the girls anyway, and I know you're looking forward to staying with Di in Reading for a few days. Shame Dylan couldn't get time off work, but in the grand scheme of things I suppose that's no bad thing, hey?

Anyway, I wanted to tell you that Abdul from Jamaica Cars is booked to pick you up at Heathrow at 7am. He's promised there will be car seats for B and K, and he knows Di's address. He'll be waiting at terminal 3 arrivals with a sign saying "WORLD'S BEST SISTER". It's true. Can't wait to see you in a few days.

Love you all lots.
Nick

In the end, once I'd helped Dad prune the weeping pear, roasted a chicken for lunch and had several lengthy post-mortems about the play, it was mid-afternoon by the time I left. Eloise had kindly offered me her and Dean's spare bedroom for a few days, but I was going to have to sort something more permanent out sharpish. As I fought my way through the packed train, eventually finding a table to myself in the quiet coach, I imagined a life of sofa-surfing ahead of me, imposing myself on one kind friend after another, until I ended up sleeping on an air vent on the Strand.

But I felt like I deserved nothing better. The thought of the next conversation I'd have to have with Nick, the one about splitting up our stuff, putting the flat on the market, and who was going to have Spanx, filled me with cold dread. But that was okay, because when I remembered the night with Gabriel, his kiss in the warm swimming pool, the drops of water clinging to his eyelashes, waking up alone in the bed, I felt a compensatory rush of hot shame.

Every part of me cringed remembering it. How, just how, had I managed to be such a dick? I could have spoken to Nick like an equal, ended things amicably and even managed to rescue some semblance of mutual respect. But I hadn't. I'd taken the coward's way out. I remembered Callie saying once that even when things with David had been falling apart, she'd been careful never to treat him with less kindness and decency than she would a friend. I hadn't done that. I'd treated Nick abysmally, leaving him with the carnage of our wedding plans, the flat filled with table centrepieces, the beautiful seating plan he'd designed propped on an easel in his office. And I hadn't even looked at it – if I had, maybe I'd have seen that there weren't three hundred guests like I'd thought, that he'd been quietly changing things to make me happy.

But then I remembered the other things, the ones that really mattered – his longing for children, his insistence that I change my name, Erica's malevolent presence, the horrible rows we'd had, the idea of him and Bethany together. I gazed mindlessly at my phone, as if Facebook would hold the answer, but it didn't. And Nick's blog didn't either – he had deleted all the posts and taken it down.

I was so sunk in gloom that I didn't realise the train wasn't moving, but after a while I became aware of an increased level of chuntering from the other people in the carriage.

"It's a disgrace, that's what it is."

"And the amount they charge…"

"I suppose it's leaves on the track again."

"Or the wrong kind of snow."

"And they never tell you anything."

Right on cue, the PA system crackled to life. "Unfortunately, owing to high winds and speed restrictions which have affected the network, this service is being diverted via Reading. Our expected time of arrival into London Waterloo is now eighteen fifty-three, two hours behind schedule. We apologise for any inconvenience this may cause."

There was a collective sigh and a barrage of tuts. I wished I'd bought the new *Heat* magazine, but all I had was my phone and a week-old copy of the *Radio Times*. I turned to an article about the new series of *Downton Abbey* and started reading it. Eventually the train crept into Reading. Through the window, I could see cross faces waiting three deep on the platform, and I said a wistful farewell to my private table for four.

The doors opened and people poured on. I put on my best 'ignore me' face and carried on reading.

"Mummy, why are there so many people?" A child's voice chimed above the general grumbling.

"Mummy! I want to sit down."

"Yes, you can, just as soon as we find… excuse me, please. Sorry. Come on girls, there's a table over there at the end."

Great. My space was going to be invaded by some poor woman with two fractious kids. At least it wasn't drunken football fans. I moved my bag on to my lap.

"Excuse me, are these seats taken?" I looked up. Shit. It was Suze. Even in her harried state, weighed down by bags, she looked impossibly glamorous, tall and tanned in a sheepskin jacket, with a knitted beanie perched on her fair hair. I know Nick's got a big family, but right now it felt like they were stalking me. I wished I could disappear under the scratchy red seat.

"Pippa!" Suze's polite smile morphed into a look of horror. I could see her weighing up the toe-curling embarrassment of sitting opposite her brother's ex-fiancée against strap-hanging for two hours with her toddlers.

"Suze," I said. "Hello. Hello Katniss, hello Bella." Like mirror images, the two little girls buried their faces in Suze's thighs, so all I could see were the backs of two identical blonde heads.

"Why don't I move?" I said. "You can have the table, I'll find somewhere else, it's fine." But the aisle was jammed solid with people. I wasn't going anywhere.

"Come on, girls, sit down," said Suze. "You remember Auntie Pippa, don't you? You've spoken to her on Skype. She was going to marry your Uncle Nick."

One of the children – it was Katniss, I could only tell them apart because of the dimple in her chin – said, "But they're not getting married any more, and Uncle Nick is very sad, so we have to be very nice to him."

"I'm going to let him watch my Dora the Explorer DVD," said Bella.

Suze mouthed, "Sorry," at me. "Yes, and you have to be very nice to Pippa too, because she's also sad," she said. "How are you, Pippa?"

"Okay," I lied. "Like you say, sad."

Both the little girls were staring at me, as fascinated as if I were a tentacled alien.

"We're not sad," said Bella, putting the end of one of her plaits in her mouth.

"Because we were going to have to be bridesmaids," said Katniss, "and wear stupid frilly dresses. And now we don't."

"We hate dresses," Bella told me, confidingly.

Suze was looking absolutely mortified. "Girls!"

"It's okay," I smiled. "Why do you hate dresses?"

"They're scratchy," Bella said. "And you have to wear stupid scratchy knickers with them."

"And firefighters don't wear scratchy knickers," Katniss said. "I'm going to be a firefighter when I'm grown up. I'm going to battle wildfires out in the bush."

"And I'm going to be a brain surgeon," Bella said. "They don't wear scratchy knickers either."

"I expect some of them do," I objected. I was sure Nick and I had watched a video once, involving an unconscious patient and two improbably pneumatic women who'd definitely been wearing frilly knickers. At first, anyway. Although possibly they were nurses.

Bella looked horrified. "No they don't! But bridesmaids have to, because bloody Grandma has to get her own way."

"Otherwise she'll throw another fucking strop," said Katniss.

Suze was absolutely scarlet under her hat. "Girls, that's enough! I'm so sorry, Pippa, they're like sponges at this age."

I started to giggle. "It's okay. They make a good point."

Eventually Suze got the twins settled down with the PettingZoo app, and once they were safely engrossed, I said, "Suze, how's Nick?"

She said, "Gutted. But he won't talk about it, you know what he's like."

I said, "I'm so sorry, Suze. You came all this way for our wedding and now it's not happening."

"Pippa, I'm not going to lie to you. I was furious when Nick told me. I called you every bad name I know, and then invented some new ones. But then I spoke to Mum, and she made me see sense."

"I'm sure she did," I said ruefully. "She must be delighted it's not going ahead."

"On the contrary," Suze said. "She's become a bit of a fan of yours recently, Pippa. She thinks you're good for Nick, and she sees how happy you make him – made him. But she says no one knows what really goes on in other people's relationships, and presumably you made this decision for a reason, so we need to accept it and help you both move on."

I was amazed at this magnanimity from Erica, especially as she appeared to have a higher opinion of me than I had of myself.

"Besides," Suze said, "If you and Nick were going to split up, it's far better it should happen now than after the wedding. Or worse, after you'd had kids. It's like ripping off a plaster, or having a Brazilian – agony, but best done quickly if it's got to be done."

Her words reminded me of my afternoon in the spa in South Africa, and having every bit of me waxed in preparation for the party, my red bikini, and Gabriel's eyes and hands. I felt like I was going to be sick. If Suze noticed my mortification, she ignored it.

"Weddings aren't all they're cracked up to be, anyway," she said. "The best thing that can happen is you have a great day and get pissed with your mates, and then a week later you're wondering why you obsessed so much about all the details in the first place. I remember having the biggest hissy fit ever because I didn't like the curtains at our venue. I sent the event planner this long email asking her to change them, and threatening to pull out and get married somewhere else. I bet she wished I would, but she talked me down. Now, if you asked me what those curtains were like, I couldn't begin to tell you. But at the time, you're reading all the magazines and they tell you the world will end if you don't have the right tablecloths or whatever, and you believe them. Looking back, I wish we hadn't bothered with it all. But it was what Mum wanted."

"It was what Nick wanted, too," I said.

"Really? But I thought…"

Before she could say anything more, there was an announcement that we were finally arriving in London, and Suze busied herself packing up the girls' things. We said an awkward, stilted goodbye, and I went off to Eloise and Dean's place in Hackney and Suze went off to my home and Nick. It all felt so wrong, and I couldn't help wondering why everyone in the world seemed to think that I'd been obsessed with planning my wedding, and I was the only one who thought it had been Nick.

"Guido's got something up his sleeve," Eloise said, as we walked from the Tube station to Kaffee Klatch together the next day. "He's told me not to put through any calls from journalists, and he's been closeted in the boardroom for hours on Skype. I haven't got a clue what's going on, but I don't like it one bit."

"Shit. Do you think the deal with Platinum Productions is going to go tits up, along with the Thatchell's partnership?" I felt cold with dread at the prospect of being out of a job as well as having no fiancé and nowhere to live.

"Zack says it's going ahead. Yes, the usual, please," Eloise paid for her cappuccino and almond croissant. "Apparently they're really pleased with the unedited footage from South Africa. You, especially."

"Really? Just a double espresso for me, please. Thanks." I wrapped a paper napkin round the cardboard cup. "I don't think I'm going to be able to watch it, I'm so scared I'll be shit."

"You weren't shit," Eloise said. "It's official. According to their last email, anyway."

Hunched in our coats against the wind, we walked round the corner to the office. I buzzed us in, just as I usually did, put my bag down in its usual place, sat in my chair and turned on my PC. It should have felt familiar, normal, comforting, even, the way being back in the office does when you've been away, no matter how much you've loved where you've been.

But it didn't. It felt wrong, somehow, as if someone had adjusted the height of my chair or moved my mouse to the wrong side of the keyboard, or something. I felt like I ought to be somewhere else. It was just post-holiday blues, I told myself, and not really knowing what I was going to be doing. But I'd have a massive backlog of emails to clear, so I might as well get on with that.

I skimmed through them, reading and deleting, and typing quick replies to the urgent things. Then I noticed a message from an unfamiliar address.

From: angelg@ananzi.co.za
To: pippa@falconis.co.uk
Subject: Awkward!

I opened it, and instantly felt the familiar flood of shame that washed over me whenever I thought about Gabriel. Why was he emailing me? Shit, shit, shit. The last person in the entire world I wanted to hear from, ever. I knew I should delete it, unread, but I couldn't.

Hi Pippa

Jeez, I've written some embarrassing emails in my life, but this one is right up there with the worst. I don't know if this is going to be news to you, what you're thinking about me, how things are with you... But I knew I needed to get in touch with you, because otherwise you might not know.

My shame turned to horror. He was going to tell me he had AIDS and we'd had sex without a condom. I was going to die. I was sitting here at my desk at work, reading my death sentence. And it was all my fault.

I heard the boardroom door open behind me, and stabbed desperately at the little X in the corner of the window to close it, as if I'd been browsing on Net-a-Porter or looking at porn or something.

"Pippa, can I see you in the boardroom, please?" said Guido.

"What, now?" I asked stupidly.

"Unless you're busy?"

Well, I wasn't, obviously.

"Sure." I got up and walked the few steps towards him, feeling as if I was floating high above the reclaimed oak floorboards, my head disconnected from my body. I was going to get sacked, and then I was going to die of AIDS and all my family and friends would know what I had done.

"Come in and have a seat." Guido closed the door behind us. I caught a last glimpse of Eloise's fascinated face. "So, how are things?"

I twisted the cap off a bottle of water from the tray Guido always kept on the boardroom table and took a sip. It didn't help – my voice still came out a husky whisper.

"Not good," I said. "Nick and I... the wedding's not going ahead. I'm not sure what I'm going to do. I stayed at Eloise and Dean's place last night but obviously I can't forever. I'm going to have to sort myself out and get a flat."

Guido shook his head. "Pippa, I'm so sorry to hear that. Do you need to take some more time off?"

"No! I don't want to make a fuss. I need to be working, I think. It'll help."

Guido looked unconvinced. "That's what I wanted to discuss, of course. But I wonder if now is the best time."

I stared at the bubbles in my water and said, "If I'm not going to have a job any more, I may as well know. And whatever decision I need to make about work might help with all the other ones. So it's probably best if you break it to me now. Try and be gentle though." I managed a feeble smile.

Guido said, "First of all, I want to reassure you that I value you enormously, and appreciate all the work you've done for me and the group over the years. I don't want you to be in any doubt about that. If you'd prefer to discuss your future here another time, that's fine. Or we can carry on?"

"Carry on."

"Pippa, what happened in South Africa was obviously deeply embarrassing for me on a personal level. But that's my problem. However, unfortunately the way it impacts on the business affects all of us. The loss of the Thatchell's partnership is going to mean restructuring, and rethinking what we do here."

I nodded again. It was the sack – I could feel it hovering over me, like a London pigeon about to dump a load of shit on my head.

"But the publicity – and almost all of it has been terrible – has had an effect I frankly didn't expect."

"What's that?" I croaked.

"Across the group, bookings have gone sky high. January and February are normally our worst months in the restaurants, as you know – it's winter, people are on diets and not drinking, money is tight, businesses' financial year-end celebrations haven't yet begun. But we've had an outstanding month so far, and it looks like continuing. Over the past year or so, I've been giving some serious consideration to expanding the restaurant part of the group internationally. When this… this news broke, I thought that would be the end of that idea. But it isn't. One of the investors I've been in discussions with confirmed yesterday that he is still very keen to go ahead with the launch of the first Osteria Falconi outside the UK."

"Great!" I said, thinking, but what does this mean for me? You won't need a glorified microwave-operator in New York, or wherever it's going to be.

"Pippa, when we were in Franschhoek last year, I got the impression that you were very keen to move back into the restaurant kitchen. I didn't mention this at the time, because the opportunity was still very vague at that stage. And besides, you had other things on your mind. But now your personal circumstances have changed, and I thought perhaps this is something you'd consider."

"What, exactly?" I asked.

"Head chef of Osteria Falconi in Dubai," Guido said. "We're looking at an autumn launch, so we have eight months to get it off the ground. That will mean you relocating in the next couple of months, initially with a lot of international travel between the UAE and the UK, then being based there full-time. The restaurant will have two hundred covers, focussing on high-end cuisine with an international theme. It will be very, very hard work, but also very rewarding, professionally and financially."

He named a salary that seemed unimaginably high.

"Do I have to decide now?" I said, with a lurch of fear.

Guido laughed. "Of course not! I wanted you to be the first to know that the opportunity is there, that's all. I'll email you a PDF with the detailed proposal, and you can think about it, chat to Helen about the HR side of things, come to me with any questions. I don't need a decision immediately. It's a huge change and a big commitment, and I want you to be sure you're making the right decision. So maybe you could let me know two weeks from today?"

The Monday after what would have been my wedding day. It felt as if there was some weird planetary alignment going on, with events leading up to this fateful day, randomly selected by the fact that a couple from Essex had decided to get married abroad instead of in Hampshire, and now their choice had linked my fate inextricably with the first Saturday in February.

I said, "I'll think about it, of course. And I'll talk to Helen. And Guido, thank you. It means so much that you think I could do this."

"Think? I know you can, sweetheart. You've proved your talent and your work ethic over and over again. We wouldn't even be having this conversation if I didn't believe you were absolutely capable of making a success of it."

"Thank you," I said again. "But... Guido, I don't know how to say this without it sounding like I don't love the idea. I do love it. But I need to know what my options are. If I say no, what happens then?"

He said, "I don't want to lose you, Pippa, you know that. But after this series I doubt Platinum will commission another. And that will mean winding down the operation here and focussing on the restaurants. We'll always need good people. There will be a place for you in the group if you don't want to move abroad, in London or perhaps in Manchester. Don't worry, your position is secure. This is win-win for you."

I thanked him again and left the boardroom. Win-win, he'd said. But heading up a shiny, exciting new restaurant in Dubai on a mega-salary versus going and being a chef de partie in Manchester sounded more like hitting the Euromillions jackpot versus winning a fiver on a scratchcard to me.

It was only when I sat back down at my desk that I realised I'd completely forgotten about Gabriel's email. Depending on what he had to tell me, I might have no decision to make at all.

I opened the email again and started reading where I'd left off.

I don't know how to say this in a way that doesn't embarrass us both. If we were face to face I'd buy you a drink and it would be easier. But maybe that wouldn't be the best plan, given that you passed out cold the last time I saw you!

Pippa, here goes. I just wanted to tell you, in case you don't know already, that nothing happened that night after you fell asleep. I wouldn't want you to think – God, I'm so sorry to have to say this – that I was the kind of guy who takes advantage of a woman who's had too much to drink. I didn't. I took your swimming costume off because you might catch cold. Your hair was really wet too but there was nothing I could do about that.

But that's not what I told the other guys. It was totally shit of me to lie but I guess I wanted to look like some kind of big man. I don't feel like one though, I just feel like a dick. I'm so very sorry.

I hope you're okay, and things are not too bad with your boyfriend. It sounds like you really love each other. I would hate to be the one to screw up your relationship and I feel really bad that things even went as far they did (not that anyone would ever regret kissing you. You're hot. And I'm digging myself deeper into a hole here, aren't I?).

Sibo gave me your email address, when I told her what really happened. Only after she'd finished shouting at me, though. She sends her love.

Gabriel

I put my face down on the keyboard and waited for the full-body blush that had swept over me to subside. God, I was a fool. A drunken, stupid fool. But mixed with my mortification was a huge sense of relief.

"Are you okay, Pippa?" asked Eloise.

"Fine," I said. "Just think I might be coming down with something. I feel a bit faint."

It was true, I did. I opened Gabriel's email and read it again. Then I sent a very brief reply.

Hey. Thanks for getting in touch, I appreciate it. I'm glad I know what really happened now.

Take care,
Pippa

I pressed send, then checked that the message had left my outbox and truly gone on its way. Then I deleted Gabriel's message and my reply. He was a sweet boy, even if he was selfish. I hoped he'd have a good life and be happy. But I never, ever wanted to hear from him or think about him again. I was double-checking that Gabriel's email had definitely been deleted and would never be seen again (unless at some point Guido gets done for phone-hacking, which seems unlikely), when another message landed in my inbox.

From: zack.wilder@platinumproductions.com
To: pippa@falconis.co.uk
Subject: Meeting

Dear Pippa

I hope you're well. Once again, thanks for all your hard work on Guido's African Safari – it was a pleasure filming with you.

Mel and I are currently working on a pitch for a new cookery show. It's around the theme of cooking with kids – how healthy eating habits and a lifelong love of food can be engendered in children and young people. We'd be going into schools and colleges, and ultimately helping a group of teenagers to set up their own pop-up food cart. Think Jamie's School Dinners meets The Apprentice, but younger and fresher in its approach.

We're keen to find someone to front the show who is relatively unknown, who can really relate to our young participants and audience, and has a warm, bubbly screen presence. Of course this is still early days and we're considering a number of potential presenters. However, the team and I were extremely impressed with your work on Safari, and would like to meet with you to discuss this opportunity, and others going forward.

Please let me know if this might be of interest, and what your availability is like in the next couple of weeks.

Regards
Zack

For the first time in what felt like ages, I had something to look forward to. Feeling considerably happier than I had done when I got out of bed that morning, I went to meet Katharine for lunch.

CHAPTER NINETEEN

From: nick@digitaldrawingboard.com
To: iain.coulson@coulsoncreative.com
Subject: Zweep pitch

Right, I'm attaching the Keynote presentation again with the amends you mentioned. I think it looks shit-hot. Let me know how it goes tomorrow – I bet they'll be blown away. Mostly because if you get it, I'll be sending you an invoice for fuckloads, haha.

And, mate? Congratulations :D

N

"I got here early," Katharine said. "This place is so popular at the moment, you have to queue for a table if you turn up after about half twelve." I could see why – the banh mi bar, with its stripped floorboards and stainless steel counter, was hipster heaven. Katharine herself looked the part, in a tartan pinafore with the kind of woolly white tights only those of gazelle-like proportions can get away with, and glasses with heavy black frames.

"Coffee?" I said, when I'd kissed her hello and asked how she was.

"Jasmine tea, please," she said. "And I'll have a five-spice chicken banh mi and a steamed pork bun if you're ordering food. I'm starving."

"So, how are things with Iain?" I asked, when I'd returned to our table carrying a tray piled with our lunch.

"He's on best behaviour at the moment," she said. "Because… well, I'd more or less decided it was over. But then I found out…" she glanced down at her tiny waist, "we're having a baby."

I gawped at her. "Wow. Congratulations. That's amazing news. When did you realise?"

"A week or so after your hen night," she said. "God, I feel so guilty, I got so pissed that night. But my midwife says as it was just the once, I shouldn't worry, and it happens to lots of people. But still. It was such a shock, because as I told you, things with Iain weren't great, nookie-wise. But there was one time when we were on honeymoon, and I guess it only takes one."

"And what about the other girl?" I asked.

"Ludmilla?" she wrinkled her nose. "She's still working there. But he says it's over. Pippa, I've been doing a lot of thinking. I'm not stupid. I don't know if Iain's going to be faithful to me, ever. Forsaking all others – it's just not his cup of tea. But the alternative seemed a lot worse. I'm not cut out to be a single mother, bringing up my kid in some poky two-bedroom flat in Stoke Newington. I want to be with Iain."

It was typical of Katharine, I reflected, to regard trendy Stoke Newington as some kind of social Siberia.

"So I decided to forgive him," she continued calmly. "I'll get a lot of practice at that in the future, I expect. I imagine it gets easier with time. And I love him, I still do, in spite of everything. He'll be a great dad, I'll get to have the lifestyle I want for myself and our kids. If there's the occasional fling with some random work experience girl, I'll deal with it. He'll always come back to me."

"Katharine, I'm so pleased you're making a go of things. I really am. But are you sure? It must have been such a shock to find out you're pregnant so soon after the whole thing with Ludmilla. Maybe you need a bit more time to think about it? To make sure you're doing what will really make you happy?"

She laughed. "Pippa, you're such a romantic. I used to be, too, but not anymore. I've decided you need to be pragmatic about relationships. I'll never love anyone as much as I love Iain, and he loves me too, in his way. If that changes, I'll think again.

"But anyway." She put her warm hand over mine, leaving a smear of soy sauce. "Sorry. Here, I'll wipe that off. I haven't been feeling a bit sick, you know, just fucking starving all the time. You and Nick. What's going on? One minute you were all loved up – and you really were, you're the happiest couple I know. Then the next thing, it's all off. What gives?"

I put the remains of my sandwich back on the minimalist square plate and sipped my Diet Coke. "God, Katharine, it's such a mess. You're right, everything was fine until we started planning our wedding, and then it all went horribly wrong. His mother's a nightmare, and she was living with us and I hated it. And he got totally obsessed with the wedding, to the point where I couldn't imagine going through with it all. And then we had a couple of massive rows, and there was the thing on his stag do, and then in South Africa I got pissed and snogged someone else, and that was just kind of the last straw. It felt like if I didn't end it and we got married, I'd be making this massive mistake. But now I think I've made an even bigger one, and I don't know what to do."

"Hold on," Katharine said. "One thing at a time. What thing on his stag do?"

"He spent the whole day instant-messaging his ex-girlfriend," I said. "And then met up with her somewhere. And I... I've always been jealous of her. It felt like such a betrayal."

Katharine burst out laughing. "That? Oh my God, Pippa, you didn't take that seriously, did you? It was really awkward, Iain says. Nick was pretty wasted, obviously, they all were. But then this woman turned up and she was more pissed than any of them and she was, like, all over him, and Nick was going, 'No, no, you've got it all wrong, I love Pippa!' And then Iain put her in a taxi and Nick came back to ours and crashed on our sofa. It was only the second night Iain had been home and I wasn't too pleased about it, but Nick didn't hang about the next day because he said he needed to get home and feed the cat."

I looked down at my plate, then up again at Katharine. I felt weirdly dislocated – as if reality had shifted. Bethany the cool girl, the irresistible woman who could take Nick from me with one snap of her fingers, had suddenly been transformed, diminished in my mind to a figure of fun and pity, a woman who turned up drunk at a stag night and had to be packed off home.

"But what did you do?" Katharine asked.

"Ugh. I was so stupid. I got pissed at a party on our last night there. And there was this guy I was working with. He was sweet, and we flirted a bit, and I didn't think anything would come of it. It seemed so safe. And then I read that thing about the stag night, and Nick and I had been arguing, and it seemed like I could either carry on with the wedding, feeling like I really didn't want to, or do something crazy to stop it, to make our whole relationship implode.

So I decided to sleep with him. But in the end nothing happened – it was just a snog really."

"Nothing happened? Well, that's your get out of jail free card, right there."

I shook my head. "No, Katharine. The thing is, I meant for it to happen. Well, I didn't really, but it could have happened, and I didn't do anything to stop it. It was just luck. And the wedding's all off now, anyway. We've made other plans."

"But you can have a different wedding!" Katharine was sounding like her old self again, the woman whose wedding was planned down to the last placecard, months in advance. "You could go abroad. You could have a small registry office wedding and lunch somewhere fabulous. It doesn't have to be huge."

I had the feeling she was about to whip out her database of alternative wedding venues. "No, Katharine. Honestly. Maybe Nick and I can be friends again, but I can't see us getting past this. It's all too shitty and horrible."

"Pippa, my husband had an affair, and I've forgiven him. Well, I haven't, totally. It's going to take a lot more time and a lot more diamonds for that to happen. But we're moving past it, because we have a future together and we love each other. You and Nick could do that too. All you've had is a disagreement over the guest list, at the end of the day. Look at my friends Neil and Adam. They argued so much before their civil partnership you won't believe. Neil wanted their labradoodle to be the ring bearer and Adam thought it was stupid – the idea, not the dog – and they had a screaming row in Selfridges and got thrown out by security. And they've been married for three years now and there's never a cross word between them. Planning a wedding is stressful."

"I wish I'd known just how stressful it would get," I said miserably. "I'd never, ever have gone ahead with it. We could have just stayed as we were."

262

"But you can't stay as you are forever," Katharine said. "Relationships change and grow. When I met Iain I thought he was a good catch, nothing more. It took him being unfaithful to remind me how much I care about him. Did he tell you what happened on Christmas day?"

I nodded, remembering Iain's account of how Katharine had flown at Ludmilla's boyfriend and stopped him from beating Iain to a pulp, in the manner of a vixen protecting her cubs.

"I love him so much I want to eat him," she said. "But then I want to eat everything at the moment, so that's not exactly news. Think about it, Pippa. Talk to Nick. I must get back to the office."

Katharine, I reflected as I watched her swish away down the street in her vintage lime trenchcoat, was a force to be reckoned with. I wished it was her who was going to talk to Nick about our relationship, not me. She could make a happy ending out of cod cheeks and bashed-up salt and vinegar crisps.

I may have been grateful for Katharine's advice, but following it was another matter. Over the next few days, I composed countless drafts of emails to Nick and deleted them unsent. I began text after text, but I couldn't find words to say that weren't, "I've been shit. Forgive me." Which, whilst true, didn't strike me as the best way to win back the man I loved. And the one time I plucked up the courage to call him, after too many beers in the pub with Eloise and Dean one night, his phone went straight to voicemail and I wimped out and ended the call without leaving a message, then took the sim card out of my phone and made Eloise promise not to give it back to me until the next day.

If it wasn't for work, I'm sure I would have been reduced to a gibbering obsessive-compulsive wreck, spending the rest of my days composing emails to Nick until eventually neighbours alerted police to a foul smell and my decomposing body was discovered, a mobile phone clutched in my cold, dead hand. But I was saved from this fate by Guido, who announced that to help me make a decision about the move to Dubai, I should spend some time in as many of the restaurants in the Falconi empire as I could, working in the kitchens and getting a sense of the culinary direction the group's chefs were taking.

I went to Falconi Familia, one of the five informal restaurants 'where good food and good friends meet', and ate braised shortrib on buttered noodles, followed by cassata sundae. I tried the nine-course menu degustation at Osteria Falconi, which had changed completely since I worked there, and was now all Noma-ed up with wild herbs foraged on Hampstead Heath and scatterings of truffle soil in the plates. I troughed pizza by the slice at Guido to Go in the Bullring in Birmingham, and heard about the new branches that were planned for Leeds and Newcastle. And by the time my odyssey ended, at Guido's Grill in Richmond, all I could face was bit of seared tuna and a small green salad – I could feel the weight I'd lost on the poached-egg-and-heartbreak diet at Mum's creeping back on. Perhaps I should write a book, I reflected, outlining a swift and effective weight loss regimen involving cancelling your wedding at the eleventh hour and eating burnt toast while lying in a single bed.

I was half-heartedly pushing lettuce leaves around my plate and wondering whether I still possessed even a fraction of the skill of the seasoned chefs whose food I'd enjoyed and admired over the past few days, and whether Guido had entirely taken leave of his senses to even consider me for the job in Dubai, when a text message came through on my phone. It was from Erica.

Dear Pippa, it's Erica here. I am sorry to bother you.

I imagined her sitting at our kitchen table with Spanx on her lap, the message written out in longhand next to her, painstakingly transcribing it on to her phone, using one finger to tap it out with agonising slowness. I rolled my eyes in annoyance, but, to my surprise, my exasperation was mixed with fondness.

It's about Spanx. He went out this morning and I haven't seen him for a couple of hours. Nick is at a meeting. He (cat not Nick) is not usually allowed out, is he? I am a bit concerned. Am going out to look for him, but think you should know. Very best, Erica.

The fondness evaporated as quickly as alcohol from flambéed brandy. What the hell was she thinking? She'd lived with us for weeks, she knew Spanx wasn't allowed further than the balcony. And despite his good looks and charm, Spanx has always been a bit of a non-starter in the feline intelligence stakes. He once tried to get to some fillet steaks I'd left on the worktop by walking across the lit stove, and I'd only just rescued him before his tail caught fire. I always had to bath with the door closed, because he'd try and drink the water and fall in. He had all the instinct for self-preservation of a hard-boiled egg. And Erica had waited – what, an hour? Maybe even two or three, before letting me know he was missing. He'd get flattened by a 188 bus on Jamaica Road for sure, if he hadn't already been.

I rushed into the kitchen and thanked Serge, the chef, for my lunch, and said I was sorry, but I wouldn't have time to try the lemon granita after all, because I was needed urgently back at the office. Then I legged it to the station and jumped on board a train just as it was about to leave, but forgot to check which one it was, and discovered too late that it was the slow one that was going to take me on a scenic tour of south-west London lasting almost an hour before arriving at Waterloo.

I tried Erica's number, but her phone just rang. I remembered that answering it generally involved hours of fumbling in her handbag and much muttering of, "Now, is it the green button or the red one? Where do I... Oh dear, it's stopped. How do I see who was ringing? Nicky, could you possibly...?" and so on. In a crisis, she'd lose what little technological nous she had altogether. I sent a text anyway, telling her I'd be there as soon as I possibly could.

Then I rang Nick. It was easy, I didn't hesitate at all, and when his voicemail picked up straight away, I found the words spilling out of me as if they'd been waiting there all along.

"It's me. I've just had a text from your Mum, Spanx has gone AWOL. I'm on my way home. Hopefully it will all be okay. I really, really hope you're okay too. If you can get away, maybe I'll see you there. If you're not, I'll let you know what happens. I'm really sorry about everything, Nick. I hope we can talk later. I can't imagine life without Spanx."

I felt myself choking up, and noticed the middle-aged man across the aisle looking at me nervously, as if he thought he'd been caught up in the beginning of some control-underwear promotional flashmob, and loads of scantily clad women were about to emerge from the toilets and chorus, "We can't imagine life without Spanx!" So I ended the call and blew my nose surreptitiously.

At last I emerged from the Tube station and dashed down our road as fast as my high-heeled boots would allow me, pausing only to look up into trees and under parked cars and go, "Spanx! Spanx!" like a woman possessed. There was no sign of him, but there was also no sign of a squashed ginger body in the road.

I was starting to feel a bit more hopeful when I passed a sign on a lamp-post with a picture of a little white ferret. I paused to read it. 'Please help us find Laurel. She has been missing since 24 January. She is a sweet, tame ferret but very shy. Our kids are heartbroken. If you see her, please call the number below or email findlaurel@gmail.com.'

I thought about poor, lost Laurel and the children who loved her, and imagined setting up a 'Find Spanx' account and all the emails we'd get from nutters and perverts, and started to cry again.

So by the time I got upstairs to the flat, I was a bit of a mess. My mascara had run and was stinging my eyes, and it took me three tries to get my key in the lock. At last I opened the door and called, "Hello?"

There was silence, but there hadn't been the moment I opened the door. I could have sworn I had heard a familiar sound, like very, very distant firecrackers on bonfire night. A sound like many threads breaking at the same time. The sound Spanx's claws made when he scratched the sofa. Then I heard another, even more familiar noise. "Bwaaarp?"

Spanx strolled nonchalantly into the hallway, then clocked me and went, "Bwaaarp!" and trotted over and started rubbing himself avidly against my boots. He looked just the same – possibly a bit fatter. He didn't look like a cat that had survived a dangerous adventure in the outside world. I picked him up and pressed him against my face.

"What's going on, Spanx? Where have you been? Why have you been hiding from Auntie Erica and driving me demented with worry, you naughty cat?"

Spanx fixed me with a steady gaze. It was like looking into a pair of orange traffic lights. "I don't know what you're talking about," he seemed to be saying. "I've been here, sleeping on my cat tree." Then he squirmed out of my arms and thudded to the floor. "Bwaaarp?" he said again, and walked purposefully through to the living room, glancing back over his furry shoulder as he went. It was a summons, and I followed.

If our cat was attempting to expose Nick's sloppy housekeeping, I didn't get it. Everything looked just the same as when I'd left for South Africa three weeks before. Not exactly immaculate, but certainly not a hovel either. There was a cobweb hanging between the ceiling and the curtain rail that could do with Erica's high-level dusting strategy – I'd noticed that for all her talk, she was as lax with the featherduster as I was. The cushions on the sofa were squashed in the place where Nick liked to sit, just as usual. Spanx wandered over to the door that led to Nick's studio, which stood ajar as it always did.

"Bwaaarp!" he said.

I pushed open the door. All the wedding things – the little zinc tubs that Erica had ordered to plant the snowdrops in, the easel that had held the seating plan, the piles of silver-bordered RSVP cards – were gone. But hanging from the wardrobe door was an unfamiliar white fabric garment bag, which bore the unmistakeable marks of Spanx's claws. He walked determinedly over to it.

"No! Just because you haven't been squashed by a bus, doesn't mean you can scratch people's things," I said. "That might belong to Erica, or Suze. Paws off!"

Spanx jumped on to Nick's office chair, tucked his tail around his chest and regarded me balefully.

"What is this, anyway?" I unhooked the hanger and pulled down the zip on the bag, and actually gasped. It was my wedding dress. The dress I'd left behind on the train in Johannesburg and given up for lost. It was every bit as beautiful as I remembered. I was holding it at arm's length, bemused, when I heard the front door open and the familiar sound of Nick throwing his bag down in the hallway.

Still holding the dress, I walked hesitantly through to find him.

He was wearing a navy blue suit, but it was covered in white fur, and there was a long scratch on his cheek, beaded with blood.

"I came as quickly as I could, Pip," he said, "but I got delayed. You see, I found this ferret…"

I started to cry.

Twenty minutes later, Nick had made tea for himself and found a can of Diet Coke in the fridge for me, and we were sitting on the sofa with Spanx between us. He was sitting upright, like an Egyptian statue of a cat, and looking distinctly smug.

"He wasn't missing, was he?" I said. "Your bloody… your mother made it up."

"I expect Suze put her up to it," Nick said. "She said she was going to the V&A today with her and the girls. I'm sorry, Pip, it was a stupid thing of her to do."

I shook my head. "She meant well. It's just a bit awkward, isn't it?"

Nick looked down at his hands, and the dimple in his cheek appeared. "We had to talk sometime. And I wasn't going to call you, and you weren't going to call me, so…"

"I tried! I tried to call you loads of times, but then…"

"You chickened out. Me too."

"But, Nick, the dress. I don't understand. How is it here?"

"Pippa, you lack confidence in modern technology," he said. "All I did was email the Gautrain lost property people.

269

Phoning them clearly didn't work when you tried it, but they responded to my email in a couple of days. Then I contacted your mate Valli on Facebook and asked him to go and collect it, which he did. And couriered it over here. All for less than a hundred quid, not counting the case of champagne I'm having delivered to his and Sanjay's wedding, but don't mention that to him, it's a surprise. You see, when you told me you'd found a dress, I didn't exactly believe you. I did at first, but then whenever Mum or I mentioned it, you got all evasive. So I thought I'd try and get this one back for you, just in case."

"Nick. And now our wedding's not even happening. Oh, God. I'm so terribly sorry."

He laughed, but it didn't sound quite right. "Yeah. I guess if I'd known, I could have avoided World War Three with Mum. I said I thought her idea of posting the wedding invitations in separate batches in case there was a terrorist attack and they blew up postboxes was brilliant, and then I made out that the cousins' batch must have got lost in the post. It didn't work, of course. I had to fess up and tell her we didn't want them at the wedding, and then all hell broke loose."

I laughed shakily. Then I said, "All the stuff about the wedding. The tomato soup and all the rest. It didn't matter that much. The trouble was, I wasn't certain, once it all started seeming so real, about us. And because I wasn't sure, I convinced myself you'd done a bad thing, a really bad thing, that something was going on with you and Bethany, and I thought that made it okay for me to do something much, much worse, because I needed to end it. But the thing is, it's partly about when things really started to go wrong, and that was a long time ago."

Nick said, "Yes?"

I said, "Is there any more Diet Coke?"

He went and fetched me another can, and I waited for him to come back, stroking Spanx, thinking that I might not see either of them again for a long, long time. When Nick came back, I told him everything: about how I'd been pregnant with our baby and not told him, but told Erica. About the blog. About how I'd felt when the plans for our wedding seemed to be turning me into a person – a bride – I didn't feel I could be. I told him how I'd used the fact of Bethany coming into his life again and my imaginings about what was going on between them to excuse the way I'd behaved with Gabriel. And I explained to him how relieved I felt when I found out that I hadn't done what I thought I had, after all.

By the time I'd finished, Spanx had gone to sleep, sprawled across both our laps, because we'd moved much closer together on the sofa.

Nick said, "Okay. We should have listened to each other, about the wedding. I thought I was doing what you wanted, you didn't tell me that you wanted something else. Or nothing. It was fucking stupid of both of us. That's partly why I started the blog – I needed other people to talk to – to enable me, I guess, to carry on with what I was doing, because if I'd listened to you, properly listened, I'd have known you weren't that keen on the whole massive wedding thing."

"Once we'd signed up to it, it got a bit tricky, though," I said. "It's kind of hard to say, 'You know that dream wedding in a castle? How about we downgrade to a keg of beer in a field somewhere?' Or, 'Marriage, schmarriage. Let's just tell everyone it's off, and live in sin some more.' It's like, once you're getting married, either you have the full-on wedding or you call everything off."

"And when Beff got in touch, I felt sorry for her. She's back in London with no husband and no job, and she needed a mate to talk to, and so did I. I shouldn't have let her get the wrong impression about how I felt, but I did, and I'm sorry.

"But the other thing," Nick said, "about whatisiname." I could tell, just looking at him, that he knew exactly what Gabriel's name was, and would remember for a long time. "That's a tough one. I'm going to have to think about that some more. Like, a lot more. It makes a difference that you didn't fuck him, I won't lie about that. I'm glad you didn't. But still, the intent was there, as they say."

"Okay." My mouth felt very dry, and I took another fizzy sip from my can of Diet Coke. "I can see why you need to think about that. I do too. It was awful, and stupid, and I wish I hadn't done it. But I got a bit carried away, not with the idea of sleeping with someone else, but with being in another world. I loved doing work that excites me again. And there's another thing. Guido's asked me if I want to go and work in Dubai for a bit. Three years, maybe five. I've said I'll think about it. It's a great opportunity. I was sure I'd take it, but I wanted to talk to you first. And now I'm not sure at all."

Nick said, "Pippa, there's no way I'm going to make that decision for you. We both need to think about this. Maybe for a couple of days, maybe for a couple of years. Maybe this is the end. I don't know. But I'm not going to do a whole, 'No! Don't go!' thing, and have you feel I'm trapping you again into something else you don't want. So we should probably leave it like this for now."

"Okay." I shoved Spanx gently over and picked up my bag. "Thanks for listening, I really do appreciate it. And I'm so glad you found that ferret. I was worried about her."

"She had a lethal set of claws," Nick said, walking me to the door. Then he hesitated, his hand on the latch. "Pip? There's another thing. Mum told me about you being pregnant. She told me after she got the email you sent her. She feels really shit about not supporting you, and letting you go through all that alone. I do, too. I wish I'd known, and been able to be there for you. If I had, I would have understood why you felt – why you feel – the way you do about having a baby."

"I could have told you," I said, dry-mouthed. "But I never did. It felt like such a huge thing to have done, when you want to have children so much." Right then, looking up at Nick's sad, serious face, I felt the strangest sensation. My eyes were stinging at there was a massive lump in my throat, but at the same time I felt a lightness, a relief. A weight I'd been carrying alone for a long time was gone, or at least shared.

Nick said, "Mum keeps saying how sorry she is about the way she behaved, Pip. She hopes one day she'll have a chance to tell you herself. I guess that's why she pulled this mad stunt today. I hope you'll be able to be friends some time, anyway."

I said, "Me, too." I made a move to hug him, and he made the same move towards me, but we both changed our minds together, and the door closed between us.

CHAPTER TWENTY

From: nick@digitaldrawingboard.com
To: caroline.travis@khanclarkegardner.co.uk
Subject: Saturday

Hey Callie

Just wanted to wish you and Phoebs a fantastic day on Saturday. I'm sorry I can't be there. I just... can't. It's all a bit too soon. I'm sure you'll understand. Let's have a beer sometime soon.

Love
Nick

Being a guest at your own wedding is a bit weird. I guess it's one of those things like Marmite or harem trousers or *Made in Chelsea* – lots of people won't even entertain the idea of trying it. But don't knock it until you do – you might end up enjoying it as much as I did.

I was woken up in one of the sumptuous suites at Brocklebury Manor – although not the ultra-swish tower bedroom, that was the brides' – by brilliant winter sunshine streaming through the leaded windowpanes. I was brought breakfast by a charming waiter. I had a long, luxurious shower, straightened my hair and put on makeup and a new frock. It was quite like my own wedding morning would have been, except it wasn't. I felt a mixture of happiness, sadness and excitement, but mostly happiness. So maybe it wasn't all that much like *Made in Chelsea*, come to think of it.

Once I was ready, I made my way up the spiral staircase to the bridal suite, and knocked on the door. Phoebe opened it, wearing a fluffy white dressing down, her wet hair hanging down her back.

"Pippa! We thought you might be the hair and makeup lady. She's ten minutes late and Callie's starting to stress."

"No I'm not." Callie appeared behind her, wrapped in a towel. "I'm perfectly calm. We've got loads of time to get ready. Come and see Phoebe's dress, it's stunning."

Phoebe held the dress up on its hanger. It was a calf-length prom dress in the palest primrose yellow, with a sweetheart neckline and a silvery-grey sash that exactly matched the colour of Callie's simple satin shift.

"That's gorgeous," I said. "Where did you get it?"

Callie looked a bit embarrassed. "I don't know if you remember, Pip, but when you were looking for wedding dresses, I mentioned the shop near home that makes them? I was worried you weren't going to find a dress, because you'd left it so late. So Phoebs and I went and had one made, just in case, because you're the same size."

"And we chose the sash to match Callie's bridesmaid dress," Phoebe said. "So it all worked out quite well, don't you think?"

"I can't believe you bought me a back-up wedding dress, you loons!" But I couldn't help laughing. "You're right, it did work out well."

Then there was another knock at the door, and this time it was the hair and makeup lady, and soon the photographer arrived, and the florist with the two bouquets she'd made instead of just one, and Callie and Phoebe's mums, and the bridal suite filled with laughter and clinking champagne glasses and clouds of hairspray.

I took my glass and sat on the chaise-longue and let the excited chatter wash over me. I ought to feel sad, I thought, that my wedding day had come and I wasn't getting married. But I didn't – it was more Callie's day than mine, it had been all along. And she and Phoebe were radiant with happiness, the most beautiful brides ever. There was only one thing that stopped it all being perfect.

At last, everyone was ready. The glasses of champagne had been drunk. The last pearl was wired into place on Phoebe's cloud of auburn hair; the last flower pinned on to Callie's sleek blonde chignon. The mums had checked their hats in the mirror for the thousandth time. The photographer said she had all the shots she needed for now. Imogen had rung up to confirm that the guests were all seated and waiting.

Callie and Phoebe posed for a photo together, holding champagne flutes, gazing into each other's eyes and looking quite serious. But anyone looking at them (or at the photo, it's up on their bedroom wall now) could see the laughter just below the surface, about to break through. For the first time that day, I felt a pang of envy. It could have been Nick and me there (well, we'd have got ready separately, but you know what I mean). It could have been me in the perfect dress, now hanging in our wardrobe in its garment bag, probably destined to be charity-shopped by Erica in a fit of altruistic decluttering. It could have been us, about to celebrate and declare our commitment in front of a crowd of people who loved us. It could have been my Mum dusting powder on her nose where it had gone all shiny from crying, and saying how proud she was of me.

But it wouldn't have worked, I reminded myself. I wouldn't have been happy and glowing like Callie and Phoebe. I'd have been white and drawn with nerves about saying such important words in front of all those people, cousins or not. I'd have been seething with resentment about the tomato soup. I'd have been fighting with every sinew not to rise to Erica's subtle gibes. I'd have been wanting nothing more than to be on my own with Nick, at home on the sofa playing with Spanx, or in bed holding each other's warm, sated bodies. Okay, the last bit I did want, right then, more than anything.

"I think it's time for us to go downstairs," said Callie at last, and down we went.

One of the dark-suited minions was hovering at the bottom of the staircase.

"There's a gentleman here," he said. "He says he doesn't have an invitation, but would it be possible..."

My heart leaped. I could see the dark head and dark-suited shoulders of a man sitting in one of the brocade armchairs, his back to the staircase.

Then he stood up and turned around.

"Dad!" said Phoebe.

"Vernon!" said Phoebe's mum.

It was the first time I'd seen this ogre in the flesh. He looked old, thin and embarrassed – not the fire-breathing tyrant I'd expected.

He walked over to Phoebe, slowly and hesitantly.

"I'll quite understand if you want to have me thrown out," he said. "But before you do, I'd be very grateful if you'll allow me to say one or two things. The first, and most important, is that I'm sorry. The second is, I've been a bad father, but I'd be a worse one if I didn't take the chance to wish my beautiful daughter and her new wife well on their wedding day. I don't have the right to give you away and I don't want to make a speech, but if there's space for me to sit – or stand – at the back…"

Callie looked mutinous, but when she saw Phoebe run to her father and hug him, smearing lipstick on his white collar, her face relaxed back into a smile.

"I think he means it," I whispered to her.

"He bloody well better had," said Callie.

And so we all trooped into the Great Hall to take our seats and wait for the brides to make their entrance.

"If Callie ever gets disbarred, or whatever, from being a lawyer, she could so go into wedding planning," I said later to Callie's brother James, as we milled around in the drawing room sipping champagne and eating canapés (I was relieved that a last-minute consultation between Callie and Hugh, the chef, had resulted in Erica's raw vegetable crudités being nixed in favour of nice, normal things like cheese straws and quails' eggs with celery salt).

"She's ace, isn't she?" said James, and we beamed happily at each other.

It was true. Callie and Phoebe had taken the remains of Nick's and my wedding plans, brought them back to life, and made them entirely their own. Okay, the pots of snowdrops might have been Erica's idea and the canopy of fairy lights Nick's, but Callie's sense of extravagant style and Phoebe's exuberance were everywhere.

In amongst the all-white colour theme were pale yellow roses to mach Phoebe's dress. Sparkly crimson hearts were dotted in amongst the fairy lights. There were bowls of 'Mrs and Mrs' love hearts on the tables and the cake topper was two brides in dresses made of fondant icing that matched Callie and Phoebe's. The Amazing Archibald proved to be an ace at table magic, and there wasn't a balloon animal in sight – in fact, he was totally awesome and I felt very guilty about how much I'd dissed him and his fluffy white rabbit. And, most impressively of all, Phoebe and Callie had managed to get a hundred of their friends and family to drop everything at two weeks' notice and be there to celebrate their wedding.

Callie had even worked her magic on the seating plan, putting me in between James (who I've known for so long it feels a bit like he's my brother as well as Callie's) and a university mate of Phoebe's called Edward, who was not only extremely hot but extremely funny too. Between the two of them, they kept me in stitches throughout the meal, and tactfully no one mentioned Nick once, which was a relief, because to be completely honest every time I thought about him I wanted to cry. The idea that I might soon be in the market for a new boyfriend, sizing up the likes of Edward for the role, didn't feel exciting in the slightest. It just filled me with aching sadness for what I'd had and lost.

Throughout the ceremony, the drinks reception, the dinner and the speeches (made by James, Phoebe's mum and the two brides), the atmosphere was just easy, spontaneous and happy. Unfortunately I missed most of Callie's speech because when James talked about his love and pride for his sister, I did start to cry great, embarrassing sobs, and had to take myself off and redo my makeup in the palatial ladies' loo. But by the time I got back, I'd composed myself enough to enjoy the celebration and witness the cutting of the cake and the first dance.

The lights dimmed, the band played the opening chords of *One Day Like This*, and Callie and Phoebe walked out on to the dance floor. If they'd had more time, they might have splashed out on a few dancing lessons, like

Nick and I were going to do, but they obviously hadn't. There was nothing choreographed about their dance – in fact, they didn't actually move much at all. They just stood together in the spotlight, staring into each other's faces like there was no one else in the room – no one else in the world. I don't think I've ever seen two people look so happy. I felt tears threatening to squeeze out of my eyes again, and James gave my hand a reassuring squeeze. Then the song finished, Callie and Phoebe were kissing each other and laughing, and everyone was rushing out to join the dancing.

I danced with James, with both the brides, with Callie's dad and Phoebe's dad, and Edward claimed me for a few slow songs. Then the band started to play *Beautiful Day*, and I couldn't keep up the pretence any more.

"I think I'll sit this one out," I said to Edward.

"Awww, no, come on!" he protested, pulling me closer.

"Honestly, I'm quite tired," I said, and it was true. Suddenly I was feeling weary and sad, my feet were hurting, and the best strategy seemed to be to find a quiet corner and a bottle of champagne and get quietly pissed by myself, then go to bed.

Then a voice behind me said, "I'll borrow Pippa for this one, if you don't mind."

I turned around, and there was Nick. He wasn't wearing a suit like all the other men – he was wearing old, faded jeans and a jumper with cat hair on it. He hadn't even shaved. But I'd never seen any man, ever, look as gorgeous.

"I wasn't going to come," he said. "But I said I'd think about things, and now I've thought, and I needed to tell you as soon as I could. I've decided that everything's better with you, Pippa. I don't care about getting married. If you've decided it's over, and you're sure, that's cool. I'll go. I don't want to pressure you. But I do want to be with you, for the rest of our lives, if you want to be with me."

"I've never wanted anything so much," I said, and Nick took me in his arms.

"Slowed-down, sexy tango with some lifts?" he said.

Perhaps if we'd kept up with Giovanna's classes we would have nailed it, but we hadn't, so we were truly crap. We were out of step and the one lift Nick attempted ended with me over his shoulder like a sack of spuds. But we didn't care. We laughed and danced and I cried again, and when the song ended we did go and find a quiet corner and a bottle of champagne, but long before it was finished we went to bed.

CHAPTER TWENTY-ONE

W hen Erica packed her bags to go back to Africa, I sneaked a cheque into her luggage to pay her back for everything she'd spent on the wedding. I would have thought that the post out in Liberia would be poor to non-existent, but evidently it's better than I expected, because a couple of weeks later the cheque arrived back through our letterbox in a padded envelope with a jar of brick-red sludge and a note.

Dear Pippa

Thank you for this gesture. I can completely understand why you felt you had to make it, but I must decline it. Please use the money to buy yourself something you will enjoy, or treat yourself and Nick to a special holiday. You deserve it, and you also deserve an apology from me. So here it is: I'm sorry for the way I behaved all those years ago, and for not welcoming you into our family as I should have. You make Nick very happy, and his happiness and yours is the most important thing in the world to me.

I'm also enclosing a jar of Liberian pepper sauce. This is the extra-hot blend. The woman in the shop told me she puts it on her mother-in-law's food when she visits. Let me know what you think of it.

Love
Erica

A couple of days later, I emailed her to let her know that the sauce was delicious, and that I'd sent the money by electronic transfer as a donation to Vision for Liberia. I was extremely tempted to end the email, "So put that in your pipe and smoke it." But I didn't. She'd extended the hand of friendship, and I wanted her to know I'd taken it.

That week, I told Guido I wasn't going to accept the job in Dubai. He said he was sorry but not surprised, and advertised the job in *Caterer and Hotelkeeper*. Loads of people applied, but Hugh Jameson got the gig. I saw him when he came to the office to sign the contract, and he told me he'd had it up to here with the unreasonable demands of fussy wedding parties at Brocklebury Manor.

Then he went absolutely scarlet and said, "Present company excepted, of course." But we both knew he was just being polite.

Preparations for the opening of Falconi Dubai are going well, Eloise says, but the last time I met her for lunch, she told me Guido has had other things on his mind. She's not quite sure when it started, but now Guido and Tamar are officially an item. There was even a picture of them together in the *Daily Mail* sidebar of shame the other day, with her apparently 'flaunting her baby bump' and much speculation about whether Guido was the father. The same day, there was a photo of Florence, 'Falconi's scorned ex', in Regent's Park with her personal trainer, alongside some gratuitously catty remarks about her muffin top and speculation that she's going to be releasing a workout DVD.

Coulson Creative didn't win the pitch for the Zweep business, in spite of Nick's awesome design work. It was terrible news for Iain. He's had to sell the Shoreditch penthouse, and he and Katharine have moved into a rented house in Stoke Newington.

Sophie Ranald

Katharine's baby is due in June. She and I have become much closer – although Callie is still my best friend, I don't mind any more that Phoebe is hers. When we met the other day for coffee, Katharine asked me if I'd be a godmother. I reminded her that I'm crap with babies, and she gave me a secret little smile and said, "You won't be crap with mine."

Her pregnancy has done a weird thing to Iain. Whenever Nick suggests meeting up for a drink, he says no, because he wants to get home early. He's even talking about jacking the agency in once Katharine goes back to work, and being a full-time father. Katharine says she's never been so happy in all her life. Nick and I think maybe it's possible for people to change.

Callie has been made a partner at the law firm where she works, so Khan Clarke Gardner is now Khan Clarke Travis. Phoebe's mum and dad have separated, but it's all been as amicable as it could have been, under the circumstances. Vernon has moved to a fourth-floor flat in a building with no lift, and apparently he says carrying shopping up the stairs is playing havoc with his back. He asked Phoebe if she could take him to the supermarket and help him carry it, but instead Phoebe gave him a fifteen percent discount code for Ocado.

The Westbourne Thespians are doing *Oliver!* this summer, and Mum's been having singing lessons for her role as Mrs Bedwin. I may not have got my cooking talent from her, but I definitely blame her for my total lack of musical ability, so the show looks like being a classic of its kind. Apparently the opening night is a sell-out already. Mum also told me that she and Dad had accepted an invitation to tea with the Alcocks, their arch-rivals in the best-kept garden competition. "Keep your friends close and your enemies closer," she said darkly. This struck me as good advice, so I sent Bethany a friend request on Facebook, and she accepted.

284

It's a strange thing, but after spending an hour or so obsessively looking through her photo albums and scrutinising her status updates, I began to feel quite differently about Bethany. She was no less tousled, blonde and cool, but she was also a normal girl. A girl whose slightly crooked front teeth showed when she smiled. A girl whose new boots got soaked when she stepped in a puddle on the way to work, and leaked. A girl who got Cersei in the 'Which *Game of Thrones* character are you?' quiz, same as me. I don't know if we'll ever meet in real life, but I have a feeling that if we do, we might not be enemies after all.

The other day, I was watching *MasterChef South Africa* on the Food Network, and there was a dining scene with a big group of guests eating barbequed fillet steak under the stars. The camera zoomed in on one of them, just as he was cramming a huge forkful of meat into his mouth. It was Gabriel. I expected to feel swamped with mortification at the sight of him, but I didn't – I just laughed.

And Nick and I?

We got married last week. I put on my beautiful dress and my wedding shoes, and we walked down to Southwark Register Office and said our vows with Callie and Phoebe as witnesses. Afterwards we all went to the Hope and Anchor for a few pints, and then Nick and I went home and ate takeaway pizza in bed with Spanx and his friend, The Amazing Archibald's stuffed bunny. Spanx and the bunny are inseparable – he carries it around with him in his mouth, which is extremely cute and also means our underwear mostly stays in the drawer where it belongs.

I've been making the pilot episode of *Pippa's Plates* with Zack and the guys at Platinum. Working with kids was downright terrifying at first, but I'm liking it more and more, and they seem to like me. The other day I was showing a group of six-year-olds how to make pizza dough, and there was one little boy with dark hair and a dimple in his cheek, and in a certain light it was easy to imagine how a child of Nick's might look, one day. When I told Zack I'd got married, he was thrilled, and announced that I'll be billed as Pippa Pickford. Apparently it's more memorable than Pippa Martin. Nick is trying very hard not to gloat about this.

All in all, we couldn't be happier. But there's one thing we can't quite agree on. Erica doesn't know yet that we're married, and one of us is going to have to tell her.

Acknowledgements

Whether I started writing *A Groom with a View*, I'd just spent a weekend away with seventeen women I am incredibly fortunate to have as friends. We were celebrating the anniversary of the second Tuesday in November 2003, when a group of us first met up to drink wine, gossip and talk about books.

Since then, we've been through marriages, divorces, births, deaths and innumerable traumas ranging from horrific mothers-in-law to what to serve the vegan who's coming for dinner. My book club friends have enriched my life so much: they are all beautiful, brilliant and inspiring, and I'm honoured to be part of their circle of fabulousness.

So I hope they will forgive me for shamelessly scavenging their lives to use in this book. I hope the snippets I've sneaked in make my readers laugh even a fraction as much as I have over the years.

Special thanks to the eagle-eyed Catherine Baigent, who proofread this book to within an inch of its life and improved it so much. Any remaining errors are definitely mine.

My wonderful agent Peta Nightingale has been unstintingly generous with her knowledge, wisdom and commercial nous since I first embarked on the terrifying journey of publication. Without her and her colleagues at LAW, this book would never have been written, and certainly not read. Thank you.

I am over the moon with the gorgeous cover of A Groom with a View. Thanks to Tash Webber for her stunning design work.

Finally, always, thanks to my partner Hopi, light of my life, who makes me happy every day and tells me to get a grip when I need one. I love you.

About the Author

S ophie Ranald is the youngest of five sisters. She was born in Zimbabwe and lived in South Africa until an acute case of itchy feet brought her to London in her mid-20s. As an editor for a customer publishing agency, Sophie developed her fiction-writing skills describing holidays to places she'd never visited. In 2011, she decided to disregard all the good advice given to aspiring novelists and attempt to write full-time.

A Groom with a View is Sophie's second novel, and she also writes for magazines and online about food, fashion and running. She lives in south-east London with her amazing partner Hopi and Purrs, their adorable little cat.

Follow Sophie on Twitter @SophieRanald, or like her Facebook page for updates and random wittering about the cuteness of Purrs (there will be pics! Even videos!).

Discover more sparkling romantic comedies
by Sophie Ranald

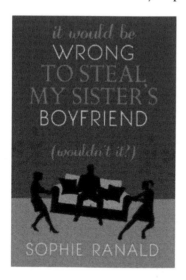

If you enjoyed *A Groom with a View*, why not read *Who Wants to Marry a Millionaire?* for FREE?

Sign up to Sophie's newsletter at sophieranald.com to claim your copy and receive updates and news of future giveaways!

Made in the USA
Middletown, DE
22 September 2020

20172384R00166